Thomas Ince

Beggar manuscripts

An original miscellany in verse and prose

Thomas Ince

Beggar manuscripts
An original miscellany in verse and prose

ISBN/EAN: 9783337132316

Printed in Europe, USA, Canada, Australia, Japan

Cover: Foto ©Andreas Hilbeck / pixelio.de

More available books at **www.hansebooks.com**

BEGGAR MANUSCRIPTS:

AN

ORIGINAL MISCELLANY

IN

VERSE AND PROSE.

—

By Thomas Ince

—

SUBSCRIPTION EDITION.

═══

Blackburn :
NORTH-EAST LANCASHIRE PRINTING AND PUBLISHING COMPANY, LIMITED,
--
1888.

Contents.

List of Subscribers.

NAMES.	ADDRESSES.
Abbott, Joseph	Kenyon Street
Abram, W. A., F.R.H.S., Editor of the *Blackburn Standard and Weekly Express*	Adelaide Terrace
Ainsworth, Thomas, Solicitor	25, King Street
Almond, J. ... ... Langho ; late,	Bay Horse Hotel, Blackburn
Almond, John	100, Grimshaw Park
Almond, Thomas ...	34, Penny Street
Appleby, Ald. Edgar, J.P. ...	Wilpshire Grange
Atkinson, John	15, Isherwood Street
Boyle, Councillor John	... Braeside, Revidge
Birtwistle, Micah	27, Harwood Street
Brierley, Jos., C.E.	... Richmond Terrace
Bailey, J. H., Borough Treasurer	Borough Treasurer's Office
Binns, James	... 24, Feilden Street
Briggs, Samuel	74, Ashworth Street
Burnett, W. H., Editor of the *Evening Express & Standard*...Revidge Road
Bispham, Anthony	Moss Street, Daisyfield
Boardman, Thomas ...	... Exchange Hotel
Blades, William ...	39, Whittaker Street
Ballard, William ...	... Whalley Banks
Bryan, Mrs. A. ...	... The Spread Eagle Hotel
Bryan, Arthur	... 88, Ellen Street
Bryan, A. O.	... 65, Larkhill
Baron, Wm., (Bill o' Jack's)	9, East Street, Witton
Baron Jos.	7, Edgware Road
Baron, John S.	Astley Gate
Ball, George, Trade Secretary ' ...	78, Eccles Street
Ball, James	The Merchants' Hotel
Backhouse, T. J., Solicitor ...	York Cliff, Langho
Barker Geo., Trade Secretary	Weavers' Institute
Blackshaw, James ...	5, Portsmouth Street
Carter, Absalom	... 5, Proctor Street
Clifton, Thos. ...	The Brewers' Arms, Novas
Cowburn, T. L.	... 55, Church Street

NAMES.	ADDRESSES.
Culshaw, A. ...	... 3, Princes Street
Crook, William ...	... 4, Mile End, Revidge Road
Cliff, R. B., Solicitor	... ... Library Street
Crossley, S., Solicitor...	... ... 1, Richmond Terrace
Cottam, Henry	... 21, Hodson street
Davidson, J. K., L.R.C.P.	... 26, King Street
Dixon, James	Ragged School, Bent Street
Dodd, Francis ...	... 12, King Street
Duckworth, John	... 73, Charlotte Street
Duxbury Thos. ...	Commercial (Temperance) Hotel, Station Road
Davies, Henry, Newspaper Proprietor	... Winckley Street, Preston
Darley, C. E., Solicitor ...	... 5, Lord Street West
Ditchfield, Wm., Clerk to School Board	... School Board Offices
Eastwood, Joseph	... 15, Richmond Terrace
Eastwood, Councillor Robt. T., (Grand Master of Oddfellows, Manchester Unity)	... ... Regent Street
Farren, Moses	... 31, Withers Street, Audley
Farrer-Baynes, Ald. Thos., J.P. ...	... ... Ash House
Fenton, Thos., Trade Secretary	... ... 63, Whalley Range
Fisher, J. W.	...183, Whalley New Road
Fairclough, R. ...	292, Whalley Range
Fletcher, John R., Solicitor	... ... 12, Preston New Road
Fox, John D. ...	"See-Saw" Cottage, Bingley, Yorks.
Gaine, W. E. L., Town Clerk, &c ...	... Town Clerk's Office
Gifford, R. Lord	... ... Salford Bridge
Graham, Wm. ...	... 61 and 63, Lower Audley Street
Graham, John	... ... 16, John Street
Grosart, The Rev. A. B., D.D., LLD.	... Brooklyn House
Green, Wm.	72, Fisher Street
Garstang, W. J.... ...	Lord Street West
Hill and Dale, Messrs. ...	... Thwaites' Arcade
Holden, Thos.	... 66, Whalley Range
Holt, Elijah, Conservative Agent	143, Whalley New Road
Hunt, Robert, Sergeant-Major ...	... 35, Mincing Lane
Holloway, F. J.	Kensington Chambers
Hughes, John ...	... Vernon Street
Hindle, Henry	... 66, King Street
Hacking Ed., Market Inspector	...Market Inspector's Office
Hacking, T. J.	... 8, Preston New Road
Hargreaves, J. R. ...	... 29, Feilden Street
Haythornthwaite, W.	... ... Cherry Tree

NAMES.	ADDRESSES.
Hayhurst, Wm.	... Lord Street
Hindle, Arthur	Richmond Terrace
Holland, W. T., Solicitor	... Northgate
Hamer, Councillor Edwin ...	Braeside, Revidge
Heaton, Thos. ...	The Nag's Head Inn
Higson, Wm.	3, Burlington Street
Hughes, Thos. ...	56, Penny Street
Irwine, The Rev. A. P., M.A. ...	... The Vicarage, Bingley, Yorks.
Johnson, R. W. ...	... 6, Hazel Bank
Kilshaw, Richard, Temperance Missionary	Shear Brow
Kinstrey, Adam.	9, John Street
Lewis, Mrs. E. A. ...	... Teetotal Mission Room
Lewis George, Chief Constable...	Chief Constable's Office
Leaver, Councillor Jas. ...	...4, Duke's Brow
Leaver, Jas., junr. ...	18, Union Street
Library, The Free	... Blackburn
McCallum, J. B., Borough Engineer	Borough Engineer's Office
McEwen, J.	70, Penny Street
Mitchell, John	The Alliance (Temperance) Hotel, Northgate
Marsh, John	95, Addison Street
Middlebrook, R.	2, King William Street
Marshall, A. ...	44, Church Street
Marshall, J.	...66, Larkhill Terrace
Martin, Isaac S....	... Granville Terrace
Martin, J. M. H., M.D.	... Arnheim, Preston New Road
Moran, Wm. ...	... ... 44, Bank Top
Norris, John, Liberal Agent	... The Reform Club
Nelson, W. H.	43, Blackburn Street
Ogden, S. R., Borough Gas Engineer ...	Borough Gas Engineer's Office
Peel, W. H. T. ...	1, Feilden Street
Panter, The Rev. C. H.	... 32, Bold Street
Pickersgill, R. ...	58, Duckworth Street
Pickup, Hy., junr.	... 68, Northgate
Pickup, Jno. ...	17, Garnett Street
Pye, Joseph ...	... ... Joseph Street
Pinder, W. H.	114, Whalley Old Road

NAMES.	ADDRESSES.

Platts, T., Solicitor ... ...Tacketts Street
Parker, Thos. ... ... 34, Ice Street

Quail, Jesse, Editor of the *Northern Daily Telegraph* ... The Mount, Duke's Brow
Roberts, James ... ... The Clarence Hotel
Rushton, J. H. ... ...Addison Street
Robinson, Wm. ... 17, Feilden Street
Ramsbottom, J. T. ... ... Russell Street
Riley, Richard, Solicitor ... ... 21, Victoria Street
Rutherford, J., (His Worship the Mayor of Blackburn) ... Town Hall
Rushton, T. ... ... The *Evening Post* Office
Ridsdale, Thos. ... ... King Street

Scott, Geo., Postmaster ... ... The Postmaster's Office
Shutt, Thos., Director Refuge Assurance Co.... Horncliffe, Duke's Brow
Scholes, Chris. ... ... Mill Hill
Slater, J. T.... ... ... 13, Ebony Street
Slater, Thos. ... ... 94, Randall Street
Shaw, J. W. ... ... 88, Whalley New Road
Simpson, A. W. R., Architect, &c. ... ... Hazel Bank
Sharples, Henry ... ... 104, Ingham Street, Higher Audley
Stirrup, Walter, Architect, &c. ... ... 6, Richmond Terrace
Stark, Archibald ... ... 14, Stanley Street, Greenbank
Southworth, Geo. ... ... 10, Snape Street

Taylor, Mrs. L. ... ... 6, Simmons Street
Tyrrell, W., Registrar of Births & Deaths...Registry Office, Simmons St.
Thompson, Jno. ... ... 50, Market-place
Townley, Jas. ... ... 29, Montague Street
Tempo, Henry, Schoolmaster ... ... 1, Holland Street
Toulmin, J. and G., Newspaper Proprietors ... The *Times* Office
Tanton, Thos. ... ... 68a, Parkwood Street, Keighley

Wright, Jas. ... ... 32, Anvil Street
Ward, Wm., Ex Chief Constable Chief Constable's Office
Walker, Gregory... ... ... John Street
Walton, William ... 13, King William Street
Wilkinson, Jas. ... ... 93, New Park Street
Walmsley, L. S. ... Kensington Place
Whitworth, Joseph ... ... 6, Abraham Street
Wilcock, James, Director Refuge Assurance Co. ... 55, Montague Street
Wilson, R., Journalist ... ...Oswald Street
Wills, J. A. ... ... 8, Darwen Street
Walkden, J. T. ... 6, Granville Terrace
Whitehead, J. W. ... ... 53, Feilden Street

AUTOBIOGRAPHY

OF

THOMAS INCE.

THOMAS INCE, the author of this book, was born at Bingley, in the West Riding of Yorkshire, on the 11th November, 1850. His father, having taken the Queen's shilling and enlisted, whilst he was yet a child he was taken along with a younger brother and sister to the Wigan Union Workhouse, where he was educated. Having been placed twice by the authorities in service—first with a collier, and afterwards with a yeoman on Sir R. Gerard's estate—through circumstances over which he had no control, at the age of fifteen, he found himself back in the neighbourhood of his birthplace, from whence he made occasional ramblings through the country, until his 25th year. He has been twice married : first, in 1875, to a Miss Wild, of Bingley, who was accidentally drowned within six weeks after the event ; and secondly, to his present wife, who was born at Haworth, but settled at Bingley also. She was the youngest daughter of Mr. Joseph Leach, who hailed from Woolwich, and whose brother Abraham (a sailor) was lost with Franklin in his North Pole Exploration. His brother died in his 20th year, amongst the strangers who had adopted him at Farnworth, near Bolton ; whilst his sister is married, and resides at Keighley. As he has never been blessed with a strong constitution, nor been taught any trade, it needs only to be mentioned that his experience of life has been anything but the rosiest. He has been honoured of late with a place in the list of "Yorkshire Poets : Past and Present," a serial work which is now publishing at Bradford, under the editorship of Dr. Forshaw of that town ; and in addition to being a frequent contributor to the Blackburn press, he has also been favoured with a letter of thanks from Their Royal Highnesses the Prince and Princess of Wales, for a poem written by him, entitled "Blackburn's Greeting," in honour of their visit to the town, on May 9th, 1888. He is at present resident in Blackburn, and has been there for some years ; living with his wife and son, and following the profession of a herbalist.

Introductory Preface.

IN presenting this work to the reader, I venture to avail myself of the liberty of offering a few remarks which to my mind appear very applicable in this connection. I refer to the extreme difficulty which bars the way to success against any humble aspirant to literary fame who may, perchance, have had, like myself, to fight against adversity from his youth up. I make no pretensions above my deserts, but I cannot refrain from thinking that the subscribers to this volume attach some little merit to my endeavours, and in justice to them I feel called upon to protest against the principle which prevents many capable but indigent writers from receiving encouragement for meritorious work. I know my own shortcomings too well—a neglected education and unfortunate surroundings have turned me out as I am, in truth, an unfinished article ; but there have been, and are still, many worthier devotees to what was and is to them—and to myself—a noble attainment, and a labour of love. The converting of genius or talent, by any process whatsoever, into hackneyed effort, is disastrous to a people's well-being ; but when instances of this kind are continually occurring, and blighted hopes and broken hearts are the peculiar spoils of genius, then, I say, that the charge is not an unfounded one. All that is truest and best in our national instincts—all that is dearest and most refined in our private sentiments—are embodied in the lives of those unlucky beings, whose hearts have warmed with the honest fervour of literary ambition, but have been often in the very budding of their genius ruthlessly despoiled by cynical, cold, and cutting neglect. Amongst local writers who have suffered in this respect may be mentioned Wildon, Nicholson, and Prince. I care nothing for the note of admiration for life services when the worker has departed hence, and gone beyond all worldly needs; for nothing can compare creditably one tittle with the evidences of the hand and brain of departed worth. Poets and writers there have also been of immortal fame, who during life had to battle with the pangs of hunger and remorse, aided considerably by the neglect of a selfish world, but whose life-work has since been used as foundations for the upraising of immense fortunes to speculators and strangers to the family. My simple, earnest wish, is then, to infuse, if possible, by my humble efforts, something more of love into the relations of humankind. The harshness of tutelage may occasion grief—the venom of jealousy may beget ill-will—the spleen of rivalry may encourage strife—but my desire is to inspire friendship. In the Spirit of Love I offer the Book, free from egotism I yield it, contented to abide by your verdict.   If, when that verdict be given, I shall have succeeded in inspiring a truer manliness of feeling for others who choose to tread the beaten track of literature, then I know that I shall feel over a thousand times repaid for any infliction which follows. The more than tinge of melancholy which prevades many of the selections, will, I trust, be excused to a certain extent, for I may in extenuation plead that a man can scarcely be expected to smile whose heart is torn and bleeding.

THE AUTHOR.

Blackburn, Autumn, 1888.

Explanatory Note.

AS the term, "BEGGAR MANUSCRIPTS," appears to occasion a feeling of surprise, and as I have no desire to screen my reasons for adopting such a title, I have to ask the indulgence of subscribers and readers whilst I tender the explanation. If the contents of a book prove satisfactory to the reader, I hold that it matters very little indeed as to what other distinction it receives ; but I will admit that if a name had to be chosen on account of the fitness of things, there is no name so applicable to this collection of writings as the one I have chosen. As an unfortunate I have played my part in life, tossed by the winds of adversity and misfortune here and there ; during such periods of distress I have penned most of the contents of this book, and forlornly I have struggled on their behalf for the recognition and sympathy of the literary world. I have begged for them to be purchased ; I have begged for publication ; I have begged for fair play and freedom ; and, begging ever on their behalf, they have *beggared* me, and are "beggars" indeed. Again, I have no sympathy with the assumptions of those who use high-sounding and meaningless titles for their efforts, and believe firmly that whilst the book may yield some little pleasure to every reader, as "BEGGAR MANUSCRIPTS," they will be no less respected. Therefore, I trust that this terse confession will give satisfaction to the curious, and in no sense detract from the good intentions and merits of

Yours truly,

THE AUTHOR.

Dedication.

AS it is necessary, now-a-days, to follow the fashions, in order to march with the times, I find it devolving upon me, therefore, to write out these paragraphs to satisfy public demands.

**

THIS is to me, indeed, a very pleasant task ; inasmuch as it enables me to speak collectively to the various friends who have, during my career, kindly assisted by their efforts to press onwards to this end.

**

THEREFORE, I do, with heartfelt pleasure and gratitude, hereby **Dedicate this, my First Book,** unto those Friends, one and all, wherever they may be, and in whatever station of life—subscribers or non-subscribers—as a very small token of my deep appreciation of their goodness, and in recognition of the charity in their hearts.

**

AND I do most earnestly trust that each one now living may be blessed with Happiness and Good Health, the best of all booms ; and that their generous dispositions may at all times prove, not only their own comforters, but a constant joy to those about them.

**

THAT each one may accept this Dedication in the kindly spirit which animates the writer is the best wish of the same, and in testimony thereof,

I am proud to remain,

Your most devoted,

THOMAS INCE.

✸BEGGAR MANUSCRIPTS.✦

The Author to the Book.

I F ever any book must cost but half so much as thee,
  Methinks it were much better lost than e'er a book to be;
Through good report, and evil, too, have I upheld thee dear,
  To prove at last a record true of many a busy year.

'Tis true, indeed, I loved too well to be thy faithful scribe,
  Though thankless was the task that fell, my *penchant* to imbibe,
A nightly and a daily toil thou recklessly entailed,
  In harvesting the varied spoil that sometimes I bewailed.

Perplexing and unkindly, too, the work has proved to be,
  Although from dangers not a few have I protected thee,
Through ups and downs, in many a guise, companions have we been,
  As though in truth thou wert a prize that is but rarely seen.

However, thou wast my delight, although sometimes a bore,
  And, but for thee a sorry plight would mine have been for sure ;
In trouble and in pleasure too, together we have sped,
  And so I will not cry, Adieu ! till memory be dead.

Lancashire: A Toast.

It has often been stated that Cotton is King,
And so of the workers in Cotton I sing.
No race in Old England hold honour more dear
Than the proud sons and daughters of famed Lancashire.

In science and skill they stand well in the fray ;
For pluck and goodwill they are noted to-day ;
In labour and love will each one persevere
For the glorious prestige of famed Lancashire.

Her daughters are modest, and faithful, and fair,
No women for beauty can match them elsewhere,
Warm-hearted and loving, in friendship sincere,
Still lending new lustre to famed Lancashire.

Her sons have for centuries acted like men,
And patriots proved with the sword and the pen ;
Ever foremost in daring and hindmost in fear,
True champions always of famed Lancashire.

Then here is a bumper unto her bright name,
And now let each friend celebrate her fair fame—
"Through the world as we go may we always revere
The beauty and worth of famed Lancashire."

The Scratchback Club.

We have heard of politicians who are leaders of renown,
We have read of clever artists who are known throughout the town,
We have listened unto orators in institute and " pub,"
But have never seen the equal of THE SCRATCHBACK CLUB.

Their rendezvous is famous as a qualified resort
Of "chappies" who have talents of a most peculiar sort.
Bel esprit is the motto which inflates them every man,
And renders the spectator to condemn them as a clan.

There are dreamers who are building airy castles not a few,
Who, in spite of being clever, are a bacchanalian crew ;
There are office-holders also, who have special work in hand,
More dignified than aldermen, and seeming twice as grand.

There are rules and regulations for the guidance of the lot,
And, strange though 'tis to chronicle, it should not be forgot,
The members all believe themselves supremely well endowed,
And keep a proper distance from the rude, unlettered crowd,

" Who are these members ? " you would ask.   So thereto I reply,
Nor dignity, nor principle, nor genius there, say I
No statesman, e'en in embryo, nor artist ever there ,
Nor yet a single gentleman could anyone declare.

Then look around, ye people all, when next ye go to town,
And notice well the braggarts who parade both up and down ;
Perchance ye may by accident your shoulders hap to rub
Against some well-dressed member of THE SCRATCHBACK CLUB.

Looking at Death.

Looking at Death from a sick man's view,
Laden with sorrow, and suffering too,
Wrung with the anguish of torturing pain,
Hoping and waiting for comfort in vain,
How great must the contrast appear pictured there,
Where Death puts an end unto blight and despair,
It may not be right to indulge in such breath,
But still 'tis consoling, thus—Looking at Death.

Looking at Death from a different phase,
A life that is blasted with sin and disgrace,
When day after day brings the end nearer view,
Distorting its horrors and adding thereto.
How utterly wretched must be such a fate,
Without one redeeming or comforting trait,
Remembering well what the Almighty saith,
How terrible thus is the—Looking at Death.

Looking at Death from the singular fate
Of one whose ambition has no future state,
Whose life without doubt may be blameless of men,
Yet ends with the beasts of the forest and plain.
How aimless and vain unto such must appear
The life of mankind when the end draweth near ;
"For why do we live, yet to gain or bequeath?"
Must puzzle the sceptic on—Looking at Death.

Looking at Death from the Christian's view,
How cheery and gladsome the prospect thereto ;
Release from a bondage of worry and strife,
To enter the portals of sanctified life ;
Nor doubting nor dreading in him can arise,
No fearful misgiving may baffle his eyes,
Nor wrangling, nor chaos, nor envious breath
Can hamper a Christian on—Looking at Death.

To my Dictionary.

A true old friend thou hast been to me
    When friends withal were none so many,
And I have none that have proved to be
    So often needed—more than any.

My lettered friend, how I treasure thee
    To my inmost heart is only known,
For thy usefulness lent aid to me
    When otherwise I had toiled alone.

How shall I sing thy entitled praise,
    Or how shall I word my tribute strain,
So thou, the tutor of all my lays,
    The highest honour may still retain.

Grant me, O Muse ! for my old friend's sake,
    A spell of thy poetic power,
Endow me now with a zeal to wake
    The echoes sweet of a tuneful hour.

Thou dear old tome, ever rich to me,
    Since Learning's sweets from thee I have drawn,
How can I fail in regarding thee,
    Companion true of the dusk and dawn.

Mere words but faintly can express
    How deeply grateful I would prove,
But my regard is nevertheless
    The yielding fruit of abiding Love.

The Death of Moses.

O'er Nebo's hill and Pisgah's height a holy radiance shone,
For Jehovah with His servant there had will'd to be alone ;
The Prophet by His order thus had travelled to his doom,
And glory from the Presence did the meeting-place illume.

The long expected Promised Land lay open unto view—
The land of plenty overflown with treasures rare and new—
The goal of man's ambition, and an Eden of delight,
Lay like a sea of riches fascinating to the sight.

The chieftain, who had served his Lord, and knew Him face to face,
Surveyed the country stretched below—the chosen resting-place ;
His six score years of age he bore, as man his natural prime,
With sight and strength as unimpaired as ever in his time.

The anxious hopes and yearnings of the troublous years gone by—
The humble, yet the faithful trust—how easy to descry !
How happy must we picture him to find his journey done,
Blessing still, yet blessed, thus to feel his rest begun.

Then spoke the God of Israel, and thus and thus said He:
" The Land whereon thou gazeth I will not give unto thee ;
" I promised it to Abraham, and unto all his seed,
" Yet thou shalt not go thither, on account of thy misdeed ;

" But, inasmuch as thou hast found great favour in My sight,
" I suffer thee to view the Land, with every prospect bright,
" For all the faithful service thou hast rendered in My Name,
" A recompense in Glory shall atone for every claim.

" Thy days are numbered, yet thine end shall be an end of peace,
" Gathered unto thy people all thy murmurings shall cease,
" Even here thou diest *now* beside the Lord of Hosts,
" A forfeit for the frailty that presumption only boasts."

Thus spoke the Lord ; and Moses then, submissive to His will,
Resplendent with the holiness His Presence did instil,
With bended knees and lowly mien, without regret or sigh,
Surrendered there his deathless soul, and thus did meekly die.

An envious death did Moses die, as doth a little child.
Fit emblem of humility, in his spirit meek and mild ;
He died an honoured Patriarch, in harmony with God,
A favoured dissolution where the Holy Presence stood.

Not all the world of schism, and not all that sages tell,
Will ever dissipate the fact that Moses' end was well ;
Promoted to communion with the King of kings in life,
He reached a higher glory when he quitted earthly strife.

And so he died ; and never man was witness of his end ;
His final resting-place unknown to every earthly friend ;
The Lord—his God and Comforter—took charge of Moses there ;
" For such an end and such a Friend ! " is every Christian's prayer.

Ube "Goös" at Ibome.

I suppose we all know something, more or less, concerning the "gods." How often other people have been amongst them I cannot say, but my own recollections of their peccadilloes and peculiarities are nearly always sufficient to inspire me with a certain amount of humour not always of the mildest type. I do not allude to any *Idol* gods, although some of them are idle enough in all conscience; so of course it is understood that I make no travesty of the sacred character. The "gods" of this sketch are of anything but a heavenly description, unless there be among them such as believe with Christians—"Heaven is our Home." The "gods" whom I particularly allude to are of so material a disposition that I venture in most instances to doubt their ethereal qualification entirely. How ever they managed to receive such an appellation at all is beyond my conception, unless it be that generally speaking they inhabit the higher regions of the places they resort to. Still, so much are they bound up in our social life, that the theatrical and musical enterprises, if not at the first of all started under their auspices, are yet greatly indebted to their patronage. If you wish to know where the applause comes from, the support comes from, the noise comes from, and the condemnation comes from; whether you care to acknowledge the fact or not, the truth is—from the "gods." Therefore, the "gods" claim a particular share of our consideration, and further still, they receive it; in proof of which, note the superior accommodation now-a-days provided for them. There is no doubt whatever about this, that the fact of them having received so superlative a distinction, in name at least, would furnish evidence sufficient to disturb the secular mind; for the logic of its implication bristles with argument. To our subject, however,—What manner of folks are the 'gods,' and whence come they?" They are not of one kind, as we know, inasmuch as they comprise male and female, old and young, decently dressed, and ragged individualities. There is, indeed, a great variety of the species, from grandparents to grandchildren, from the patriarch down to the street arab. There are "gods" from choice, and "gods" from necessity, decent "gods" and rakish "gods;" forming altogether, for the time being, a combination powerful for either one thing or the other, but more generally *for the other*, if that other be rowdyism or fun.

When a stillness as of death pervades the building, and a sudden sound as of the falling of a heavy body, accompanied by a chorus of execrations occurs, it is ten to one upon the interruption emanating from the sweltering, excited, or mischievous "gods." When the most pathetic and tender portion of a play is being enacted, and every sympathetic soul and kind-hearted listener is enthralled with its intensity, any sudden outbreak, rush, stumble, clash, crash, and shriek that rudely breaks the charm, is a most certain indication that the combative instinct has been roused amongst the "gods." Or, when the vocal accompaniments of a pugilistic "set to," with all its attendant stumbles, awake the echoes, and also the ire of the whole "house," you may, in ninety-nine cases out of every hundred, stake your last penny that the "gods" are *in evidence*, and enjoying themselves immensely. And by degrees we become imbued with the same characteristic ourselves; perhaps in a more refined fashion at first, but surely ending in a resigned spirit of large-hearted toleration, sympathy, and brotherhood.

And, in fact, there is ample evidence, as managers can testify, that the proportion of respectably-clad and fairly comfortable members of the "godly tribe" has largely increased of late years; and, with that addition to their numbers and character, a more critical and exacting spirit prevails, so that, perhaps, it is no light task or compliment to satisfy the "gods" in these times. The *unfortunate* female, minus a shawl or other head-gear, side by side with the more fortunate miss or matron in all the glory of superior toggery, and who is accompanied by a sturdy helpmate or protector, together with the very small specimen of humanity whose occupation of street-vending or begging is for the time neglected, whilst he or she as the case may be, perseveringly endeavours, and at last manages, to cheat the "checker" at his post, and to sneak in unseen; along with the careless and broad-shouldered loafer, the strong tobacco odour from whose clothes and gums seems to permeate the building, and whose frequent ejections of tobacco juice are a standing (or sitting) joke and terror alternately—these constitute the better known part of that original mass of humanity somewhat incongruously designated "the gods." Add to those, just here and there, a dreamy and sallow-visaged youth, or a pale love-sick maiden, with anything but classic features, although of most romantic disposition; whose tearful demeanour, and at times audible outbreaks of sympathetic feeling are the standing jokes and butt for the comic element, then you have something like a fair description of what may pardonably be termed as Britain's left wing—" the ' gods ' at home.

The corner-man, or bully, is very rarely to be seen amongst the fraternity, for being of a more beastly, unnatural, greedy, and vicious type, he finds his quarry in the drinking dens of low repute and other haunts of iniquity. I make bold to say that were one of this class to commence his devilment amongst our "gods" he would share the fate of his satanic superior who was driven out of Glory ; and possibly he knows this quite as well as we do ourselves. There is at the bottom, even amongst the "gods," a certain modicum of love for British fair play, and any corner-man would find himself " in the wrong box," as it were, did he commit himself unnecessarily and intolerantly amongst them. And this it is which provides for an *artiste* the opportunity for applause and distinction, and in contra-distinction proves the downfall for incompetence. The true "gods" are of a lively, rakish, buoyant, careless, discriminating, and comfortable stamp, as different from their poorer or more disreputable allies on all other occasions as could fairly be conceived. Taken all round, as a class, we may therefore describe them as being a far more preferable essential of society than those whose reputation is identical with police or criminal annals. It is now quite common to see in a crowded assembly of the "gods," dozens of them eagerly and seriously discussing the columns of some evening newspaper, " between the acts," so that such a circumstance of itself entitles them to a fair share of our respectful consideration ; for it is an infinitely better means of employing themselves than either rushing off to some beer vaults, or beclouding with tobacco smoke the means of entrance and exit. If we except the untimely and too frequent exits and entrances, the noises made by too clumsy peregrinations after the ever-favoured cheap gills and pop bottles, the orange-peel and nutshell assaults with which they playfully disport themselves, and the small rivulets of tobacco-juice which besmear the seats ; I say, if we can ignore or put up with such drawbacks, we may possibly find that the haunts of the "gods," so far as sight and comfort go, are in reality the most convenient part of the building. So that, after all that can be said about them, if either Dick or Sarah, Jack or Gill, possess enough robustness, strength of nerve, love of mischief, or selfish bravado, with the requisite ability for self-protection ; there is no real reason why they may not with considerable profit enjoy an occasional night in our entertainment temples amongst "the gods at home."

The People.

What shall I say to the people ?
How shall I reach to their hearts ?
   Had I the wisdom of sages—
   Had I the records of ages—
A clarion tongue from a steeple—
   I lack in enacting my parts.

What can I say to the many,
That fortune may turn to their good ?
   Happy, indeed, to befriend them,
   Gladly my all I would lend them,
For sadly, say I, there's not any
   But better might be if they would.

Why are they always dependent ?
Why ever sad and downcast ?
   Why are they browbeat with money ?
   Why should the bees have no honey ?
For Unity's need each defendant
   Will bleed till salvation is past.

When will the toilers use reason?
When will they show common-sense?
Image of God, like the master,
Travelling Heavenwards faster;
Now is the chance and the season
To thwart the usurper's pretence.

Then, on to success and renown!
And forward to freedom and right!
United your sway shall begin,
You only need will it and win;
So band yourselves well in each town,
And organise meetings at night.

A Workman's Home.

Let lordlings sing, and ladies cling, to wealth, and fame, and place,
Let Handicraft and Science vie, to deck them out in grace;
Amidst a round of gaieties though daily they may roam,
They lack the blessedness within a honest labourer's home.

Besieged with state—betokened great—possessed of wealthy hoard—
Surrounded by the flunkeys who attend their bed and board;
Yet, though they shine and look so fine, and pleasant seems their lot,
There's a greater charm, and hearts as warm, within a humble cot.

Around the workman's hearth, at night, when daily toil is o'er,
The loved ones sit with spirits light—dull care without the door—
The children's glee is good to see, whilst the elders' happy mien
Excels the studied graces that with affluence are seen.

The schoolboy's task; the baby's care; the dangling father's knee;
The mother's work; the granny's chair (where granny loves to be);
The pleasant chat; the cheerful play; the free and homely joys;
The evening meal; the prayerful kneel of youngest girls and boys.

A later hour—with freer power—of devotion fond and true;
Domestic schemes, and loving dreams what Father Time may do;
Perchance some news, awhile amuse in passing night away;
Then off to bed, with reverent head, to rest till coming day.

'Tis little, I know; but who can show a happier lot than this?
Or who could wish for better fare, when such imparts a bliss?
The rich may boast possessions, but contentment beats them all;
So ye who would enjoy the boon, respond to duty's call.

An Old Man's Story.

So you think I could tell you a story, that is, if I felt so inclined,
An'l only because I am hoary, and show an intelligent mind;
You credit my years and my reason, and truly you judge not unwell,
And so that you suffer no treason, a brief simple tale I will tell.

'Twas in days long ago, then remember, not many years short of three score,
On one cheerless night in November, a stranger did come to our door,
I lived with my father and mother, a few miles away from the town,
With only a sister and brother to accompany me up and down.

The stranger was handsome and clever, with a style captivating and bold,
And his equal, till then, I had never, beheld in a man young or old;
His age was, perhaps, five-and-twenty, somewhere not so far from my own,
And of wealth he was 'customed to plenty, as any might easy have known.

He had called on a matter of business, and father invited him in.
And of course he accepted the welcome, because of the brightness within.
He got introduced unto sister, and also to brother and I,
And soon he became quite familiar, and time glided pleasantly by.

Our dear sister Alice was pretty, not so-so, but something more rare,
And he was uncommonly witty, with a presence commanding and fair,
And soon—very soon—she was captured, by him and the arts he possessed,
While he, I could see was enraptured, by the charms her sweet beauty expressed.

She was only a child, please remember, whilst he was so polished and smart,
And before but the close of November, the stranger had stolen her heart ;
For he made one excuse and another to call many times after then,
And the darling, in spite of her mother, beguiled him again and again.

Dear sister, we could only scold her, but sternly forbade him the house ;
'Twas then that, indeed, she grew bolder, and stole to his arms like a mouse ;
We felt that she was not his equal, and dreaded that harm would ensue,
And, sir, if you notice the sequel, you'll find our suspicions proved true.

They carried on thus until Christmas, and then on that festival morn,
Whilst joy-bells were ringing so sweetly, the message that Jesus was born,
We found the dear girl had departed, and fled from the home of her birth,
Leaving each one gloomy-hearted, and driving all gladness from earth.

We loved her so well, and she knew it ; for she was the family's pride,
We could not imagine she'd do it, though sorely no doubt she was tried ;
We thought her our one pretty flower, so lovely, so gentle, so kind,
And to think of that one fatal hour makes justice appear almost blind.

Ah, well ! she eloped ; and, believe me, she crushed us each one by the deed,
And sometimes to speak does relieve me, for now my old heart seems to bleed.
We saw her no more for a year, when she wandered back homewards to die,
With a sweet little baby so dear, she gave us, and whispered, "Good-bye."

It was something that all had expected, but it broke our old parents down,
To hear how she'd been neglected, by the scamp who allured her to town ;
He robbed her of honour and virtue, then left her to starve in the street,
And as sure as there's justice in Heaven, some day he that justice will meet.

Poor darling ! I hope she's forgiven, for although 'twas a terrible sin,
Her beauty was worthy of heaven, could she get admittance therein,
She died for her sin like a martyr, heartbroken, repentant, and young,
A victim to frailty and folly, misleading, degrading, and wrong.

Before many months had passed over, from that very sorrowful day,
We buried both father and mother, near Alice, beneath the cold clay,
Her baby, that nothing would nourish, just wasted in spite of all care,
Whilst nothing we had seemed to flourish, but trouble grew harder to bear.

So, sir, you will know what we suffered, all through a gay libertine's whim,
Who only, when told of what happened, looked on with indifference grim ;
He knew that his wealth and position secured him from personal harm,
And, reckless of future condition, he scoffed to behold our alarm.

Then quickly we left the old homestead, to fight in the battle of life,
And since then I have been in far countries, and joined in adventurous strife,
But though I am now old and feeble, and my journeying reaches its close,
My memory clings to sweet Alice, and the place where my loved ones repose.

So now is my sad story ended, but in leaving you just let me say,
Such a time I had never intended, upon this occasion to stay.
I thought a great deal of my sister, and if maybe you have one yourself,
Remember the fate of young Alice, and protect her from even herself.

Dabbling.

Next to sneaking hypocrisy there is nothing so despicable as "dabbling." The man or woman who habitually turns up to everyone's inconvenience, who meddles with other people's affairs, and who constantly ventures opinions unasked, are at best only mean, useless, and contemptible creatures. A trickster or a gossip should always be avoided, for they only make merry when other folks are sad. Love of mischief—their sole virtue—is to honesty the greatest vice ; the same people, after tendering their solicitude with a dying man, would actually execute a dance o'er his tomb. Dabblers in trade, dabblers in law, dabblers in religion or in politics all men should shun ; and, whenever troublesome, put their foot upon and expose them. Dabblers exist everywhere, and, insidious as they are, Society is corrupted and pestered with them. Be wary of them, whether in friendship's garb or sheep's clothing ! Resent always officious solicitude ! In public, on the stage, on the street, or in your home give them their just deserts and no favour. A dabbler is a braggart, a braggart is a coward, a coward is a cheat, a cheat is a knave, and knaves are scoundrels. Be just and firm, and dabblers cannot harm you. Merit never dabbles, and dabblers never merit—only the disgrace that eventually finds them. Heroes are not dabblers, and dabblers never make heroes. Look to it, then ! for all backbiters, cowards, gossips, and knaves are despicable dabblers.

A Daily Prayer.

Thou who knowest all our failings
And the inmost of each heart,
Guard us, Lord, in all our dealings,
That we ne'er from thee depart.

Make our thoughts and acts more holy,
Lead us to Thy heavenly throne,
Teach us to be meek and lowly,
And accept us for Thy own.

Help us to withstand temptation,
Cheer us with Thy gracious love,
Grant us, Lord, Thy true salvation,
Fit us for a home above.

God of Mercy ! God of Justice !
Deign Thy servant's cry to hear !
God of Love, and God of Goodness !
Listen to a sinner's prayer. Amen.

Gleeson's Luck.

In a quiet, respectable street
Stood a house which was marked No. 4,
In the track of the constable's beat,
With a knocker attached to the door.

There the occupants, seven in all,
Who had once been esteemed well-to-do,
Reconciled unto poverty's thrall,
Resided with comforts but few.

Surrounded with plenty and pride,
They might have been strangers around,
Since all of their neighbours denied
Acquaintance, with hauteur profound.

Yet open, and honest, and brave,
  Was each one within Number Four ;
And rather than favour to crave,
  Each one would have perished before.

Mr. Gleesom the father was called—
  A fine-looking man of two score—
By hardship he ne'er was appalled,
  Though poverty he would deplore.

A city man—once he had friends,
  Who stayed while his fortune ran high—
For riches a false glamour lends
  To the selfish and indolent eye.

'Twas then he could well entertain
  His friends and acquaintance at will,
For he, be it said, had a brain
  Attractive to good men and ill.

But an evil day came all too soon,
  And stripped him of all that he had,
Till drudgery turned to a boon
  For which he was thankful and glad.

With his family long he had tried
  Full bravely to hold up his head,
But often they had to decide
  To go barely clad to get bread.

Yet year after year they contrived
  Amidst carking care to exist,
Till the much dreaded climax arrived
  When this simplest diet was missed.

The younger ones struggled in vain
  To help in the making ends meet,
But children sometimes prove a pain
  And tend to make anguish complete.

Untrained and untutored in trade,
  No match for their fellows were they,
Although honest efforts each made
  To earn a few coppers some way.

Pretty Mary and Algernon tried—
  As always good children will do—
To aid them and comfort, beside
  Denying necessities too.

But cupboard and shelving were bare,
  And the fire had died in the grate;
Not a crust or a morsel was there
  To save them from hungering fate.

The mother tried hard to caress
  And quiet her youngest in arms,
Imploring the good God to bless
  And shield them from direst alarms.

The father sat still with bowed head,
  And tears trickled down his sad face,
For if ever the heart of man bled,
  'Twas Gleesom's just then with disgrace.

Their sobs and the ticks of the clock
Were the sounds that could only be heard,
When a sudden unusual knock
Impelled them to note what occurred.

'Twas the postman's "rat-tat" at the door;
"For Gleesom's—a letter!" he said ;
And the father received it before
He had scarcely erected his head.

Then he started to read, and he saw
That an uncle had made him his heir,
Whilst the writer—*a limb of the law*—
Desired his commands then and there.

And a cheque—a remittance—fell out,
Which Algernon caught as he stood ;
Whilst Gleesom walked strangely about,
Exclaiming : "*My uncle ! my God !*"

And the wife and the elder ones next
Got the letter, and read it in turn ;
So startlingly sudden a text
With gratitude caused them to burn.

Then the parents and children all,
The very first thing that they did,
Was down on their knees each to fall
Unto Him from whom nothing is hid.

And there, as they solemnly knelt,
Delivered from longing and strife,
They prayed Him in language heartfelt
To grant them His guidance through life.

And thus did their care pass away,
And Gleesom's have riches again ;
Good Samaritans all, from that day
They lived well-beloved of men.

The Cat and the Mouse.

A cat, once in a house,
Caught a very little mouse,
As it crept from behind an open door ;
Then began with it to play,
Till it slyly slipped away,
And bolted through a crevice in the floor.

"Ah, ah !" then said the cat,
"I must take a hint from that,
"For I can't afford to throw a chance away ;
"I must change my way about,
"Or be bound to go without
"The comforts I require every day."

So reader, in your turn,
A lesson you may learn :
To let no opportunity pass by,
But engage them as they come,
And deny them not, like some,
Who through neglect at last neglected die

My Old Friend James.

Of the many I have met, whom I never can forget,
There is one my grateful memory proclaims
As a very friend in need—in his thought, and speech, and deed—
And I gladly Hail—my old friend James

No sanctimonious knave, so impiously to rave,
Is he whom now my admiration claims,
Yet it should be understood—an undoubted "child of God"
Do I love to deem—my old friend James.

He owns no large estate, and is neither rich nor great,
Possessed withal of truly modest aims ;
He loves a comely dame—and contentment, just the same,
A philosopher is—my old friend James.

He enjoys the doing good—as a honest nature should—
Though such as he the niggard ever blames ;
Yet is he valued more, and is truer than before,
For a gentleman is—my old friend James.

He could never yet succeed, nor he ever will, indeed,
For he practises no underhanded games ;
Yet, he struggles "like a Turk," and unceasingly does work
Alack-a-day—my old friend James.

He is good at repartee, and a "*point*" can deftly see—
Most learnedly in discourse he exclaims :
He can picture like a book, and will read you with a look –
So peculiar is—my old friend James.

Then here's unto my friend, may he have a peaceful end,
Untroubled by the glare of tort'ring flames :
May his manhood bear him well, and his record ever tell
To the credit of—my old friend James.

Poesy and Art.

One morning, as over the world's barren waste,
  Two Sisters went slowly along,
The one exercised her harmonious Taste —
  The other burst forth into Song ;
Both the high and the low were enchanted full soon
  And under their influence fell,
Till none but the lost ones could fail to attune
  With charms beyond man to excel.

Oh, hard is the heart ! unresponsive and cold,
  Denying the beauty and grace
Of either the Sisters, whose worth is untold,
  In giving true riches a place ;
For the acme of grandeur, refinement, and worth
  Alone by their aid is pourtrayed,
And all the routine and the foibles of earth,
  In comparison, sink in the shade.

So let us endeavour these Sisters to woo,
    In charity, honour, and truth,
Regardless of what any scoffer may do,
    Or fashion may threaten, forsooth ;
We are proud of the past, and will welcome the day
    When man, recognising his part,
With dual devotion can feelingly say :
    "All hail, unto Poesy and Art !"

For One Night Only.

To the reader of dramatic and musical tastes, whose acquaintance with professionalism is above the average, there will doubtless appear, in connection with this heading, a stereotyped brusqueness which is quite as familiar as in this instance it is misleading. I have nothing to recite of Thespian reminiscences or of footlight surprises—my theme is altogether unconnected with the achievments of lovely debutantes or successful prima donnas—and it is, in truth of so opposite a character that I doubt if, after all, I shall be forgiven for the liberty I have taken in thus arresting attention. Descending, however, from this lofty pedestal, I must crave your indulgence whilst I briefly but faithfully become introduced to your notice. I need not disclose every particular of my past life and experiences ; it will suffice to state that I am not yet forty, and that I hail from within a couple of hours' ride of Manchester. When I refer to my home I imply the neighbourhood of my late abode, for, as the appended remarks will show, my homestead is a memory, and my home is *non est*. Had it been otherwise, these remarks would never have appeared, and I should have been a happier man ; for they faithfully represent an actual occurrence, and are true in every detail. Therefore it is that I wish you to pay particular attention to the narrative, for the profits of life are divided so finely that none can tell what their share may be. As you may have observed that a child without toys is lonesome, so adult life without corresponding joys is a misery; and it is correct to say that no joy so corresponds with adult life as the joys attending the married state ; and I am a married man, and a father to boot ; so you will understand that whatever may now appear, and however irascible you deem me, having once possessed a home and family, I *have* been a contented and happy man. It is the remembrance of such happiness, indeed, that imparts to my present state and surroundings an appearance they perhaps would not otherwise have possessed, for at this present moment I am utterly disconsolate. It matters very little how I managed to lose my home, or that I only lost it yesterday—sufficient for now is the evil thereof—but it does matter very much that within the space of twenty-four hours, a man with his wife and child, should be driven out into the world, houseless, friendless, and penniless. Yet such is the fact ; and whether it matters or not, or whether we like it or not, we have to endure it as best we can. And so, as there was no help for it, we had to turn out at very short notice, and with a very small bundle of clothing—saved from the wreck—which we were *allowed* to take with us, we faced the alternative. I do not think it could honestly be laid to my charge that I ever was a hard or illnatured man, or that my poor wife ever denied charity to a deserving case ; but I do know that never did any beggar feel more bitterly neglected than I did then. Respectable acquaintances we avoided, and as some occult witchery seems to enlighten the understandings of our more influential and also prosperous friends of our impecuniosity whenever we are unluckily thus afflicted, none such as these were encountered ; and we had recourse to that very common but no less praiseworthy expedient amongst the poor, of "*raising the wind,*" by "*pledging*" the slenderstock of apparel that we fortunately had allowed to us. Shelter we were compelled to have, and in desperation we hurried into a back street and very quickly bargained for it. I had hopes of being enabled on the morrow to surmount the chief difficulties of our position, or I should not so unthinkingly have run into the place I did. The two rooms I had bargained for, when at last I was shown into them (which was not until I had innocently paid in advance), resembled nothing so much as a dilapidated outhouse below and an old ruined barn-loft above. If ever there was a curiosity in connection with architecture and design, that place was one, I am assured ; and, barring the severity of our condition, there could not possibly have been a more motley or ludicrous offering for risible contemplation. No sooner had the "*landlady*" departed into her own domain than we commenced to stare in bewilderment, first at each other, and lastly around the premises. As badly situated as we were, and although the tears were scarcely departed from my dear wife's visage, yet it was next to impossible to repress a smile at our surroundings. There could not have been less than fourteen varieties of wall-paper adorning (!) the walls below, and some of the patterns were extremely gaudy and highly-coloured, whilst others were dull, dark, and greasy ; not to mention the variations in design, which were opposite as almost could be. The pictures on the walls, which were really cuttings from very old illustrated papers, and framed in most bulky fashion, had a thick coating of dirt each ; so that what with the frames being covered with tissue paper, or what had once been so before the change took place, and the glass being besmeared abundantly with more than one dirty deposit, they were fit objects for destruction. The flooring was uneven, and in many places broken up ; two corners were thoroughly dripping from a cesspool just outside in the yard corner, which slowly but surely oozed onwards, into, and through the walls right inside the house, and ultimately disappeared through the interstices of broken flags. Two ricketty chairs, a three-legged stool, a broken table, and a wretched cupboard, with its criminal assortment of crockery ware, together with a rusty old fender and a spacious ashes receptacle, in which the poker lay half hidden, constituted the full complement of furniture at our disposal. Not that we were the only occupants of the premises, either; for, before the lapse of many minutes, we were most disagreeably startled and disgusted to observe the bold but none the less measured progress of three or four cockroaches and a cricket across the hearthstone. With these we commenced reprisals, and for fully the space of two hours we were frequently engaged in the work of extermination; for no sooner did one lot get massacred than several others seemed ready and willing to appear on the scene. The smile, which at first tarried upon our lips, very quickly gave place to an opposite expression, and for my own part, I felt in a very melancholy condition. As for my wife and child, I could not appease them, try as I might, and verily to attempt thus to do seemed like adding insult to injury ; so I refrained, and to put an end to our discomfort, proposed retiring to sleep ; thinking also thereby to benefit for the morrow. The demon of mischief must surely have prompted me to such a course, for if the below stairs was wretchedly furnished, the bedroom was if possible more so; and we quickly decided not to undress ourselves. Fortunately, being provided with a piece of candle, which was stuck into the neck of an ancient beer bottle, we were enabled for a time to watch by its twinkling aid the various accessories of our dormitory. Were I to describe each one in detail I am sadly afraid that my word would be doubted, for of a surety it was never—previously, nor since—my lot to meet so rickety and horrible a state of things. Words would fail in describing the utterly lost and poverty-stricken condition of the whole interior, for it literally swarmed with filth and vermin. The walls, which had once gone through the process of "blueing," but which were now highly variegated in colour (owing to the high death-rate of the bug tribe, whose gore and mangled carcases were so plainly *en evidence*), were crumbling away with age and dampness. Three or four large butcher's hooks which were suspended across the ceiling, and across which cords were strung, hinted hideously at the convenience of self-murder, and to my fevered imagination, as it were, awaited grimly my acceptation. Mice and other vermin scampered in and out of the hollow walls, almost careless of our presence ; whilst bed-flies and house-flies held undisturbed holiday. I had as many coppers left me as would purchase candle-light until morning, so I thankfully hurried outside to a corner store for the boon, determined if possible never to close my eyes in sleep upon the premises. With my family that was impossible, for what with fretting and crying, and nervous exhaustion, neither the child nor his mother could keep awake ; so resigning myself to the inevitable, for one night, at all events, I persuaded them to lie down on the bed-covering, whilst I seated myself on the bedstead rail. To make matters worse than they were, it was terribly close and stifling, and although the window of the room was half open, yet breathing was a matter of much difficulty; and I felt half choked. Poverty is dreary enough of itself, in all conscience, but when saddled with every horrid accompaniment of pestilence and misery, then indeed is it a grievous burden. Of all the nights that ever I spent disconsolate in my life, never before was this night equalled. Well might the Poet sing in praise of balmy sleep ; for long before dawn I felt thoroughly undone with my weary vigil and its attendant evils, and a prospect of rest seemed the embodiment of perfect bliss to my tortured mind. What with my endeavours to keep the sleepers unmolested : my huntings after the biting disturbers of their peace ; my clumsy efforts to keep a steady light burning ; my adventures with a few of the boldest mice, who were audacious enough to leap occasionally upon the bed ; and my weary eyes and heart ; my lot was indeed a truly wretched one. I must at last have succumbed unto circumstances ; for being somewhat startled at the sudden noise made by some passing carts through the streets, I lost my balance and fell head over heels on to the room floor. This was the last point of my endurance, for daylight having arrived, we arranged our clothes and general appearance as best we could under the circumstances, and hurriedly quitted the premises ; determined never again to trust our health and persons to the vagrant mercies of a_ *back street lodging house.* And, God willing, I never shall ; and in conclusion I trust that no reader, gentle or simple, will fail in extending their kindliest sympathy to any belated person whose experience brings them at any time within such a shelter, if even " for one night only."

A Kiss.

What rapture in a lover's kiss,
What concentrated store of bliss,
What happiness, what passion keen,
What love, what joy, a kiss can mean.
A soul to soul, a heart to heart,
What fulness doth a kiss impart ;
A signature of homely birth,
A bond of truest friendship's worth ;
A taste of nature's native bliss,
And purest ransom—is a kiss.

A seal of love, a compact sign,
An emblem of a troth divine,
An union meet, an issue won,
A token sweet and dual boon.
The kiss of innocence and faith
A world of restful comfort hath ;
The kiss of fond possession means
A harbinger of blissful scenes ;
A kiss at worst expresses most
Achievement better won or lost.

A kiss can grant a lease of life,
A kiss presents a truce to strife,
A kiss can bind a wayward soul,
A kiss can travel pole to pole ;
A kiss of love or kiss of joy,
A kiss of pride without alloy,
A kiss of welcome well bestowed,
A kiss of God speed on our road,
A kiss of pleasure, how'er given,
Yields a spicy balm of Heaven.

The Ways of Peace.

How well it is to see the ways of peace,
  And view the sweets of innocence and joy,
To gain from anxious care a brief release,
  And taste the boon of rest without alloy.

To see the people toiling in content,
  And join their homely pleasures day by day,
To cultivate such cheerful sentiment
  Unfettered by ambition's restless sway.

To help the poor and needy in their lot,
  To soothe the sick and comfort the oppress'd,
To rescue those the world may have forgot,
  And yield the wretched wanderer a rest.

To train the rude and ill conditioned mind,
  To foster and encourage learning's boon,
To profit by example to mankind,
  And teach the world with Nature to attune.

How happy then to witness this indeed,
  And mingle with such usefulness and love ;
How better still in sowing such good seed,
  And labouring the harvest to improve.

Then "onward" let your watchword ever be,
  Ye peaceful workers whereso'er you roam,
A Heaven here on earth ye cannot see,
  But Heaven at the last will be your home.

To a Bird in Summer.

Chirp on, sweet bird, and let thy lay
  Bespeak thy joyful plight :
Sing on, and gladly hail the day
  That brings thee life and light.
Let every note be full of praise,
  And every trill be glad :
Sing on, and revel in thy ways,
  And nevermore be sad.

Sing on, and let the joyous song
  Thy timid nature cheer ;
Sing on, and in thy strength be strong,
  A stranger unto fear ;
Let every blade and every bough
  Sufficient harvest prove ;
Sing on, and let the Maker know
  Thy gratitude and love.

Chirp on, and may the sunshine be
  A pleasure to thy need ;
Sing on, and prove thy loyalty
  For mercy small indeed.
Sing on, and let all human-kind
  Such lessons from thee take ;
In everything some good to find,
  For God the Giver's sake.

"Crookie Bland."

Come, listen all, both great and small, whoever you may be,
And I will tell a story of a man of low degree ;
He was not rich nor famous quite, as you may understand,
But a simple individual we knew as "Crookie Bland."

Now, this was not his "Christian" name, though many folks forgot,
But "Crookie," ever humble, thought a nickname mattered not ;
He only was of ugly build, a strangely shapen elf,
So people called him "Crookie," and he answered it himself.

The creature never had a home to call his own in life,
And bare existence proved to be an ever constant strife ;
He sheltered in a lodging-house, well noted in the town,
And earned his scanty livelihood by job work up and down.

Sometimes he earned a shilling, and again he might earn more,
Sometimes he could not earn at all, and so was very poor,
But whether he had work or no, he never used to growl,
And never was induced to steal, or covetously prowl.

It is the truth that I relate about poor "Crookie Bland,"
His nature was as upright as the noblest in the land ;
So long as he could earn a crust, or yet a trifle spare,
Some other poor "unfortunate" was welcome to a share.

His clothes were like himself—as strange—and never nicely fit,
He had to wear what he could get. and get them bit by bit,
Sometimes, indeed, he loooked a "guy," a most peculiar sight,
Which caused the thoughtless urchins to exclaim with wild delight.

Now, "Crookie" was but human, and no relish had for scoff,
He knew his imperfections well, but could not shake them off ;
He knew that his was not the blame for ugliness of form,
And grieved to be molested by the ragamuffin swarm.

However, he contrived his best to get along each day,
And season followed season, until years rolled away ;
His hardships and his failings he endured as he could,
Although his lot, when happiest, was anything but good.

He had his friends, as who has not, whoever they may be ?
But his especial favourite was little Nellie Lee ;
Her father and her mother both lay in a parish grave,
And so the rugged "lodgerhood" a willing succour gave.

She really was a lovely child, just bord'ring six years old,
And prattled on through every day delightful to behold ;
The roughest men and women there would listen with delight,
For all beloved the little one, who rendered life more bright.

A trifle here and a trifle there—all round they did their best—
Maintaining little Nellie, now her parents were at rest ;
Her lovely eyes and witching face, and busy prattling tongue,
Withheld the mad behaviour of that rudely sorry throng.

And Nellie dear would love them all -as little children do,
And yet, their special favourites, have little children, too,
And Nellie's ripe affections were, as all could plainly see,
Accorded to poor "Crookie," all unstintingly and free.

And, O ! what happiness it raised within that rugged form,
To feel a love that kept his heart, unfrozen too, and warm ;
He struggled through his bitter lot as only heroes can,
And outwardly though like a beast, within him lived a *man*.

An apple or an orange, or a cunning little toy,
Ofttimes bespoke the fullness that poor "Crookie " did enjoy ;
A merry little pastime, or a very pleasant chat,
Were preludes unto Heaven that no other work begat.

Poor "Crookie !" though his worth was small, his wealth of love was great,
And hour after hour he would list to Nellie's prate ;
If ever in a pet and cross, or if she was unwell,
It was only unto "Crookie" that her troubles she would tell.

And so the days, and weeks, and months, took wings and flew away,
Whilst Nellie unto "Crookie " was the lodestar of his way ;
Just like a child the man became, when seated by her side,
Contented to remain her slave, and wait on her with pride.

That " beggars can't be choosers," is a saying trite and true ;
Discomforts of a many kinds they bear with spirit too ;
Too often, now, to be forlorn, is counted as a crime,
And Justice is discounted, to keep headway with the time.

Upon a rough-and-tumble bed, upon the attic floor,
Young Nellie with the children lay, the poorest of the poor ;
Whilst "Crookie " had a space within the second floor backroom.
And often thought himself in luck, such quarters to assume.

    *   *   *   *   *   *

'Twas on a night in winter, when the household were asleep,
And every inmate also was enwrapped in slumber deep,
Poor " Crookie " was awakened by a suffocating smell,
Whilst blinding smoke that filled the room a horrid tale did tell.

An instant more, and only one, ere "Crookie " up did start,
And "Fire ! Fire !" loudly roared, with all his voice and heart ;
One instant more, and then he forced his way unto the door,
And shouted, " Fire !" once again, more loudly than before.

In less than half-a-minute then the house did ring with cries,
As falling sparks and angry flames did greet the slumberers' eyes ;
The oldest and the youngest there were filled with wild affright,
As nakedly they rushed without, that bitter winter's night.

The fire-engine quickly came, on Mercy's errand bent,
And through the hose full quickly then the cooling stream was sent ;
Room after room the gallant men—disciplined, cool, and brave—
Explored 'mid dangerous flame and smoke, some lingerer to save.

Among the falling timbers, and amidst the smoky gloom,
Brave " Crookie " did himself engage in rushing to each room ;
Here and there, and everywhere, his crooked form was seen
Assisting old and young to flee in safety from the scene.

And soon, indeed, the news went round that every one was safe—
Each strong-limbed man and woman, and each harried little waif—
When suddenly the cry arose, " Was Nellie safe and sound ?"
But, to the horror of them all, the child could not be found.

Then, like an arrow from a bow, and with an awful sigh,
The hunchback leaped upon the stairs to rescue her or die ;
With solemn earnestness he prayed, in deep distress of mind,
"May God direct my footsteps till the little one I find."

His hair was burned, his face was scorched, but onward yet he strode,
Risking life at every step where fiercest danger glowed.
He gained the door at length, and groped, amid the stifling fume,
Then, seizing on her senseless form, he struggled from the room.

The angry flames leapt round the pair as if to burn them down,
But still the hero staggered on with neither faint nor frown ;
His strength had well nigh left him, when, with one exertion more,
He crawled beneath the window where the water in did pour.

Thank God ! a fireman saw them then, and quickly grasped the girl,
For at that fatal moment, "Crookie's" form was seen to whirl :
The floor fell through—and he went too—an instant only late,
And thus was lost a Hero who deserved a better fate.

Poor "Crookie !" ugly and deformed, possessed a manly heart ;
The lordliest of Britain's sons could play no nobler part.
True chivalry a champion lost that spiritland did gain,
When he for love laid down a life that bore no shameful stain.

In vain we look for heroes in a set and chosen place ;
In vain examine rank and wealth, or quality and race ;
They rise promiscuously round the surface of the land,
And never win regard until, they end like "Crookie Bland."

Who can tell ?

Who can tell what load of sorrow
Daily fills each bed of pain,
Where a victim for the morrow
Watches hopefully in vain ?

Who but these can tell the story,
Fraught with suffering, care and grief ;
Young and tender, old and hoary,
Sadly longing for relief !

Helplessly each vigil keeping,
Stung with gnawing pain and woe ;
Fitful slumbers, sighs and weeping,
Only such can ever know.

Trusting, maybe, that a brighter
Dawning be for them in store ;
So the burden may be lighter,
And the dread suspense be o'er.

Who indeed can guage the feeling
Rife within each troubled breast ;
Manifold of thoughts revealing,
Still at war or calm at rest !

Let us not unkindly judge them,
Rather let us render aid ;
Never favour once begrudge them,
So their lot be better made.

Proud mankind may vaunt religion,
    As the safeguard to the soul ;
But, alas ! 'tis often sickness
    Paves the way into the goal.

Broken, bruised, and weary hearted,
    See the sufferer lie enchained ;
Strength and pleasure all departed,
    All the world's resources drained.

How embittered then the anguish,
    Like misfortunes to endure ;
How could any help but languish
    With such helplessness in store.

Prate no more of vain enchanters,
    Biblical or classic lore ;
Pain and crime are master ranters,
    Which disturb the conscience more.

Dread remorse and meek repentance,
    Point the pathway to the fold ;
Passion's slaves discard rebellion,
    Once the beacon they behold.

Well sometimes it is to suffer,
    If it check a wayward mind ;
But the man's an arrant duffer,
    Who would wilfully be blind.

Why should any wretched mortal,
    Strive against the Supreme will,
Whilst a blessed heavenly portal,
    Proffers balm for every ill.

Turn again, ye heavy laden,
    Start anew and lose no time ;
Comely youth and beauteous maiden,
    Celebrate true manhood's prime,

Let us yield the sick ones succour
    Whilst our health be unimpaired,
And with true devotion utter
    Pleas that each to God be spared.

Love, Rank, and Riches.

There are three simple words which are known unto all,
    Love, rank, and riches ;
And yet how important in truth may we call,
    Love, rank, and riches.
There lives not a man in the world's wide domain,
But of one or the other must ever retain,
Some keen recollection, come joy or come pain,
    Oh, love, rank, and riches.

Three simple words, big with meaning and weight,
    Love, rank, and riches ;
Swaying the Universe early and late,
    Love, rank, and riches,
What though it be either one of the three,
The others full soon in attendance will be,
And rivalry royal betwixt them we see,
    Oh, love, rank, and riches.

Beggars, forsooth, may be swelling with Love,
    Sans rank and riches ;
Noblemen, t o, may dejectedly prove
    Sans love and riches.
The wealthy *parvenu* so vulgarly low,
In seeking alliance, perforce has to go
And forfeit all Love to ennoble his show ;
    Oh, love, rank, and riches.

Which is the mightiest one of the three,
    Love, rank, or riches !
Of weightiest import which shall it be,
    Love, rank, or riches !
Enough and to spare is true Riches indeed,
And Rank cannot soar beyond Honesty's creed,
But to Love and be Loved is a laudable need ;
    Oh, love, rank, and riches.

Cold is the heart that is hardened 'gainst Love,
    'Midst rank and riches :
Titles and wealth only emptiness prove
    Vain rank and riches ;
Mankind would be wiser and better by far,
Did riches and rank never happiness mar ;
But love and its rivals are ever at war,
    Oh, love, rank, and riches.

"A Reminiscence."

Watching by the cradle side
    Of our infant treasure,
Listening the while it tried
    Its breathings hard to measure.

How my heart went out to him,
    To see him rack'd with pain,
Words would only picture dim,
    Description is in vain.

I loved him with so deep a love
    To rest him I'd have died,
And yet such selfishness did prove
    A foil to all my pride.

So helpless and so frail withal
    It seemed a bitter fate
That he, my precious boy, my all,
    Should lie in such a state,

The dearest thing on earth to me
Was he, my darling joy,
And oh, it was so hard to see
My helpless baby boy.

The tortured limbs and fevered brow,
With anguish rent my heart,
Too well I worshipped him I know
Nor thought I e'er to part.

But when the time so dread had past
And hope from me was riven,
I found it better at the last
For baby rests in heaven.

Eclipsed.

He was stylishly clad you could see, and resembled a man well to do, his demeanour was easy and free, and his eyes glistened fearlessly true ; he seemed to lack nothing at all of the comforts and pleasures of life, his form was commanding and tall, and his features betokened no strife. His quite elegant whiskers and dress, bespoke a peculiar style, and none could have fancied him less than favoured with fortunate smile ; his linen, too, quite *comme il faut*, immaculate, clear, and profuse, outvied, with some jewels to show, a model for masherdom's use. As he sauntered along through the street, a magnet for envious eyes, both the lowly, the wealthy, and great, regarded him all with surprise ; a strut, or a stare, or a halt, betrayed each inquisitive mind, and mem'ries for once were at fault, his identity seeking to find. Some lordling, or rich millionaire, each knowing one thought he would be, for who with him else could compare, or bear such a carriage as he. Thuswise they discussed as they passed, and the stranger strode grandly along, till the vulgar obstruction at last, enticed the police to the throng ; and the sergeant, a knowing old hand, full quickly the magnate espied, and hastening on did soon stand, very close to the gentleman's side ; just a moment he rested his eyes, upon features that paled to his view, and then to the rabble's surprise, he uttered one loud "*So it's you.*" He handcuffed his man in a trice, and smiled a peculiar smile, then gripped on his arm like a vice, retracing his footsteps the while, and somehow the mob got to know that the fellow was not a grandee, but a criminal vicious and low, and few were so daring as he. Then arrayed in his grand superfine, the magistrate's sentence he heard, never more in such plumage to shine, but uttered he never a word ; like a star he had burst into view, but as suddenly vanished away, without even one brief adieu, unto those who beheld him that day.

Hope.

What cheering magic in the word,
The blessed thing called Hope,
Exhorting mortals to attain
A welcome goal of joyful gain,
Indeed, it is a bliss ;
A bliss to sooth a drooping heart ;
A bliss that sweetens sorrow's part,
A precious boon is this.

A beacon of the dawning light,
    A treasure in the dark,
The one thing needful in the storm,
A shield that baffles all alarm,
    What shall compare with Hope?
Hope will steer us through the fray,
Hope will help to win the day,
    Cling to blessed Hope !

What matters though in direful need,—
    And troubles fill the air ?
Live on, plod on, the tide will turn,
Joy will come to those that mourn,
    And sadness find relief ;
Relief with double strength and grace ;
Relief that time will ne'er efface ;
    Hope on through every grief.

Hope is a lamp, a light, and friend,
    That saves us from despair ;
The faith of innocence and love,
A cheering sunbeam from above.
    To pilot us ahead ;
A pilot true, when tempest toss'd ;
A pilot true, when all seems lost ;
    A quickener of the dead.

Alone with the Dead.

[Occasioned by a calamity which befel the author's wife, who was drowned accidentally within six weeks after their marriage, and in her twenty-fourth year.]

'Twas a cold winter's night, and my friends had departed,
    I sat quite alone in the darkness and gloom ;
I thought of my loss, and I felt heavy hearted
    To know that my loved one had met such a doom.
The joy of a lifetime had left me for ever,
    The hope from my heart had remorselessly fled ;
The dream of my youth I thought nothing would sever,
    But I sat there awakened—alone with the dead.

'Twas only a year since first I had met her,
    And but a few days since I made her my bride ;
Yet she was devoted, and I'll not forget her,
    For life was worth living with her by my side.
She lay cold and still, in her robes calmly sleeping—
    I wished, as I gazed, that I lay in her stead ;
But useless my wishing, or thinking, or weeping,
    I sat broken-hearted—alone with the dead.

Young though I was, yet it brought me a sorrow
    More lasting than all I have met with in life ;
And the joy of to-day is a burden to-morrow
    Perchance I remember my lost little wife.
She brought me no wealth, but her love was a treasure,
    A stake for which I would undaunted have bled ;
And though she is gone, yet in moments of leisure
    My fancy will paint me—alone with the dead.

Runawayisms.

Some people may perhaps think there are no such things as runawayisms, but there is; and if you wish to make their acquaintance, always run away from a temptation to do wrong ; run away from double dealing and hypocrisy. All such are solid and tangible *isms*—contemptible plagiarisms—that never made a man respected, or led a soul to heaven. If you cannot grasp in your minds the fairness of anything which comes within your notice after reasonable consideration, run away from it, have none of it ; for it is manifestly unsafe to tamper further. Always remember that nothing upon earth is so plain as honesty, and nothing so open as merit. The light of day—like the hand of time—exposes all things, and not every infernalism attending life or death can stand against it. The *isms* of life are stumbling blocks to a man's feet ; if man will only trust his Maker, let his conscience lead. There is an entity in the conscience apart from the mind, and where there be an inclination to wrong doing, the conscience rebels. Isms are born of diplomacy, and diplomacy lives by circumvention. From every *ism* of doubt or wrong, run away ; and then will conscience applaud you. A peaceful contentment surpasses all and under difficulties or with success uprightness wins the day.

Written to Order.

One afternoon on business bent, I hurried on my way,
Scheming how I best could earn some wages for the day ;
A wife and child were left at home, who awaited my return,
Whilst I, unskilled in any trade, knew not which way to turn.

At length into my muddled brain there entered an idea,
So quick to give it vent I strayed to a neighbouring area,
And in my distant mind I saw, dear reader, you must know,
A gleam of luck if I would try my Genius to show.

In Poet's haunts I'd ventured oft, and wandered many a time,
And sentiments in verse I'd penn'd, producing lots of rhyme ;
My soul was fired with glory, and elated was my pride,
And I fancied that for Poesy like a martyr I'd have died.

So, furnished with a sober mien, across the road I strayed,
And entered in a busy store where boots and shoes were made ;
The master asked my errand, which I scarcely could explain,
But when I did he laughed aloud—then looked and laughed again.

Then laughing still, he closer came, and gazed into my face,
I felt abashed and humbled, for it looked a hopeless case ;
But after he'd enjoyed his stare, said he, "young man, 'tis true,—
For I pretend to study heads, and see the '*bump*' in you."

Contented then I made myself, until he spoke again ;
"I understand Phrenology, but do not think me vain ;
It is strange indeed to hear a man discourse on such a text,
And whatever in the world," said he, "will people come to next."

Unto him then I did not dare to make a bold reply,
For appearances against me went, a fact I don't deny ;
Seedy-looking clothes I wore, with old boots on my feet,
And boldness then would never do if I with him would treat.

So quietly I answered that my errand I could do,
But he needed no such service, and I had no cause to rue,
For he chatted with me cheerily, on topics rich and rare,
Confessing full belief in what the Spiritualists declare.

A blank to me were subjects like to that he had in hand,
And, truth to tell, I must admit, I ne'er could understand
What interest there was in such, the people to excite,
But whilst I listened, he explained the case in better light.

"Spiritualists believe," said he, "that people never die ;
"That mother Earth does claim her own is what they don't deny ;
" But the living conscious entity can never waste away,
" For how can Immortality relapse into decay.

" We know that people still appear, fanatics claim as dead,
" Although the bodies may depart, their influence has not fled.
" We know that in another sphere, and in another frame
" Intelligence does prove that they are one and both the same.

" We reckon that the Bible is the best book in the world,
" The truest narrative of facts that ever was unfurled.
" Its histories and precepts both, prove our belief is true,
" And if you are not bigoted you must believe so too.

" We do not tell you this is true, but this is what we prove,
" So come, examine for yourself, as truth no one can move
" I'll meet you here on Sunday next, and come just as you are,
" For what thy hand can find to do, that do and always dare.

" We know that people preach us down, we know we've black sheep, too,
" We know that knaves and hypocrites, will any mischief do,
" But still we trust to common sense, for what is just and right,
" You'll find it no delusion if you come on Sunday night."

When he had finished speaking thus, I stood in mute amaze,
And still he stood to look at me with fervent, honest gaze,
Nothing I had heard before, and read in papers, too,
Had laid the case so clear and plain to my untutor'd view.

I told him so, and then he asked, if I would think it o'er,
Declaring if I did, that I would wish to study more,
But we left the subject there and then, and pleasantly did smile,
For I had not thought my precious time he would so well beguile.

So back unto my visit's cause, we started once again,
And thoughts of home and family, brought me a tinge of pain.
We talked the matter over, and I vow his words were true,
When he described my failings, and informed me what to do.

Said he, " I do not advertise just so as you suggest,
" But to further your endeavours, I will give to you a test,
" And the purport of this interview, between yourself and me,
" Write down in twenty verses and your banker I will be."

So I came away, and cannot say, I left with merry heart,
Although he'd aired his eloquence and repartee so smart ;
Yet are these lines a record of my willingness to try,—
To earn expenses for the time so spent 'twixt he and I.

And now I reach the twentieth verse, completing this my task ;
From every one that choose to read, some interest I ask,
I may not meet each person's views, and such I don't intend,
For I have written to order, and I hope to please my friend.

A Hymn of Praise.

Christians, all with one accord,
Join in praises to the Lord !
Sing with heart and voice to Him
Who is King and Lord supreme.

Laud His praises to the skies,
Let your Hallelujahs rise
Humbly to the Judge of all,
Plead His mercy ere you fall.

Sound the grateful, happy song,
Till it reach the Heavenly throng ;
Loud Hosannas all proclaim,
Sing with joy the Saviour's Name.

Praise Him all with joyful cry,
King of Heaven! God Most High !
While the echo sounds again,
Every heart respond "Amen."　Amen.

The Days Gone By.

I cannot check a sigh when I think of days gone by—
　Of my boyhood, when the future seemed so bright and fair ;
How I played with childish glee, from all anxiety free,
　And never knew aught of sadness or of worldly care.
Then all was joy and mirth, but like everything of earth,
　They could not last for ever thus, and quickly they did fly ;
And now, when I am alone, I often grieve and mourn
　The loss of the many joys I had in the days gone by.

Many sights since then I have seen, and in many places been—
　In search of pleasure I have rambled far and near —
But the pleasure that I find can never give peace of mind
　Like youthful joys that warm the heart and banish fear ;
And while I roam through life, amid its scenes of care and strife,
　No matter what befalls me, still I never shall deny
That of all the days I have seen not one to me has been
　So endearing as my boyhood's days, now long gone by.

On Freedom.

" Who cries Freedom ?" know ye not,
　There is no freedom 'neath the sun,
The calls of Duty are forgot,
　When freedom holds our duty done.
'Tis freedom only to progress,
　To prove by action and endeavour,
A people's claims deserve no less,
　Where duty regulates them ever.

"What is Duty?" can we say
Man has not an obligation
To redeem himself each day
By a code of preservation.
How can manhood live and thrive
In the midst of self-abasement,
Freedom's sons must ever strive
Unto Tyranny's erasement.

"What is Nature?" doth it mean
A sympathy of kindred forces,
Or, alas! as hath been seen,
An union by forceful process?
Away the thought of vengeful mien,
Which clashes with good human feeling,
True Nature at its best is seen
When gentle effort 'tis revealing.

Thus Nature, Duty, all indeed,
Within mankind of thought and action
Creates a truly noble creed—
The Liberty of satisfaction.
'Tis this which animates the soul,
And fires hearts albeit lowly
In martyr'd ranks their names to roll,
And perish in a cause so holy.

Resignation.

Safe with the holy Lord I place
My every hope and trust;
In Him my soul can surely trace
A righteous God and just.

Although temptations hem me round,
And troubles try me sore;
Yet is my faith in Him profound,
And shall be evermore.

'Tis meet that He should try His own,
And strengthen with His care;
For true foundations are unknown
Without recourse to prayer.

And if my soul should turn away
To more alluring scenes,—
It hastens but the evil day—
A wicked portion gleans.

The righteous man God loveth well,
For righteousness is He;
Uprightness He can truly tell,
And it pleaseth Him to see.

Then will I leave my care with Him
And trust in His good grace;
For feeble though I be, and dim,
Yet shall I see His face.

What does it matter?

What does it matter although you be poor,
If still of good health and your strength you are sure,
You toil and you live as an honest man should,
When some of your *betters* are not half so good.
Beware, and take care, that no evil thoughts mar,
Your comfort and prospects if lowly they are :
There are many who pass you in superfine clothes,
Would gladly exchange with your humble repose.

What does it matter, because and betimes—
Grim poverty seems just the blackest of crimes :
Though the sun reigns aloft and illumines the earth,
Yet a duty well done gives true happiness birth.
Contentment's a flower no money can buy,
The fruit of well doing which none can deny ;
So sing while ye may, and be true to your kind,
Then quickly you leave discontentment behind.

What does it matter to you or to me
Because there are others much richer than we,
Each one has a duty on earth to fulfil,
With wealth or without. or for good or for ill.
Do the best that you can, whether wealthy or poor,
For none can do better than that we are sure,
And though we may never with Fortune succeed,
The highest good fortune is ours indeed.

Chronicles of a Clan.

(A POLITICAL DISQUISITION.)

Attend to me, whoe'er you be, for just a little while,
And I will tell to please you well, in brief and homely style,
The story of a doleful band who wander through the town,
And by report are of the sort that mean to earn renown.

Now understand, this doleful band, in solemn conclave met,
Not once or twice, but more than thrice— the numbers I forget,
They met in " holes or corners " where each made his trouble known
Bold champions of a purpose which made selfishness its own.

By energy they did contrive to build themselves a cause,
And inwardly did swear to kill the blight that gave them pause ;
They were not ragged pariahs although they felt the ban
Of excommunication keen that blackballed every man.

The members had distended minds, well versed in surface lore,
Each thought himself a Solomon and higher could not soar ;
But sad to tell, with all their skill--the drawback of each life
Was this indeed, that caste decreed, an ignominious strife.

Now I like a man—who is a man—to have a good backbone,
To show his mettle by some deeds that make his virtue known ;
A man whose goodness proves his worth, whose merit gives him place,
For such an one is useful unto all the human race.

The policy of " *by hook or crook* " appeals to narrow minds,
It may attract the reckless ones, but upright people blinds,
And yet these celebrated men whose foibles I relate,
Resorted to such tactics in vain hopes to change their fate.

Diplomacy, perfidious art ! was not more cute than they,
They first secede, and thought to bleed attention by such way ;
O'er one thing and another then they agitated loud,
And formed a combination to attract the vulgar crowd.

So glaring did this action seem, it fairly took one's breath.
For a head without a tail is doomed full soon to certain death ;
But a very special friend they found to bear the brunt of all,
And find the needful, don't you see ? to trundle on the ball.

This master stroke of policy kept each one in full view,
And automatous speeches were reported through and through,
Themselves supplied the talking for it pleases little minds,
And one did move, and someone prove, a plaint of many kinds.

Alas ? indeed, for all their schemes, a failure was the game,
For people got disgusted at the mention of each name,
And the very special friend himself—a much respected man
Got a very costly bill to pay for joining such a clan.

No earthly use—however small—was gained by such a *coup*,
Sans honourable mention then they knew not what to do,
A base ingratitude did seem to hang about the town,
For many thought they had been sold, to buy the Clan renown.

The *Barrel Organ* next went wrong, if what they said was true,
The wonder is, it went so long, without rebellion too ;
They rated it and threatened it, then from it did depart,
And ever since, as people say, 't has turned with better heart.

Another question then arose, to which they did attend,
And fate, so cruel hitherto, again beseemed a friend ;
But all their boasted knowledge proved a blunder and a sham,
And showed crass ignorance to be synonymous with "damn."

And thus enraged with everything they sent abroad for aid,
Which not refused did rally them that they were not afraid,
They charged again in bold array, and this is truth I tell,
They got another routing and it made their passions swell.

Failures thick on every hand discredited them each hour,
A simple body could but think such fate would turn them sour,
But still once more in very truth they tried their hand again,
And pleaded hard for allies, both with specious words and pen.

Those allies sure, knew what was best, for both themselves and us
And heeded not the sorry tales the Clan did fuss and buzz,
They pander to self benefit and personal renown,
And never cause will prosper that they pilot in the town.

So people all, both great and small, take notice what I say,
Avoid this clique as best you can, and eye them well each day,
They speechify and write reports, that help their purpose on,
But seek of them a favour, and you'll find them giving none.

Give me a Slasher, far away before a whining cur,
At least we understand him, and what is to do he'll dare,
He is free from pettifogging, and we know he's blunt and true,
And hole and corner fancying will find him nought to do.

Then fellow men, look round you well, for members of this band,
Their troubles they must bear alone, pray let them understand,
They rant and rail and agitate, they twist and strut about,
But where they thrust their noses in, you dearly get them out.

On Friendship.

O, is it not exquisite joy to clasp a loving palm —
To mark the fervour in the eye, and taste of friendship's balm —
To note the cheering, kindly tone, and feel the welcome given—
To know a heart beats with your own—in unison of Heaven ?

What in the world can half compare with Friendship's happy lot ?
What can so well defy dull care, or make each care forgot ?
What boon of earth is half so cheap, and yet what boon so dear ?
What chasms will not friendship leap ? What heart will it not cheer ?

Be manly and let Friendship prove the true love of the soul,
For love is strong enough to move the world from pole to pole ;
Its influence goes everywhere, whilst Friendship jogs apace,
A foil to every darkling care, and helper in life's race.

Grant fully, then, this precious boon, and let its virtues spread ;
With virtue it doth well attune, or else is virtue dead ;
A friendly clasp or kind embrace—a simple word or kiss—
Possess a charm and honied grace, that renders sorrow bliss.

"The March of Genius."

[BEING A SUMMARY OF THE PROCEEDINGS AT AN EXTRAORDINARY MEETING OF THE

NOTORIOUS "SCRATCHBACK CLUB."]

The occasion of the 100th meeting of this assembly was an event in the annals of our town, for public interest had been excited by an announcement which had appeared in the *Weekly Scorcher*, the pet organ of the club, and read as follows :—

FIRST ANNUAL SOIREE and 100TH MEETING of the SCRATCHBACK CLUB. — SPECIAL ADDRESSES by NICODEMUS PODGE, F.O.G.Y., and LITTLE INFLATOUS, M.U.G. Subject :—"The March of Genius." Chair to be taken at 8 p.m.—A. BOUNCER, Secretary.

Such an important occasion could not be considered other than extraordinary in our neighbourhood, and as a natural consequence there was an unusual muster of members and their friends on the night in question, to the number of about three dozen souls. When it is remembered that each one present either was, or expected to be, an authority amongst his fellows, the dignity attending such a distinguished gathering may easily be surmised.

Punctually to the appointed time (within twenty-five minutes, during which certain and sundry refreshments of an alcoholic nature had been freely imbibed) the Chairman—who happened to be Mr. Inflatous—together with the orator announced for the occasion, ascended the rostrum, and immediately sat down. It was very evident that both gentlemen had exceeded the bounds of discretion, for they indulged in a playful familiarity which could not fail to be noticed. However, at exactly half-an-hour behind the time advertised, the Chairman called attention to business, and, after a rough ovation had been accorded him, he commenced as follows : —

"Brother Scratchbacks,—We are assembled on this special occasion to celebrate the 100th meeting of our society's being and progress -(hear, hear)—and also to listen to the inspiriting oratory of an illustrious member of our ranks. Although the subject chosen for to-night has hitherto baffled the understandings of the highest and most learned societies, I am proud to say that it will now receive, in this room, an exposition and unravelling that will at once and for all time render the modern name of 'Scratchback ' a blessed memory. (Great applause.) If you will pardon me for saying it, I would embrace this opportunity of suggesting that from this time henceforth our beloved institution be considered and styled the 'Premier gathering of noble minds that periodically assemble in this our town :' for it is undeniable that *we are*, in truth, gentlemen, the only real and local embodiment of true Genius. As you are well aware, we already number amongst us some wonderful lights of learning, in the shape of poets, novelists, scientists, &c. ; and it is true to say, that although the great world of literature have in their ignorance failed to recognise that fact, nay, more, have actually laughed at our efforts ; the grand time is coming on when the said world will be not only compelled to admit the same, but will be proud of the distinction of our alliance. (Cries of " Bravo," " Good lad," and applause.) It is true, indeed, that our poets are only *Spring* poets ; it is too true that our novelists are unappreciated ; and, gentlemen, between ourselves, it is beyond dispute that our scientists are in any but an advanced state. But that is no disgrace, gentlemen. I merely mention the fact in order to reveal in open assembly the correct nature of the rare resources at our disposal ; and, I say it proudly, my brothers, we never, never, under-rate our achievements. (Applauding cries of "Good old man," &c.) To-night, Brother Scratchbacks, the subject is ' Genius,' and as every one of you understand it perfectly—bearing its stamp on your brows, in fact—I need not ask the question : ' What is it ?' One thing I can vouch for boldly, and it is this : if there be any such thing at all as Genius in man's composition, assuredly its home is here. (Disturbance in the staircase caused by the replenishing of glasses, &c.) If I am to have order, I will proceed, but if not——(cry of " Here's luck," and applause, during which the rest of the sentence was lost). Well, gentlemen, I am not presumptuous enough to trespass further on your time—for I want my glass as well as you—but I strongly believe that if I had to deal with the subject under discussion this evening, I could do better justice to it than Mr. Podge ; but, as in order to maintain our dignity we must scratch each other's backs in a friendly style, I have great pleasure in giving him the job, and beg leave to join in your carousal." (Great applause and uproar, in the midst of which the renowned Mr. Podge grandiloquently rose to address the meeting.)

This gentleman, whose voice betrayed a certain huskiness, and whose gestures were remarkably dramatic, commenced by referring to the self-esteem of his friend, who had preceded him, as a special characteristic of a Scratchback, and expressing himself willing on that account to excuse his loquacity, he proceeded :—

"My Friends,—I am to-night placed in a proud position -a position which my qualifications merit—but a position, after all, which only true Genius can adequately fill. Having once had the distinguished honour of shaking hands with the worthy editor of our enlightened *Weekly*, and having also been invited to tea by that functionary's better half, I am fully confident that most of you will support me in the inference, that in honouring me this evening, you likewise honour yourselves. (Cries of " Question.") To-night I address you upon Genius, and I venture to ask each one present the startling question, ' What is it ?' Is it merit ? Is it learning ? Is it craft ? I say, emphatically : *No !* it is Genius, and Genius only. Then, what is Genius ? Is it a combination of art and wit, or is it in reality only another name for science ? I tell you, plainly, it is neither. Never shall it be said that this advanced assembly did not understand the term, when every " Man-Jack " of you is a Genius in himself. Genius is marching along, and nothing can prevent it. In the far away future, when each of us shall have passed away, who can tell, my brethren, what may or may not happen? Lifting the curtain of that distant period, I can clearly see that no name of that age exhibits such bold relief as the even now celebrated name of "Scratchback," and everywhere in that day are *we*—the pillars of this greatness—renowned for our Genius. Like an Indian on the warpath, Genius is marching on! Like an Arab crossing the desert, Genius is marching on! Like the earth revolving on its axis, Genius is marching on! What is Genius, I ask again? Is it wisdom? *No*. Is it pride? *No*. Is it conscience? *No*. Then, I say that it is something vastly different to what the world—not our world—esteem it. Should any man, not a member of this our Learned Brotherhood, ever aspire to it, we will attack him. Should any advanced stranger contribute to *our Weekly*, we will assault him in the rear. Should any man refuse homage to our light and leading, we will slander him. Should anyone criticise us unfavourably, we will destroy his peace and comfort, and smile at his discomfiture. In short, comrades, in one brief word I will admit it: a Genius is a Scratchback, and only Scratchbacks are *Geniuses*. (Loud applause, and disturbance occasioned by a couple of inebriated brothers having a friendly wrestle in a corner.) In conclusion, my Divinities, as I see that a few of you, through a series of potations, are developing a certain wildness of aspect, and as I know from experience what a clannish lot you are when aroused, I would state, if you will give order—(cries of "Shut up," &c.)—that for the honour of this assembly—(noisy interruption)—for the good of this house—("bosh")—for the character of the famous 'Scratchback Club,'—for appearance, and my health's sake—I will now retire and leave the premises."

Mr. Podge rapidly retires from the place, after a refresher at the bar; leaving the late Chairman hugging the table-legs most affectionately in a kneeling attitude, whilst the rest of the "*Geniuses*" are settling matters in a peculiarly rough fashion of their own.

At 11 p.m. arrives the landlord, who, knowing the wayward character of his friends, very kindly besprinkles them with cold water, whilst his "*thrower out*" proceeds muscularly and scientifically to clear the room.

And then indeed was seen, in a somewhat startling fashion, how truly erratic is the "MARCH OF GENIUS."

—— ——

A Good Old Song.

How well I love the singing,
   Of a really good old song:
With sweetest echoes ringing,
   Treasured memories among.
It fills my soul with gladness,
   And my pulses quicken fast,
Until its tuneful sadness,
   Leads me back into the past.
O happy is the sorrow by some goodness sanctified,
And bitter is the morrow of such happiness denied.

How truly mem'ry keeps us
   Always evergreen and young,
When hearts become enraptured,
   By the strains of some old song.
Recalling in one moment,
   Other days of long ago.
Our sympathies are chastened,
   · And with deeper vigour glow:
I love the tender feeling, ever masterful and strong,
Our nobler self-revealing, when we hear a good old song.

A good old song I like it
For the glimpse it yields so free
Of days now past for ever,
That are always dear to me.
It seems to lend a fragrance,
And an essence all divine,
Commingling with the mem'ries
Of the happy *auld lang syne.*
I would not miss such pleasure, though it may be fringed with pain,
And, whilst I have the leisure, let me listen once again.

Latter Wit.

It's a wonderful world that we live in, my lad, you'll find as you travel along,
One half of the people are gloomy and sad, who hardly get clear of wrong,
The other half seldom take heed of their lot, but pass them unthinkingly by,
And so, 'twixt the two, I declare unto you, 'tis as irksome to live as to die.

When I was a lad, and that's sometime ago, things were different then, by the mass !
We had all room to breathe very freely, you know, without interference with class,
There were not so many to keep then as now, and nine out of ten earned their share,
And each one to fate would contentedly bow, and harboured nor mischief nor care.

There wasn't such scheming and trying to cheat, as there is in the world now-a-days,
And folks were not useless as now, I repeat, and had less extravagant ways,
A working man then left to more moneyed men the business we term "Legislate,"
And so the world wagged, and in blessedness dragged, to its length undeterred by its
fate.

All around were green fields and most beautiful lanes, for exercise, frolic, and health,
There were comforts in store for the humble and poor, as well as for those who had
wealth ;
There was work to be had, and poor folks could be clad, without "*striking*" and
suffering long,
And none but the worst could become so accurs'd, that a life was a burdensome song.

But take notice now, what a hubbub and row, there exists 'twixt the rich and the poor
And only reflect what a curious creed, does equality teach, to be sure ;
The new-fangled schemes may be much in advance, of jog-along methods of old,
But, believe what I say, we're no better to-day, although more inventive and bold.

Just look what we drink ; an old body would think we surely don't know our own
minds,
For with milk and with tea, other mixtures we see, and not always the safest of kinds ;
Our food is the same, and whom are we to blame, the buyer, or dealer the most ?
'Tis a nice state of things that this modern life brings, if only we counted the cost.

Concerning Religion, too, look what a tribe of strange sections now can be found,
But in my younger days we united in praise without such dissension around.
There were Church folk and Papists, and Wesleyans then, with Ranters and Quaker
folks, too,
And, as old as I be, and from all that I see, full quite as much good did they do.

There were not such fashions as now in my youth ; there was more sense of modesty
    then,
And people behaved, I can say it with truth, like sensible women and men ;
The boys and the girls, just remember it, please, were kept under proper control,
And modernised " Masherdom " could not appease the weakness of one little soul.

We then had our sports for all seasons betimes, such as Maying and Carolling too,
The Peace-Egg, and Mumming, and Bonfire games, creating much hullabaloo,
We had annual Feasts and good Statute fairs, where sweethearting had its full bent,
And we fared none so bad, I can answer, my lad, had people remained in content.

To-day, 'pon my word, though it sounds so absurd, Life seems but a tiresome race,
And those who would last, to avoid getting pass'd, must accustom themselves to the
    pace.
'Tis a moil and a toil, and it makes my blood boil, to be hurried and worried like this.
And if nought will atone but departure, I own, there are times when departure seems
    bliss.

But yet after all, I can never recall, those days that are past long ago,
Though I oft feel it hard, that I cannot retard the march of events you must know,
Had I only foreseen, what has happened and been, I declare I would never have
    stayed,
But I'll stop whilst I can, that each woman and man, may see that I am not afraid.

A Brief, in Extenso.

O, who can tear aside the veil that shrouds the mortal mind,
Or render yet one brief detail or portraiture defined
Of what is known or what is felt of either sight or sound,
Or of anything that may indeed indulge a thought profound.

Ah, why indeed, should mortals seek to wield immortal power,
And pierce through the solemn state encircling death's sad hour,
It matters little what the views that tend a dying state,
So that the work of life portends a happy blissful fate.

Poor narrow minds, that christen Faith a weakness of the brain,
Because, forsooth, they will not stoop to grasp immortal gain ;
How true it is that all the might and force of logic's sway,
Supports the right of reason to yield faith its natal day.

The stubbornness of self-willed minds too truly may impede
The welfare and the progress of a simple life and creed,
Dissenting and disputing through a wretched fear of trust,
Will never sight the Beacon or the Refuge of the just.

What boots-it that a something seems to favour Unbelief,
It is not right we should presume to fathom and conceive ;
We feel, by force of reason, that our faith is good and grand,
And, therefore, can content ourselves, with things we understand.

The warrior and the statesman, with the sage and genius too,
Are but a portion of the host who prove the maxim true,
That light and reason animate whenever duty calls,
And faculty becomes supreme where even death befalls.

Then why refuse to exercise this sound and simple view,
Since every exigence of life proclaims it good and true,
To think that men who live and die, or stand or fall in turn,
Begrudge a full belief in this, compels my wrath to burn.

To a Dead Bride.

Short indeed has been thy journey,
　　Soon thy race of life is run,
Never did we dream, dear Mary,
　　Thou so early wouldst be gone.

When our cup of joy was brimming,
　　And our loves were strong and true,
Little heed we gave to dreaming
　　What the future might not do.

But, alas ! my heart's devotion,
　　Death has claimed thee for his own ;
Bitter grief remains my portion,
　　I must journey on alone.

Brief has been our part together,
　　Swiftly hath it sped away,
But its sweetness shall not wither,
　　Till of life my latest day.

Once again, my darling Mary,
　　We shall meet in realms beyond,
Joined in bonds of love eternally
　　Midst the heavenly hosts to stand.

Keen and bitter is this parting,
　　Bitter more than words can tell,
Keener still it is to murmur,
　　This—my loved one—this farewell !

This is the Land.

(PATRIOTIC SONG.)

This is the land our fathers trod,
For which they fought and died ;
They heeded not the despot's rod,
Nor danger yet denied,
Theirs was a great and noble cause,
No baseness could they brook ;
Their struggles were but freemen's wars,
To break the tyrants' yoke.

CHORUS.

Then raise the flag of Freedom !
Long may it wave unfurled !
The glory of Britannia,
And envy of the world.

True Britons yet of freedom boast,
They honour still the brave ;
And though array'd 'gainst many a host
They won't desert the slave.
To tyrants and oppressors still
Each true heart is a foe ;
They must submit to British will
Or quickly be laid low.—CHORUS.

Then rouse ye all of British blood,
From duty never fly ;
But try to do your country good,
And like true Britons die.
Then will the nations envy ye,
When strife away is hurled ;
And Britain's sovereign ever be
The monarch of the world.—CHORUS.

Visions of Home.

A SONG FOR SAILORS.

When sailing at night o'er the fathomless sea,
The fairest of pictures of home come to me,
In fancy I see the beloved ones there
And hear gentle voices for me breathe a prayer.
Softly, sweetly, soothingly come,
Welcome and beautiful, visions of home.

When Nature's exhausted and calmly I sleep,
Lull'd by the wild waves of the wonderful deep,
True blessings from heaven so bounteous come
In touchingly tender memories of home.
Softly, sweetly, soothingly come,
Welcome and beautiful, visions of home.

Though danger surrounds us, still I love the sea,
And whilst I've a choice, yet a sailor I'll be.
With a hope that wherever fate bids me to roam
I shall often be favoured with visions of home.
Softly, sweetly, soothingly come,
Welcome and beautiful, visions of home,

Checkmates.

Say what we will, there is nothing so unwelcome as checkmates. In whatever guise they appear, there is no denying the fact that none of us relish their intrusion, and yet, in many instances, how often we might, by the exercise of a little forethought, guard against them effectually. It is very hard to be checkmated at every turn, and yet we cannot improve our circumstances by repinings. To be checkmated in wrongdoing is commendable, even if it be unacceptable ; but checkmating honest endeavours is detrimental to both morality and position. In the battle of life, never tread upon the weak and lowly, for it often occurs that circumstances change the nature of things entirely, and everyone in a more or less degree is subservient thereto. Charity, when properly exercised, yields more pleasurable results than any other virtue ; and, blessed indeed, are the charitable. For your manhood's sake, have charity. Never check a noble aspiration ; never discourage a manly bearing. Be no willing hindrance to an earnest and striving effort. Check all greed and selfish tendencies, prevent every unfair attempt at down-treading, but never give a helping hand to check a deserving cause. This life of ours is weary enough for many poor souls as it is ; there are already sufficient evils without adding to them. The curse of poverty, the burden of bereavement, or the drunkard's folly, checkmate with loving sympathy so far as lies in your power, but never under any circumstances, by either aiding or abetting, prove a party to hinder any upright effort. Be a man or a woman in daylight and in darkness, and you will have the satisfaction of feeling that no one can justly discredit you ; and if there were no further result than this, it is undeniably the brightest adornment of our nature to feel that we are living in practical sympathy and at peace with all the world.

Love Song.

Fair as the stars that shine above,
All radiantly bright,
Thou art to me, mine only love,
My heart and soul's delight.
No monarch ever loved his crown,
Or held his country dearer,
Then I love thee, my peerless one,
My beautiful Louisa.

Believe me, dear, believe me now,
That I am only thine,
And most sincerely here I vow
No other shall be mine.
For weal or woe, where thou shalt go,
I only wish to please thee,
And loyal prove, to thee, my love
My beautiful Louisa.

No tempting wiles, or rivals fair,
　Shall change my love for thee,
Devotion unto thee I swear,
　My bride if thou wilt be.
Then why withhold thy glad consent,
　Or longer let us linger,
Yield now, I pray, and name the day,
　My beautiful Louisa.

An Address to a Cat :

BEING A LOGICAL DISSERTATION ON MATERIALISM, ETC.

Come hither, my Tabby, I'll talk unto thee,
Whilst lazily taking thy ease on my knee,
Though only a cat, yet I value thee more
Than many whom fortune attracts to my door.

I wish to have silence from thee for awhile
That wink of thine eye is a wise-acre's smile ;
Any contrary work will make us disagree,
And caterwauls surely provoking will be.

Thou well knowest, Tabby, how once thou wert weak,
How plenty good fare made thee comely and sleek ;
A twist of thy tail or a short plaintive mew,
Expresses thy wish as to what I should do.

Thou art but a brute and yet thankful withal,
In receiving attentive response to thy call,
Content on the hearth ever trustful and free,
What better if any could any cat be !

And yet what a little it is to receive,
So little indeed it is hard to believe ;
But stranger it is that mankind are so blind,
Only few are contented when fortune is kind.

Then patiently listen to what I relate,
Contentment's a boon, and a boon truly great,
A brute such as thou purring low on my knee,
Is richer and happier than thousands like me.

'Tis true thou art weak and dependeth so much
Upon all that in reason we tender to such,
But for just what thou art and doth daily receive,
Thou hast reason to smile beyond any to grieve.

Enough and to spare from each morning till night,
Sufficient from then till another day's light,
A sleep now and then with some frolic between,
Completes in good faith all thy daily routine.

Nor hunger nor trouble e'er come to thy lot,
Misgivings of fate never enter thy cot ;
Whenever for change thou art truly inclined,
Some innocent pastime is easy to find.

Compared with us mortals how vast is the change,
Since mind is a master that freely does range
Away through the earth and far over the sea,
Without any respite wherever we be.

We boast of good sense with a heart and a soul,
We prattle of hell and a heavenly goal ;
We bolster religion and politics too,
Then wonder next moment at mischief they do.

We rave and we argue, or vow and blaspheme,
We crave and we cheat, or we dote and we dream ;
We grumble and sigh at the drawbacks of life,
But augment them daily with worry and strife.

No wonder that men with such minds are so strange,
No sooner they settle than sooner they change
Each whim or each fa cy with which they're possessed,
Or leads them or drives them as fancy seems best.

They vaunt and command or they fume and they rave,
Very cowards betimes and sometimes they are brave ;
They are skilful and clever, or giddy and weak,
And blow hot or cold as they interest seek.

But thee, my own Tabby, I understand well,
Whatever betides thou hast nothing to tell ;
Whilst nations and rulers experience throes,
Yet thou art contented as anyone knows.

'Tis true that sometimes thou dost make a great noise
At a seeming neglect or a too stringent voice ;
Although when thou seest a quarrelsome mood,
Thy instinct impels thee to hide and be good.

But there ! thou are only a cat after all,
Without an endowment unless 'tis thy "*call;*"
Diplomacy never was study of thine,
And as true as I live 'tis no study Divine.

The arts it employs are but fitted for men
Or women, or both having need of a brain,
And even with such they oft-times prove a curse,
When instead of panacea they make panic worse.

And thus thou art blest in thy own lowly sphere
And calmly exists quite regardless of fear,
A lesson pourtraying in minding thine own,
Since men seldom leave other's business alone.

And yet how indifferent thou to thy fate,
Not caring nor troubling concerning thy state ;
Debarred from a prospect of heavenly place,
But safely secured from hellish disgrace.

A lord of creation with both heart and soul,
Who boasts of eternal or infinite whole,
Although he be blest with a far seeing mind,
Thy brutish contentment he never can find.

The bliss that is born of an ignorant state
Can ne'er be attained by the wise or the great,
For low condescension will ne'er reconcile
Presumption whenever united with guile.

This then is the truth that thy kind same as men
Are creatures of impulse at best now and then,
But such must obey whilst mankind regulate
Dame Nature's resources to suit their own state.

So Tabby we reach the old topic again,
That vexes the learned and startles the vain,
A topic that bristles I own with much point,
But as nicely digestive as pudding or joint.

The topic is : "Whether is matter or mind
" Superior agents in ruling mankind ?"
And this I will say that if matter they prove,
Mankind will be levelled to thy brutish groove.

I do not speak lightly, for rather I'd weep
Than jest at the folly such reasoners keep,
No reason I'm certain exists in the plea,
That Materialism gives reason to me.

Matter we grasp, but the mind we can trace,
Or else had my logical rhyming no place :
For matter lies dead until mind gives it life,
Or matter would never be groundwork for strife.

Here is my simple body, such matter as that
Is like unto thine although only a cat,
Yet deeper and further than matter of weight
Is a difference reasoners cannot put straight.

How comes it that I can well estimate thee ?
How is it thou always art subject to me ?
Why ever should I thy necessities please ?
Or what dost thou care about minerals and trees ?

What knowest thou too of the heavenly sphere ?
Or what comprehension of joy or of fear ?
Discover thy ancestry, tell me thine aim,
What carest thou, too, for a good or bad name ?

Bah ! It is nonsense to ask thus of thee,
But yet I'll explain how the subject strikes me ;
We cannot account for each thing that we know
By reason that nature has rendered us so.

We know for a truth that the mind can explore,
We know its resources are boundless in store,
We know that each object is handled as plain
As any the feelings can measure again.

And why do we know it ? because we can feel
A tangible grasp as of metal or steel ;
The eye of discernment that reason employs,
Accords with the senses that make it the voice.

And not only thus is it reason can feel,
For reason can grasp what it cannot reveal ;
As for instance, the soul it can bring into view,
Although undefined and invisible too.

We know it and feel it by faith and by force
Of reason and logic which none can divorce,
Accepting a doctrine of reason and right,
Then faith is the offspring first-born to the sight.

We cannot have reason unless we believe,
We cannot believe only that we can feel,
We cannot have feeling we cannot conceive,
And can only conceive what the mind can reveal.

So Tabby that's why we are just as we are,
And nature is so that we never should dare
To call into question one little doubt,
Of end, or of aim, or our mission about.

We are not immortal although we are wise,
Corruption can ne'er incorruptible rise,
The same as the brutes we return unto dust,
But they, unlike us, have no future in trust.

By virtue of virtues with which I am blest,
In lieu of right usage I now stand confess'd ;
A forfeit is made of a glory beyond,
And I merit a future of torment to stand.

So run away, Tabby, I've settled my mind,
And feel rather better, I'm eased of the kind ;
For studies like this prove uncommonly hard
For mortals to practise with faithful regard.

The Call of Duty.

When a nation's honour lies at stake, and a country's in dismay,
When hearts and nerves their tension break to mingle in the fray,
When hearths and homes the strain abide, and subjects suffer long,
When ruination stalks beside the struggling, patient throng ;
'Tis just in such a moment that the mind asserts its will,
'Tis then a nation breaks restraint o'er burdens that can kill
When leaders falter, heroes rise, to throw the gauntlet down
And daring to the action, thus the daring wins renown ;
So, in the hour of danger, let this your watchword be :
" For the honour of my country, and the cause of Liberty !"
Trust the God of Battles e'er yet the strife's begun,
Then, up and do your duty, till the victory is won.

When hearts are sad, and blackness seems to hover through each day,
When anguish torn with scenes and dreams that seldom pass away,
When loved ones weep and children wail, for better days to come,
When troubles deep, each adverse gale is wafting nearer home;
Be still, be calm, be brave, be strong, just face it like a man.
The worst will soon be over if you grapple best you can ;
'Tis cowards only court defeat, and fortune meets the brave.
For while there's life there's hope at hand, to decorate the grave ;
Then up, arouse yourselves, and strive to live with better grace,
When bad is worst, the worst at least may bear a smiling face.
Be ready for the conflict, and respond to duty's call,
Then duty in the doing yields a pleasure through it all.

Misfortune ever proves itself a most unwelcome guest,
The tug of war 'twixt it and self conduces slow to zest,
But surely men need never shirk the doing what is right,
Or else, indeed, the wasted work will aid a bitter plight.
Be up and doing, stir yourselves, stand well unto your guns,
Respect your obligations unto all the weaker ones.
Be loyal, just, be firm, be true, put all your armour on ;
Tarry not, but struggle through, until the work is done ;
Nations, countries, men apiece, each one and all have wrongs,
One and all must do their best, or singly or in throngs ;
The task may be a hard one, and the duty may give pain,
But duty still is duty, and but duty will remain.

The Last Wish.

I feel very much for either the man or woman who has never listened to the sweetly-mournful strains of the musical gem bearing the above title. Composed by an ardent musician, hailing from the Throstle nest of Old England, as a part of Airedale, in Yorkshire is proudly called, I never wonder indeed at the eminent Londoner's enthusiasm, when he frankly declared that this one, grand, simple effort of genius, was far more sublimely musical, than all his own celebrated compositions put together. The mournful ring, the tender pathos, and gentle, melancholy cadence of the music, cannot fail to impress itself upon any intelligent listener's imagination ; for it truly conveys to all intents and purposes, a last good wish very dearly expressed. But it is not of "The Last Wish" itself that I am going to speak just now, but of an incident which the strains of this touching requiem always bring fresh to my recollection.

Originally hailing myself, from the village above-mentioned, but more often in the exigencies of life wandering away from it, it fell to my lot, one cold winter's evening, to find myself after a weary day's march, at a country place in one of the Midland counties. As usual in those harassing times I was in great straits, and upon that occasion my sole possessions were a very few pence in my pocket, and the rather seedy-looking clothes upon my back. I entered a lime washed lodging-house, which was a familiar resort for needy pedestrians in those days, and at once bargained with the landlady for a night's shelter. The place was almost filled with the resident lodgers who worked in the neighbourhood ; and most of them were then engaged in preparing the evening meal. Having no means of indulging my own appetite, and feeling the pangs of hunger very acutely, I at once made my way into a far corner of the room, and entered into conversation with a late comer like myself. Curiously enough, our conversation was of home reminiscences, and interchanges of sentiment took place between us. One of the young men residents happening to hear us mention my native village, turned very sharply round and gruffly demanded "what we knew about it ?" He was a strong, muscular fellow, of the medium height, black and grimy from his work at the forge, with a cut of features and general appearance that denoted a reckless and bold disposition. He was busily engaged at the fire, superintending the preparation of what, by its fumes, represented a savoury supper. He was a man, in truth, whom, when you see such, you instinctively avoid as dangerous to the peace ; but of course having been asked a question, it was only common civility to return him an answer. So I answered him quietly that I knew every nook and corner of the village, and moreover, every grown-up resident there. He grew more interested and became more civil, and asked me further of many people and places that I remembered quite well. I grew more interested myself, and wondered what was going to happen next, for I could judge by his knowledge and vernacular that he was intimately connected with the village somehow.

" Did ta ever know 'Owd Peter' there ?" he queried after a time.

Now as it happened, I had always been on very good terms with the old man, and had spent many hours in his company. In fact, no one was better known than "Owd Peter" was, for he was foreman of the largest works in the village for half-a-century, and he suffered besides from a terrible impediment in his speech. Perhaps it was this impediment which rendered him so notorious, for nothing delighted the village *harum scarum* so much as an exhibition of his weakness. Again too, he was well known on account of the achievements of a wild runaway son of his, and because of his own campanological distinction : so that altogether old Peter was common property, and I answered that I knew him quite well.

However, the victuals being cooked and ready for discussion, the young man bade me cheerfully to draw up to the table, and get a 'bit o' summat to eit,' a request with which I willingly complied, seeing that I was in a famishing condition almost.

When we had eaten for a little time, he banteringly said—

" Awl tell thi what it is, owd lad, but tha doesn't talk sich brooad Yorksher nah as tha once did," and, continued he after a pause, " thers varry few folks as ud know wheer tha comes fro."

I assented to that cheerfully, explaining my peculiar associations and proclivities, but owning a great regard still for " my native twang."

" Well, awl tell thi summat," said he, " whenever tha sees owd Peter ageon, just tell him tha's seen his bad lad ; an say awm all reet, wilta ?"

I promised him gladly that I would do so, and pictured to myself the surprise with which the old man would hear the news. I cannot deny but that the confession rather startled me, for the youth's reputation was a bad one, and to be at such close quarters with him was far from being desirable. However, I noticed from that moment that the man's voice was broken, his eyes were dim with tears, and his food lay untouched.

It is not agreeable to see a strong man wrestling with the agony of pent-up remembrances, and when I saw the tear-dimmed eyes, I felt that even the most rugged heart is not wholly inaccessible.

" Nah, mak thisel a good meal," he enjoined, after composing himself a little, " aw don't feel mich int eiting way misel somehah to-night, but tha'rt welcome to owt at aw hev."

I thanked him heartily for his kindness, but his only reply was—

" Don't mention it, but think on nah, an tell towd chap ; an say at aw wish him weel." And I promised.

I was away early next morning upon my travels, and so did not see him again ; but the changed features and gentler tones as he gave me his loving message, will never be forgotten. I was only in a very sorry plight myself at the time, but it is really wonderful what a little sympathy will do. And some months afterwards when I returned to the dear old home, I did not forget to keep my promise to him ; for, meeting old Peter in the main street, I acquainted him word for word with his son's remembrance and good wishes. And how the old man's features relaxed when I told him everything ; how his eyes dimmed ; how brokenly yet kindly he ejaculated " Poor lad ! Poor lad ! God bless him !

I can tell you, reader, whoever you may be, that I felt repaid ten thousand times for any trouble it might have cost me, when I saw the loving unison of heart and sympathy exhibited in both father and son : although in distance and appearances so wide apart. How good indeed is it to see such sympathy. There may be tears and sadness : there may be sacred yearnings and painful memories ; but every tear, every thought, every look and every word, is doubly sanctified thereby, and I felt glad because of my part in the occasion. It may be doubted, nay, it often has been, that tender feeling can be manifested in humble life, and by the pariahs of society ; but the loving instinct, it may be, is far stronger in the despised ranks than is often credited. The old man was not looking so strong and hearty as was his wont, and I felt as a consequence that his son's tearful good wishes were all the more appreciated. He shook my hand heartily before we parted, but could not express himself in words, and it was not so very long after then that he succumbed to affliction, and found relief in death.

Who can say that it was not easier for him to die with his wild son's loving message than without ? Hearts can keenly feel, and responsive love and sympathy yields comfort even in death. There are few people indeed in our own locality, but respected the old man, for half-a-century of usefulness will tell its own tale ; and so, as he had officiated at many funerals and weddings in his day, it was decided by the neighbours to yield him a public funeral in return. And finally, in return for the many peals he had rung for the villagers, they decided to ring a peal for him ; and whilst many hundreds of them crowded the beautiful grounds of the little cemetery on the hillside in honour to his loving memory, his comrades at the grave-side, with uncovered heads and muffled handbells in their grasp, feelingly and harmoniously rang their adieu, to the pathetic and mournfully solemn strains of " The Last Wish ;" the composer of which music the old man had known personally.

It was about two years afterwards, when in improved circumstances, and going a journey south, I again saw the young man, and was enabled to repay him the kindness I had received at his hands. His appearance was much the same as when I had seen him before, except that he seemed more careworn, but his first words to me were :—

" Did ta tell mi fayther what aw tell'd thi ?"

So I told him everything as it had happened, and I shall never forget whilst I live, his happy, tender and tremulous appearance, when I related how his father had blessed him. I do verily believe that if his redemption could be traced to any one cause more than another, it was owing to his father's love. And he broke down completely when I detailed the last sad scene of all at the grave-side ; how the whole village had turned out in his honour, and his comrades had played " The Last Wish." He could not say what he wished to say of thanks, but he grasped my hand ; and with bowed head, he wept until his feelings were relieved.

No other thanks would have expressed half so much. Hearts are often caught at the rebound, and I ventured to suggest a turning point in his life and actions, pointing out the unprofitableness of a reckless and dissolute career. He said very little at the time, but that he had considered himself well has since been amply evident, for he returned home, became sober and thoughtful, and has now succeeded in earning the respect of the neighbourhood. We are good friends still, and often comfort one another ; and now having become respectable, his own best wish and mine is, that he may remain so, and prove a worthy son of a dearly loved and honoured father.

Unexpected.

Within a large hall in a northerly town,
   Not very long since, you must know,
Along with a neighbour and friend—Mr. Brown—
   I sat for an hour or so.

The room—quite a large one—was very well pack'd
   With children of every degree :
Whilst some, who had further in life's pathway track'd,
   Attended to listen and see.

'Twas a temperance meeting was held on that night,
 And such as a man loves to see ;
For that is the side which is safest and right,
 And where all true men ought to be.

The simple addresses were brimful of truth,
 Condemning the drunkard's great sin ;
The moral of each was to prove unto youth,
 What folly it was to begin.

At length there arose a sedate looking man
 Whose manner was earnest and strong,
He started at first where a drunkard began,
 And followed his course right along.

And he told us a tale of a bright little boy
 Whose father had seen better days,
But who, through the drink, was a stranger to joy,
 Since the habit he could not erase.

He also described how the wife had to plan
 To get for them all daily bread,
And how people jeered at the once happy man
 Who then was a drunkard instead.

And Johnnie —a smart and intelligent lad—
 Was father's particular pet,
For his heart was not ruthless and viciously bad,
 But only when drink he would get.

And it happened one night, when he started from home
 To mate with the foolish and vain,
He heard little Johnnie entreating to come
 A " tata," with father again.

He felt very sad as he looked at the boy,
 For the question cost him a pang,
But roughly he bade him not thus to annoy,
 And passed through the door with a bang.

His desolate wife keenly felt the disgrace,
 Well knowing no money was there,
And tears trickled freely adown her sad face
 In bitterest grief and despair.

Then brave little Johnnie—the youngster—uprose
 And tearfully still did insist ;
Then quick through the door after father he goes,
 While she—well, she couldn't resist.

And he followed along through each by-way and street
 For the lad could not well understand
But the tavern where father his comrades did meet
 Must own some attraction quite grand,

So he followed him on, through the cold and the snow,
    To the place he had hurried within,
And he crept in the room where his father did go
    To drink beer, or whiskey, or gin.

And nobody noticed the youngster pass in,
    Being each one stood up at the bar,
But being so cold, and a fire within,
    He child-like did warm himself there.

But after a time, an old customer there,
    Espied him, as proudly he stood,
And he wondered indeed to see the lad dare,
    As though none but customers should.

Then he called out aloud, in his rough, drunken tones :
    " Holloa, lad ! what is't brings thee here ?
" Tha stan's up so cleverly roasting thi bones ;
    " Tell t' gaffer to fill thee some beer."

But the bright little chap saw his father stood by,
    And he answered, as bold as could be :
" My dada comes here ;" and then heaving a sigh,
    " I want to stop with him and see.

" My dada declared that they didn't take boys
    " To such kind of places as this,
" But if I can stay I won't make any noise,
    " Nor do anything that's amiss."

And his parent stood there, and he heard every word,
    And thought of the sin and the shame ;
And his good honest nature resolved, as he heard,
    No longer would he be to blame.

And he picked up his Johnnie, so lovingly true,
    Whilst manliness shone in his face ;
Then, kissing him, said, " My brave boy, it is you,
    " That shall save me from further disgrace."

And there—at the counter—he vowed to his God
    That he never would taste any more,
Declaring for ever he threw down the rod,
    And passed with his child through the door.

And Johnnie went home with his father that night,
    Which his mother did wonder to see,
But she wondered yet more at the far stranger sight,
    That her husband was sober as she.

Then he kiss'd her, and gave her the money he had,
    Relating what Johnnie had done,
Explaining that rather than injure the lad,
    Conversion in him had begun.

And his wife—poor woman—grew instantly rich,
    And her heart sent a prayer up above ;
Her needle was stayed in the midst a of a stitch
    To praise Him for mercy and love.

The fulness of joy overspread her wan face,
    As Johnnie she pressed to her heart ;
The goodness of God had averted disgrace,
    Disclosing a manlier part.

And the parents together with gratitude swell,
    And offered thanksgiving to God ;
Whilst mercy heartfelt, beyond mortal to tell,
    Enshrouded their humble abode.

*   *   *   *   *   *   *

The speaker that night told the story so well—
    His picture was shown to the life—
Disclosing the depths to which drunkenness fell,
    And the heart-rending grief of a wife.

And then, when he mentioned the scene at the bar,
    His acting was earnest and true ;
I vowed to myself this description I'd dare,
    Exposing the drink curse to you.

And many a tear and a sorrowful face,
    Betrayed how his efforts told well ;
And the purest of wishes arose from the place,
    To save the poor drunkard from Hell.

The Might of Right.

The acting aright in life, is, and should be, a great power for good.   It may not, and does not in every case receive the world's adulation, for this is a selfish world ; but to those who act rightly it yields a settled conviction and peace of mind, that the world can never give.   They who act aright never need to fear, but the evil doer always will.   The might of right has a nobility, a strength, and a candour, that wrong doing can never give.   It is a mighty power, and all the world of wrong in battle array, cannot rob it of its charm.   They may assail, they may attack, they may kill even, but right must ultimately prevail.   Do then that which is right, stand by it and maintain it.   Doing right gives a peaceful mind—beyond the transgressor's comprehension—and wrong, however powerful, cannot prevent it.   Right is above temptation, and baffles Hell.   Nature is with it, Heaven is with it, and conscience demands it.   The battle may be fierce, its light may be hid for a time, but its force justifies it.   It alleviates pain and sorrow, it soothes adversity, and sanctifies the doer.   If there were no other benefits, it is its own justification and reward.   Be honest, be true, be manly, be strong ; and in time your strength and innocence becomes so plain, and so contagious in its efficacy, that verily none but fools shall dare to dispute the exceeding power, the sublime majesty, and the truly wonderful Might of Right.

The Voice Beyond.

(SUGGESTED BY A MIDNIGHT VISIT TO A GRAVEYARD.)

Halt thee, mortal, cease thy tread,
　Let thy eyes around thee gaze,
Dare not to disturb the dead,
　But return to thine own ways.

Let the evidences round thee,
　Sacred to departed worth,
Prove, if only to confound thee,
　All the fickleness of earth.

Bid thy simple wits to serve thee
　But to hold a brief review ;
If, indeed, they don't unnerve thee,
　Yet some service may they do.

Note the costly slabs erected,
　Side by side with lowly mound,
Vanity thus-wise detected
　Even in the burial ground.

Blots upon the face of nature,
　Monitive of worldly pride,
Each a too convincing feature
　Of its emptiness beside.

What is man that he should flourish,—
　Vainly thus his puny might,
Since himself he cannot nourish
　To prevent his manhood's flight

Tide and time the while o'ertake him,
　In a ceaseless hurried flow,
Still doth his presumption make him
　Yearn to mastery below.

Why will he parade his weakness,
　Or his vanity display,
When his conscience prompts a meekness
　Which befits him day by day.

Hear me, thou audacious mortal,
　If thou would'st attain the goal,
Death is but the hidden portal
　For the transit of the soul.

Life and death are *ldent* together.
　In accord with God's design,
Nought of science can untether
　Or unravel things Divine.

What is His is far above thee,
What is thine belongs to Him,
If he did not dearly love thee,
Then in truth thine eyes were dim.

Go to, then, and let thy reason
Lead thee to the better path,
Live anew thy life's brief season,
Mindful what thou art and hath.

An Acrostic.

IN HONOUR OF THE BAPTISM OF BLACKBURN'S "ROYAL" BABY, JUNE 21ST, 1888.

A fter many days, when Womanhood shall reign,
L ong though it seems—yet it is but a span,
E ven then, we hope that life within its train
X cells in beauty this harmonious plan.
A lthough we know that Fortune's added years
N ever can wear the harmlessness of youth,
D oubtless there may in place of bitter tears
R emain for her sweet Innocence and Truth,
A nd so rest with the loved one love and ruth.

M ay, laughing May, sweet harbinger of joy :
A llied to Hope, untrammelled with alloy,
Y ear after year thy Sylvan grace employ.

A uspicious day ; may each succeeding June
P rove fitter still with Nature to attune ;
P eerless though ever the Royal Sponsor be,
L et loyal friends and neighbours tender Love as free.
E re yet the cares of life come crowding round :
B e this the charm whence happiness is found,
Y ea, this the shield 'gainst all unholy sound.

Invoking the Muse.

Come, inspiring Muse ! and bring another moment's joy,
My heart is sad within me, for my life seems all alloy,
The road is rough and thorny, and I know not what to do,
So lend again thy kindly aid, to cheer my journey through.

Full often have I thee invoked in times of sore distress,
Yet often though I've needed thee, I need thee now no less ;
I cannot find another friend that I hold half so dear,
Nor do I wish for other aid, while thou remainest near.

Let sophists and philosophers disclaim thee as they may ;
Let fools of thee make ridicule, and brawlers have their say,
Still I can fully value thee, because I understand
A friend in need, thou art indeed, with ready, helping hand.

Then aid me now whilst unto thee my woes I strive to tell,
For here I vow I never could, did I not love thee well ;
My head is bowed with sorrow, and my heart with anguish sore,
More care have I than man can bear, and never man had more.

My life's a burden, yet it is to me of little weight,
Troubles lurk in every path, I cannot travel straight ;
Penury and sickness too, with endless pain and care,
Combine to make me wretched, for 'tis more than I can bear.

Bereft of home and comfort, and of kindred heart or friend,
Remain with me, O Muse, and cheer my journey to the end,
I'm stricken and faint-hearted, too—full disinclined to strive—
For man to man is so unjust, some fall where others thrive.

Then come, dear Muse, and favour me, with thy protecting care,
Endow me with forgetfulness of all that I must bear ;
Gloss again my sorrows o'er, and prove a faithful friend
And pilot me o'er life's rough sea, unto a happier end.

With thee the moments I enjoy, with thee I ease my pain,
With thee will I take comfort now, and stand erect again ;
I'll try to be a man once more, with purpose well unfurled,
And meet unflinchingly my fate, in battle with the world.

One Little Year.

Only a year !   And yet what a change
    Just one little year has brought ;
Fancy could never so recklessly range
    Away from all reason and thought.
The life that was brightest is nothing but gloom,
    The hope that was highest is gone ;
Both victor and victim are laid in the tomb,
    And shadow and substance are one.

Only a year.   Alas ! what a span
    Of suffering, worry, and crime,
One little year discloses to man,
    Though 'tis but an atom of time
Great joy may be changed into comfortless grief,
    And happiness turn to despair,
Yet the days seeming long are in truth only brief,
    For swift is the flight of a year.

Only a year ! How well may we say
  'Tis like to a vain empty boast,
For quickly indeed doth it hurry away
  When life is entwined with it most.
A breath, or a page, yet mankind cannot tell
  The changes that time ever bring,
But each may assist their good fortune to swell
  By watching whilst still on the wing.

When Men are Sad.

When men are sad instead of glad,
  And all things seem awry,
How easy then, for wayward men,
  Precaution to defy ;
Because some plan goes wrong, forsooth
  And trouble looms ahead,
We reel along like giddy youth
  In 'wilderment and dread.

The world is not (though oft forgot)
  A palace of delight ;
And men must work, and cannot shirk,
  A share of common blight ;
A childish mood attains no good,
  Nor wins a steadfast friend,
And halting ways can only raise
  A sad regretful end.

How happy we might only be,
  Did we but estimate
In better light, what to the sight,
  Displays a vast estate
Of nature's gems and diadems
  Implanted for our use :
Examples all, inspiring gall
  To follow their abuse.

What boots it then, I say again,
  In this haphazard life,
To build despair, and hasten care,
  By drifting into strife ;
Let each enjoy, and well employ
  The good things at command ;
And just as free and earnest be
  To meet reversing hand.

So have good cheer, and give your ear
  Unto this homely strain ;
The day will follow evening,
  As the sunshine follows rain ;
Stand firm to every duty,
  And with righteousness shod,
You will rise again in beauty,
  And be nearer unto God.

Sulks.

Never employ sulks. If they were not cultivated they could not exist. They always prove harmful, and under no circumstances is it possible to be otherwise, for they are at best an unnatural and ineffective method. Nature may attune with humanising efforts, but artifice cannot compete with it. Sulks are artificial. If you have a grievance, out with it, and let it air itself. Nothing like ventilation for giving satisfaction; secrets and sulks go together. Freshen your grievance, and exposure will drive it. Sulks are unmanly and treacherous in the highest degree. Harbour no secrets, do nothing underhand, or fretting and sulking will never cease. Sulkers are cowards, for sulks are unfair. Sulks are selfish, and in truth often cruel. Speak out your sentiments ; affirm or deny, but never sulk. Mischief, uneasiness, and sorrow are ever the offspring of sulks. There cannot be love in sulky people. Curb your wilful temper, if you have such an incumbrance ; and bear meekly your deserts. Give up all peevishness at once. Put away childish views and habits, and try to be happy. Be open, mingle with your kind, and do everything above board. Be cheerful, and never sneak, and I'll wager a trifle that you never sulk.

A Midnight Soliloquy.

When Night's sombre mantle Creation is clouding,
    And Nature is still'd into deathly repose ;
When silvery Luna is hid by o'erclouding,
    And all things around bespeak the day's close :
How well to reflect on the greatness and wisdom—
    The infinite Majesty throned upon high :
The grand and mysterious rulings of Heaven
    Encompassing earth with an Omniscient Eye.

What mercy and grace : how vast and how tender—
    How deep and how mighty the Power above ;
What wonderful goodness that can so well render
    All things around to accord with His love.
O, Infinite Being ! the Source and the Fountain
    Of Love, and of Hope, and of Time without end :
Designer of all, even ocean and mountain,
    How rich is poor mortal in calling Thee Friend.

How well is God's wisdom displayed in His power,
    How ample His mercy dispensed to mankind ;
How tenderly precious in life's darkest hour
    They only that serve Him can gratefully find.
The stars and the heavens, the earth and the ocean,
    All things created and breathing with life,
Proclaim a Supreme and Omnipotent Motion,
    One Almighty Ruler in peace or in strife.

O, when will poor mortals yield Heaven the glory,
    Discover God's goodness, and yield Him the praise ;
Since all things around us proclaim the same story,
    The Lord's the Arbiter that numbers our days.
The earth is the Lord's, and the fulness within it,
    The bright starry Heavens His own resting-place ;
His hand is revealed upon everything in it,
    And blessed are we to partake of His grace.

Beautiful Things of Life.

The beautiful things of life,
  How little in value seem,
Though manifold and rife,
  We pass as in a dream.

Ungrateful even in thought,
  How thankless are mankind,
Remembering as we ought,
  The Source from whence design'd.

The priceless boon of Health
  With many comforts given,
The joys of love and wealth,
  Encrowned with hope of Heaven.

The trees and plants that bloom,
  Luxuriant and fair,—
With food or sweet perfume,
  Proclaim Almighty care ;

The treasures of the deep
  And wonders of the sea,
Our gratitude should keep
  Both evergreen and free.

The birds that skim the air,
  The glories of the skies,
All Nature full and fair,
  Bids thankfulness to rise.

Then let us always prove
  How thankful we can be,
Abiding each in love
  And peaceful amity.

Enjoying to the full,
  The blessings all around,
However bright or dull,
  In kind, or taste, or sound.

Poor mortals may not trace
  The Maker's wise design,
But full in every place
  His care and goodness shine.

The lowliest of earth,
  In life, in heart, or mind.
A purpose had in birth,
  If only we might find ;

Complete in each detail,
 The rough becomes the smooth ;
Man's artifices fail,
 Divulging each, forsooth ;

So let us take to heart,
 The while we live our days,
That manhood's better part
 Is to render grateful praise.

Watching 'em off.

Many a time in my rambles through the streets, near to the Police Court or the Railway Station, has my attention been directed to the motley groups of people, who, by some strange meandering of fate, always seem to congregate thereabouts. If there be any one time more than another when they abound, it seems to be when the necessity of a Prison Van is most useful and convenient. Why this should be so to the extent it appears, is not so clear to my reason—unless it be that tastes and inclinations are more morbid in their character than is generally supposed to be the case—but certain it is that the fascination exists in a most surprising and general degree. The particular time when *the van* has to make its appearance at the prison gates seems to be very widely known, and consequently the assembling of those who know serves as a magnet to attract greater numbers of spectators, and lends greater consequence to the occasion. Therefore it is that the ceremony of *watching the prisoners off* has obtained generally here-abouts, and as they are escorted from the assembly-room to the steps of the vehicle in waiting there is nearly always an interesting but very mixed type of conversation carried on between the prisoners and their friends or acquaintance in the crowd. Upon these occasions there does not seem to be any manifestation of bitterness on the part of the police towards their charges, as a rule ; and certainly it is well on the whole that such should be the case, for it would only provoke retaliation in a more or less degree, from either the public or the press. This conversation is carried on by many voices at one time, and, as the time when it occurs is limited to a very short span indeed, it has sometimes happened that the prisoner could not discover his correspondent's identity, much less to carry on and maintain a healthy and satisfactory dialogue. However, as the wits are sharpened in the case of *old hands*, for such an emergency, and terribly blunted and paralysed in the unlucky new ones ; as much is probably "made out" as serves for the purpose ; and without a doubt sufficient will have been said to either appease, disturb, or annoy, as will last each one of them for some time to come. There can be no denying that the receptions usually accorded to one or another, as the case may be, constitute to some others a very grievous form of punishment indeed ; and, doubtless, many a poor soul would consent to have his or her term of imprisonment doubled could they only escape the "exhibition" torture ; and for such unfortunate wretches it is a very hard lot indeed. It is not such a difficult matter to distinguish the different types of character, and I have sometimes thought that if the positions were only reversed, and a few gaolers were placed in the same predicament, they would in many instances fail in exciting a similar amount of sympathy. But, as we know—and the detective force know also—appearances are often deceitful ; and so we will not attempt to judge upon that head. We must admit, that generally speaking, the class of delinquents who face the Bench are much of a "sameness," as the saying goes ; and there is seldom any need for much study, deep research, special attention, or any great share of wisdom or legal lore ; so that it may well be that magistrates of experience are in truth the very best judges of all that should command their discretion in connection therewith. At any rate, if they possess any true manhood at all, most assuredly they will prove so. There are now and again a few prisoners who step jauntily enough into the van, and who seem to relish the whole matter as a labourer would his holiday. These are altogether characterless as regards morality, and it is only on account of physical self-benefit that they thus seem to embrace the unenviable notoriety. This class is largely composed of females of the lewd type, and as they well know that dissipation has it penalties, they have just sufficient sense left them to enable them to appreciate the virtues of enforced chastity, cleanliness, and temperance, knowing, as they do, that they will emerge from "durance vile" in a hearty, vigorous condition, ready and fit for the old life and habits. Of all vile offenders against society, these surely are the vilest. We may rail against the drink traffic as we like, but it is such offenders as these—whose doings, in a measure must be winked at by members of the police force in our large towns—who are the chief manufacturers of crime in the country. Choosing as their associates the most reckless and abandoned of their once-a-day dupes, they hound them on by their hellish artifices into greater crime, until they hold their liberty as it were in their hands. Then, should the man not have become lawless enough to brutalise and bully the intemperate victims of their decoying arts, he is betrayed into the hands of the police for some petty misdemeanour previously undiscovered, and so is often made through such means the vicious and villainous pest of society that he is. How misplaced, indeed, is the pity engendered of their prison plight ; only God knows how many ruined homes and broken hearts can be laid to the harlot's charge. But enough of such. Safely cabined in the prison van, away scour the crowd, or the main portion of it, through the streets at full run towards the railway station, there to have one last glimpse of the poor wretches descending from the vehicle to run the gauntlet of the whole assemblage there present, idlers, passers-by, and passengers included. What a crowd it is, too, to be sure ! One would suppose by their features, demeanour, and apparel, that at least two-thirds of the spectators had already made acquaintance with the same establishment that the State-paid and manacled travellers are journeying to. How pinched, how woe-begone, and how cunning are their visages ! How painfully interested do they seem in the welfare of those, who, although deprived of their liberty, do yet enjoy ten times over a more beneficial restraint and protection than their erstwhile chums. But who can imagine the grief — the deep consuming grief—of the poor unfortunate prisoner, as the case may be, who, from sheer inability to pay the fine and costs incurred for having had his house-chimney on fire, or even to pay his rates, must perforce be linked to and marched along with some low despicable vagabond, or worse still, with a hardened criminal. God help such unfortunates, say I ; and may the law not fail in helping them also, ere long, I am sadly afraid that we think too little of these things whenever we are brought into close proximity to our Police Court victims, and that, somehow, the best part of our attention is directed to the more audacious members of the degraded fraternity. It would hurt our feelings, jar upon our nature, and enlist our sympathies too greatly did we allow ourselves to be occupied with a study of these wretched beings and their fate ; and so, like the vultures we are, we let them severely alone, and consign them unmercifully to the oblivion of forgetfulness. That is the truth, I am sorry to say ; and in our humble behalf we may fairly urge that little practical good could possibly attend our single efforts in so morbidly melancholy a direction. There they are, however, the best and the worst of them ; and, could each of them only know it, it is far better to be resigned to their lot, and endeavour, bad as it is, to extract from it any grains of comfort there may be hidden, than to busy themselves with regretful or revengeful brooding. Some of them do this, poor souls ; and the straightened shoulders, the erect mien, and the steady stride bear witness thereto. It cannot be expected that any prisoners would laugh loudly and long, for that would certainly be enigmatical conduct ; but a cheery word, a smile, or a pleasant nudge are manifestations both feasible and proper ; and so some of them endeavour thusly to comfort each other. Some, indeed, are anything but satisfied with such innocent arts and wiles ; and for these, a piece of twist tobacco, a fully charged and burning pipe of tobacco, or a last drain of beer or whiskey, represent truly the objects of their most tender solicitude ; and occasionally they are gratified therewith. "Ta, ta, Liz !" cries a voice in the crowd ; "Cheer up, Tom," says another ; "Keep thi pecker up !" bawls a third ; and from amidst the surging and struggling mob who crowd the pathway, the police hurry their prisoners along to the platform like driven cattle ; whilst the handcuffed crew, with many brave efforts to nod, smile, or sign a farewell, tramp on at a quickstep, and are soon out of sight. The prison van hurries back unto its accustomed shed ; the police return to report progress ; the mob break up and disperse ; whilst we ourselves wander away homeward, sentimental and glum, through "*watching the prisoners off.*"

Dedication Shakesperian.

[Being a Greeting to the Founder of a Shakesperian Banquet, at the Shakespeare Hotel,
Huddersfield ; he being a Shakesperian actor, by name Shakespeare Hirst.   April, 1881.]

Hail to thee of ready voice, attuned to minstrel lay,
Hail thou troubadour, and grant this liberty I pray :
Namesake of a master mind, and friend to humble bard,
Hail thee, Boniface, and yield the writer thy regard.

What matters it if until now we twain have never met,
Are we not enamoured both, and serve without regret—
Sweet Poesy, the gentle muse ; that ever and again
Enliveneth the drooping heart with varying refrain.

Then hail, thou fond remembrancer of Avon's peerless bard,
Press on with all devotion, and betoken thy regard,
Flourish yet thy darling hope and hope to flourish still,
Give votaries true welcome and befriend them with good-will.

Let the festive cheer be spread as in the days of yore,
Charge and pledge fidelity and friendship evermore ;
Bid each saddened heart be glad, and start its life anew,
For darksome days are best forgot, where comforters are few.

Read again the sober verse that token learning's staff,
Tell again the merry tales, that listeners may laugh ;
Bid the company be gay, and push a pleasant theme,
Let the hours speed away as in a pleasant dream.

Teach alike to old and young the duties of their sphere,
Entertain with portions neat of records fitly dear ;
Prove alike to every one his seasons of the mind,
An eloquence and wisdom both engaging and refined.

'Tis meet for every living soul, and good for bodies too,
The sad, and merry, or sublime, are well displayed to view ;
The high or low, or good or ill, whatever be man's lot,
Is pictured fair, with skilful care, and never point forgot.

Then hail thee, friend, and take from me this token of respect,
Though humble, yet I ne'er disgraced nor man, nor creed, nor sect ;
In simple parlance I bestow, although in guise the worst,
My wishes strong, for comfort long, unto thee, Shakespeare Hirst.

The New Estate.

We have read and we have pondered of the mischief born of caste.
We have studied long and wondered o'er the history of the past ;
We have gathered and digested all the records up to date,
But cannot find a paragraph about—The New Estate.

Conservatives and Liberals we had thought we understood,
And extreme Whigs and Tories, too, we rated as we should ;
Even Rads and Independents we had learned to tolerate,
But own to being puzzled, over this—the New Estate.

A Tory once was known to be an advocate of class,
Who firmly clung to privilege and hardly let one pass ;
The Church and Constitution he held big with his own fate,
But never tolerated any upstart—New Estate.

A Whig, too, was a gentleman who played a useful part
In preaching up economy with opposition smart ;
In the revenue and taxes, too, his interest was great,
And so would not demean himself with any—New Estate.

The Radicals, of course, we know have very forward views,
And will, in spite of Closure, still obstruct and still abuse ;
They bait and bite, and angle well to drive a bargain straight,
And possibly have interests in this—the New Estate.

Of Independents, 'pon my word, I scarce know what to say—
There certainly is such a class in Parliament to-day.
They seldom rise sensational, and know well how to wait
Without, indeed, a stirring need to start a—New Estate.

Who are they then ? What is their aim ? Of what extraction they ?
The people certainly should know what underlies their play.
Are they true-hearted democrats and agitating well,
Or is the Democratic cry a swindle and a sell ?

Conservatives, we know it well, are joining in this cry—
Liberals too, have struggled hard for all they would supply.
There surely cannot be a breach in ought but ways and means,
Then why not put in Conference, an ending to such scenes ?

Come, Democrats, declare yourselves and tell us what you mean—
Say, are you on the people's side, or making that a screen ?
Is this a trap for privilege, or do you stand for right,
Pray tell us that we may esteem and prove your honour bright.

Hard Lines.

'Twas in the merry Christmas time,
    When all is joy and love,
When bells from every steeple chime,
    In praise to God above ;
When all the earth in gladness meet
    In pleasure's sweet accord,
And each with hearty welcome greet
    The Birthday of the Lord.

Upon this bright auspicious day,
    When hearts should all be glad,
A humble cotter's daughter lay
    In bitter plight and sad,
A wasting, lingering, fatal ill
    Enchained her to her bed,
Defying love and care, and skill,
    Creating grief instead.

'Twas very cruel each one thought
    To suffer fate so hard,
To lose the comfort life had brought,
    And reap such a reward.
A prettier or a gentler lass
    Had never joined in play,
And yet the verdict forth did pass,
    To die on Christmas Day.

Imagine, each one, if you can,
    The sad, depressing scene,
The broken and unhappy man
    Who had contented been ;
Imagine, too, his weeping wife,
    So weary, worn, and sad,
The stricken daughter losing life
    And all that makes life glad.

A frail young creature, well endow'd
    With every sense and care,
So very soon to wear the shroud
    For lifeless clay to wear.
Consider then, the parents' woe,
    And bitter, deep distress,
To see their only darling so
    In utter helplessness.

And yet the Christmas bells rang on
    With merry, joyous peal,
And bands of choristers sang on
    In 'thankful, happy weal ;
And all around them, far and near,
    The festive tidings spread,
And sorrow lingered only there,
    In constant fear and dread.

It had not been so long ago,
    Since she with all the rest
Of youthful friends in playful show,
    Could gambol with the best.
Her mother's pride and father's pet,
    Enfreed from aught of harm ;
Her simplest wish was gladly met,
    To shield her from alarm.

And there she lay—a shattered wreck
    Fast hurrying away ;
Their hearts did almost seem to break,
    Upon that holy day,
And whilst they tended her so well,
    Her playmates sang outside,
And tearfully in song did tell
    Why Jesus lived and died.

They sang about His blessed birth,
    And all that did attend,
Of how He also lived on earth,
    And proved the sinner's Friend.
They sang about His precious love
    And sufferings on the cross,
Of His translation up above,
    And gain for every loss.

And whilst they sang, each trembling limb
 Her pleasure testified,
For she had learnt to trust in Him
 Who had for sinners died.
Yet still the tears trickled down
 Her wan and wasted cheek ;
'Twas hard indeed with dear ones round
 The last farewell to speak.

Her playmates kissed her one by one
 And bade the "long good-bye,"
And when each one away had gone
 She burst in fretful cry :
And thus she lay with saddened heart
 And tear-bestreaming eyes,
'Twas hard indeed with all to part,
 And never more to rise.

Full anxiously her parents tried
 To soothe her deep distress,
And each essayed with loving pride
 The darling one to bless ;
And then she gently went to sleep,
 Entwined in fond caress,
To wake no more from slumber deep
 Till Gabriel sounds to bless.

 *   *   *   *

The bells still rang ; and all around
 Was joy, and peace, and love,
And everywhere was heard the sound
 Of praise to God above,
But when at length the worthy pair
 Again stood by her bed,
She had release from every care,—
 The Cotter's child was dead.

And soon they carried her away
 Into the old churchyard,
Assured at the Judgment Day
 Of Heavenly reward.
Then quietly they settled down,
 Bereft of child and pride,
Remembering she gained a crown
 The Christmas Day she died.

On Criticism.

There are several passages of Scripture which have a direct bearing on this subject, notable amongst which are : " *Judge not, lest ye be judged ;*" and " *Let him who is without sin cast the first stone.*"   It is so easy at times to under-rate or over-rate another, that a man must indeed be very careful lest a thoughtless action or malicious feeling predominate over what is just and right, Learning or experience alone should ever be the guiding principle in a critic's work, for without such competence, folly will ensue. Honest criticism is uprightness, false criticism is cowardice, and none may lightly essay the task ; for so surely as that sunshine follows storm, it is, that the fruits of criticism —good, bad, or indifferent—will inevitably appear in due course. Fault-finding is not criticism, for it blinds us to the virtuous side; and favouritism fails likewise. No man should attempt to criticise that which he is ignorant of, if so, it is damnatory in its rebound. Surface minds cannot yield honest criticism, and criticism without qualification is slanderous. If every critic would remember that his own decisions receive criticism, there would result more honesty. Place, bluster, and wealth, are no qualifications of a critic; for such an one is sure to be ridiculed, and his decisions reversed some day, alive or dead. True criticism is humanity proper, and a touch of nature or friendship should animate the ruling. In unprincipled hands it is a dangerous power for evil, in humane ones a great lever for enlightenment. So let each one try in the opportunities of life, to remember always that none are so good that they cannot be better, and none so bad that they cannot be improved. Thus everyone can be benefited; and there cannot be a truer and straighter method employed for that end, than the upright and downstraight action of honest criticism.

Life as it is.

(ALLEGORICAL.)

Once on a day, in a fertile resort,
　Where wild flowers grew in profusion, and free,
And Nature in splendour maintained her Court:
　A stranger young Blossom there happened to be
Transplanted, untended, bedraggled, and bruised,
　Not boldly nor vain—but full meekly it lay,
Desirous withal to be only excused,
　For daring to live as unfortunates may.

By little and little the blossom did thrive
　Albeit neglected and low,
While all other flowers united, contrive
　Not one sign of love to bestow.
Nor feeling nor friendship did any disclose—
　Divided they seemed past recall;
Yet bravely surmounting the list of its woes,
　It flourished in spite of them all.

It struggled along till its usefulness gained,
　A place in the heart of the crowd:
But just as the same it had duly attained,
　Again were the murmurers loud.
And when by-and-bye it discovered a friend,
　Who dared to unburden his mind,
The shriek that was heard was so madly absurd,
　New friends did the blossom then find.

And truly 'tis so in the battle of life:
　A man may be wretched and sad.
He may also be hamper'd with worry and strife,
　But jealousy wishes him mad.
And the worst of it all, is that slanderous blows
　Are cowardly dealt in disguise—
For a Cur never dare to intrude but his nose,
　Lest punishment open his eyes.

A Bully.

If a man on this earth be dishonest and mean,
To take an advantage be known or be seen,
If he in his heart be a coward, I ween—
    That man is a Bully.

If a man strike dismay into peaceable mind,
By sad misbehaviour and mischief combined ;
If he is both selfish and cruel, I find—
    That man is a Bully.

If a man of his strength make a brutal display,
Abusing his manhood by night or by day,
If he's dissipated and idle, I say—
    That man is a Bully.

If a man make a boast of a virtuous part,
The while being stony and vicious at heart,
If his life be a lie--his pretensions apart,—
    That man is a Bully.

If a man be unkind unto children, 'tis true,
It proves him a cur who would meaner things do,
If he lorded it over a poor woman too,
    That man is a Bully.

If a man lend himself to the working of ill,
And lives so that none can extend a good will,
If he be unworthy his station to fill,
    That man is a Bully.

Kindly Deeds.

Who can guage the tender measure,
    Or the force of kindly deeds ?
Telling how each heart doth treasure
    Such attention to its needs.
Truly is the language spoken :
    " Blessings fall in double store ; "
Since to heal a spirit broken
    Sanctifies the healing more.

In your heart, as in your dealing,
    Let each one be kind and true,
Ever offering fellow-feeling,
    As ye would each should to you.
Never let a paltry action
    Stain a conscience good and clear
There is deeper satisfaction
· In upholding honour dear.

Though the world mayhap deride you,
　And you lose a seeming gain,
Let uprightness ever guide you,
　If respect you would attain.
Kindness never fails in blessing ;
　Sympathy sheds peace around ;
Ever in the conflict pressing,
　Prove a man in honour bound.

Why should any be so cruel.
　E'er to wish his fellow harm ;
Life, at most, is but a duel :
　Death deprives of every charm.
Better far it is to wander,
　Always gentle, simple, kind,
So that in our journey yonder,
　No regrets disturb the mind.

Peace, and Love, and Understanding,
　Far surpasseth worldly store ;
Conscience ever is commanding
　Each to love his neighbour more.
Oh ! if men would only cherish
　Purity of thought and deed,
Rivalry would quickly perish,
　Yielding to the better creed.

Strayed.*

(IN WEST YORKSHIRE DIALECT.)

It wor dark as I turned aat at haase
　Just to smook and parade abaat t' street
An' all wor as quiet as a maase,
　Exceptin' mi own noisy feet.

So I trailed away carelessly graud,
　Just as I oft used to trail,
Contented as ony in t' land
　Crawlin away like a snail.

I hedn't a care nor a thowt
　At could cause me a trifle o' pain,
Mi conscience wor burdened wi' nowt
　In t' shap of a troublesome stain.

So I smooked an' I trailed at mi ease,
　An' felt what it wor to be free,
I'd nobbut mi own sel to pleeas,
　An' noabdy felt leeter nor me.

* For Glossary of words employed in this and the succeeding rhyme, see Page 76. The pronoun *I* is used purposely in preference to *ee* in this poem, in order to prove clearer to the reader's comprehension.

I wanted for nothin' to eit,
　An' nothin' to drink or to spend,
I'd nobbut to keep misel straight,
　An' wor certain o' mony a friend.

So I smook'd and I strutted away
　As cheerful an' breet as a lark,
An' as heedless as though it wor day
　For all it wor ommost pitch dark.

I could see nowt but stars intut sky,
　As they twinkled and shone all so breet,
And I noticed 'em twinkle an' fly,
　An' thowt it a glorious seet.

An' I wondered an' stared sich a while
　Till mi een gat quite dazzled an' dim,
An' I'd sauntered away hauf a mile,
　Takken up wi' mi studious whim.

Then I thrust mi owd pipe in mi coit,
　An squared misel up like yo've seen,
I wor capp'd at I'd fon sich a toit,
　For I hardly knowed wheer I'd been.

But I stood for a while wheer I wor,
　Just to sattle misel in my mind,
An' I'm blest if I hardly durst stir,
　For I'd stared misel varry near blind.

But after a while I coom raand,
　An' bethowt me to toddle back hooam,
When I yerd all at once a strange saand
　At startled me rarely, by gum!

Then I yerd it agean quite plain
　An' mi hair peeakd straight o' mi heead,
I wished I wor back hooam again,
　For I thowt it wor summat fra't deead.

It worn't like a shaat or a screeam,
　If it wor I should easy hev known,
An' I'm certain I worn't in a dreeam,
　Just as certain as that wor a moan.

But I hasted to get aat o' t' gate,
　For I wanted no bother wi' nowt,
An' I knew it ud be raither late,
　Though I hedn't gien time any thowt.

So I framed misel ontut road back,
　An' started a gooin' at full run,
But not bein' certain o' t' track
　I slacken'd as sooin as begun

An I heeard the varry same saand
  'At I'd nobbut just noticed afoor,
An' I turned varry sharply araand,
  Ther wor mischief abaat I felt sure.

But I thowt just for once in mi life
  At a secret I'd try to finnd aat,
'Twornt oft as I mixed up wi' strife,
  But I meant it if strife wor abaat.

So I waited to yer it agean,
  An' bith mass if it worn't cloise by,
It saanded full waikly wi' pain
  Just like a young moorcock's cry.

An' mi heart fairly louped wi' surprise,
  An' I trembled in every limb,
I wor freetend to oppen mi eyes
  For all wor so dismal an' dim.

I knew there wor no help for me
  If some mischief wor plannin' araand,
But I waited for owt ther mit be,
  An' I heeard the self and same saand.

Then I heeard it again and again,
  Till I wondered whatever's to do ;
I felt as it couldn't be men,
  An' determined to follow it through.

I thowt happen somedy's in pain,
  So I sooin fon a match and a leet,
An' I hunted araand me and then
  I leet on a wonderful seet.

A poor little youngster laid theer,
  In't turnin' just off at roadside,
Wi' nobody ony where near,
  To soothe it whenever it cried.

It wor cruddled ameng t' tufts o' grass,
  An' wor lapp'd varry snugly an' dry,
But hardly left room for to pass
  For ony 'at chonced to go by.

Besides, it wor lat on at neet,
  An' it must hev laid theer some while,
It wor nearly heart-brokken wi' freet,
  Au' couldn't give one little smile.

An' t' poor little thing fairly sobb'd,
  An' its cheeks were as cowd as could be ;
To find it of comfort so robbed,
  It wor almost heart-burstin' to see.

Its poor little een oppen'd wide
  An' they looked sich a look in mi face,
I felt as if I could hev cried,
  To see sich a pitiful case.

It would hardly be four years owd,
  But it seemed to be middlin' an' strong,
Yet it couldn't hev missed bein cowd,
  Through liggin' in t' oppen so long.

I had plenty o' matches bi chonce,
  So I managed to keep up a leet,
An' I started to coax it at once
  Because it wor flade so o' t' neet.

I wiped it its nice little face,
  An' stroked daan its bonny black hair,
I straightened its clooas into place,
  An' acted with every care.

Then I kussed it an' kuddled it oft,
  Just soas it mit tell I wor glad,
But I felt varry sheepish an' soft
  When it started o' callin' me " Dad."

So I lifted it up off at grund,
  An' foulded it into mi arms,
Determined I'd noan be behund
  In shieldin' it 'gainst all alarms.

But mi heart wor as full as a fitch,
  For I felt what good luck it had been,
I'd hev faced oather giant or witch
  To sarve mi poor innocent queen.

I didn't think haa it would end,
  But I helped it an' did what I could,
For I felt at it wanted a friend
  An' resolved what I could do I would.

I'm sure at I felt varry glad
  In seein' haa things hed turned aat,
But I thowt after all it wor sad
  To hev littend so strangely abaat.

So I kuss'd it again and again,
  Tryin' hard for to mak it content ;
I lapped mi coit raand it an' then,
  Towards mi owd homestead I went.

An' I carefully threeded mi way,
  An' gat intut roadway to walk,
An' t' mooin comin' aat breet as day,
  Caused t' youngster to prattle an' talk.

An' it hodded as breet as could be
    To leet us back home to mi cot,
An' t' bairn wor a beauty to see,
    In spite o' t' exposin' it got.

But just as we landed tut street,
    I seed such a bustle abaat,
I thowt we'd be best aat ot seet
    Till I know'd what me'l people be aat.

So I axd of a chap comin past
    Whatever hed stirred 'em like that,
An' he said " Ther's a youngster ats lost
    " An' nobody knows where it's at ;

" An' its mother's near aat of her mind,
    " For thers nobody knows wheer to goo,
" They've tried all their utmost to find
    " Yet nobody knows what to do."

But as sooin as he spak I rushed aat
    An' hurried tut middle ot craad,
An' for all I geet jostled abaat,
    I shaated for t' mother reight laad.

An' I showed 'em mi charge safe an' saand,
    An' it laughed as they shaated wi' glee,
An' varry sooin t' news spread araand,
    'At t' babby hed landed wi' me.

Then its mother coom cryin' like mad,
    An' I gav her it safe in her arms,
She stroked it an' kussed it so glad
    To finnd it wor free fra alarms.

I thowt at shood never give ower
    Booath laughin' an' cryin' in turn.
But it cheered me rarely, I'm sure,
    To watch her so feelin'ly yearn.

An' she thenk'd me wi' tears in her een,
    As I stood like a dunce in a schooil ;
It wor t' nicest seet I'd ever seen,
    But it made me feel same as a fooil.

I followed 'em homewards just then,
    Till I saw t' little darlin' all reet,
Then they started to thenk me again,
    So I left 'em an' wished 'em good neet.

An' I hurried straight back to mi home,
    As pleeased an' as praad as a king,
For all mebbe different to some
    Mich liker to whimper nor sing.

But t' poor little lass took no harm
For its thrivin' as weel as can be,
An' it allus possesses a charm
At mi een are oft gladden'd to see.

An' I hope it 'll live in content,
An' keep happy hearted an' true,
For 'twor Providence certainly sent
Salvation to t' bairn an' me too.

Witty=schism.

(A WEST YORKSHIRE DIALECT DITTY.)

Mony whimsical mottoes aw've heeard in mi time,
  At saands raither natty an' true,
But whether they're oather in reason or rhyme
  Aw'm backard at praisin a few.
An' when aw wor nobbut a bit of a lad,
  Aw sattled when aw geet a man
Aw wodnt hod aat for owt shady or bad,
  As aw want to do reight if aw can.

CHORUS.

So allus do reight if yo can,
It pays ev'ry woman an' man ;
Ne'er heed what folks say, it's mich better each day
To allus do reight if yo can.

Ther's a motto aw've heeard allt days o' mi life,
  " In Rome do as all Romans do :"
An' aw think it breeds endless o' fratchin' an' strife,
  Deceivin' an' ticein folks too.
For if a chap's honest an' oppen hissel,
  An' starts to fall in wi' this plan ;
What's likely to happen ther's noabdy can tell
  When he moant do reight if he can.—*Chorus.*

Agean, ther's another, aw've oft heeard said,
  " A Romany once, an' for ever ;"
An' should anyone wi' sich humbug be led,
  It never can prosper him— never.
If once yo'v gone wrong, ther's no reason to think
  Yo cannot get back like a man ;
An' it wodn't be nice for a poor chap to sink,
  As wants to do reight if he can.—*Chorus.*

Aw'l mention one moor, at's weel known to yo all,
　" A rowlin' stone gethers no moss ;"
An' this one aw think everybody 'll call
　As waik as them tothers, or woss,
Ony shallow-craan knows, if he ligs hissel daan,
　He'll never turn aat a rich man ;
For a chap needs to venture sometimes fra a taan,
　As wants to do reight if he can.—*Chorus.*

Aw believe if aw tried, aw could goo on awhile
　Explodin' sich owd-fashioned wit :
For nah-a-days childer can venture to smile,
　Baat gaunin such rubbish a bit.
Its just on a par wit' t' owd Latin and Greek,
　Of a past but a time-honoured clan ;
But aw'l try not to give ony impident cheek,
　For aw want to do reight if aw can.—*Chorus.*

GLOSSARY OF DIALECTISMS

Employed in the Rhymes entitled, "Strayed," and "Witty-schism."

COMPILED BY THE AUTHOR OF THE BOOK.

DIALECT.	ENGLISH.	DIALECT.	ENGLISH.
Aat	Out	Coax	Fondle or nurse
Abaat	About	Clooas	Clothes
An'	And	Chap	Fellow
'At	That	Craad	Crowd
Ageean	Again	Comed	Come
Afoor	Before	Craan	Crown
Araand	Around	Childer	Children
Asd	Asked	Deead	Dead
Allus	Always	Daan	Down
Allt'	All the	Eeas	Ease
Aw're	I have	Eit	Eat
Aw'm	I am	'Em	Them
Aw	I	Een	Eyes
At's	That's	Fra't	From the
Aw'l	I will	Finnd	Find
		Freet	Fear or fright
Breet	Bright	Fon	Found
Bethowt	Bethought	Flade	Afraid
Bother	Trouble	Fowlded	Folded
Bith	By the	Faced	Met, defied
Brokken	Broken	Fra	From
Bein'	Being	Fooil	Fool
Behund	Behind	Fratchin'	Quarrelling
Booath	Both	Freetened	Frightened
Bairn	Child	Grund	Ground
Backard	Backward	Gate	Way, road, passage
Baat	Without	Gi'en	Given
		Geet	Got
Cowd	Cold	Goo	Go
Coit	Coat	Gac'	Gave
Capped	Surprised	Gooin'	Going
Coom	Came	Gethers	Gathers
Cloise	Near	Gaumin'	Noticing
Cruddled	Snugly placed		
Chonce	Chance		

DIALECT.	ENGLISH.
Hodded	Held
House	House
Hev'	Have
Hedn't	Had not
Hauf	Half
Heead	Head
Hed	Had
Haa	How
Heeard	Heard
Hod	Hold
Hissel	Himself
Hooam	Home
Int'...	...In the
Intut'	Into the
Impident	Impudent
It, applies to anything helpless or inanimate.	
Knowed	Knew
Kissed	Kissed
Kuddled	Squeezed caressingly
Litten'd	Had let, happened
Loupid	Leaped
Let...	Let and light
Lapped	Wrapped
Lat	Late
Liggin'	...Lying
Laad	Loud
Ligs	Lies
Middlin'	Fairly, just nice
Mebbe	May be
Mouse	Mouse
Mi	My
Misel...	Myself
Mony	Many
Mit	Might, may
Med	...Made
Mooin	Moon
Mich	Much
Moan't	Must not
Moour	...More
Neet	Night
Nowt	Nothing
Nobbut	Only
Noab'dy	Nobody
Noan...	None
Natty	Smart
Nah	Now
O' t'	Of the
Ony	Any
O'	Of
Owd	Old
Ontut'	On the
Oppen...	Open
Owt	Ought, anything
Oather	Either
Ommost	Almost

DIALECT.	ENGLISH.
Peeak'd	Reared, perched
Pleeas	Please
Raand...	Round
Raither	Rather
Reight...	Right
Rowlin'	Rowling
Smook...	Smoke
Sheap	Shape
Sel'	Self
Seet	Sight
Sich	Such
Sattle	Settle
Summat	Something
Sooin	...Soon
Saand...	Sound
Sooa	...So as, so that
Sarve	Serve
Spak'	Spake
Shoo'd...	She would
Schooil	School
Sud	Should
Some'dy	Somebody
Thowt	Thought
Takken	Taken
Toit	Hobby
Toddle	Steady walk
Ther	There
'Tworn't	It was not
Ther's...	There is
Theer	There
Tords...	...Towards
Tut'	To the
'Twor	It was
Theak'd	Thanked
Threeded	Threaded
T'others	The others
'Ud	Would
Varry	...Very
Wes	...We shall
Wor	...Was
Wi'	With
Well	Till or while
Wheer...	Where
Whoam	Home
Wern't	Was not
Waikly	Weakly
Whimper	Cry
Wodn't	Would not
Weel	Well
Waik	Weak
Woss...	Worse
Wi' t'	With the
Wod...	Would
Yo	Ye
Yerd...	Heard
Yer	Hear
Yo've...	...You have

By the Way.

When you sit at home in comfort, round your hearthstone, snug and warm,
With your dear ones all around you, safely guarded from all harm ;
Do you ever give one moment's thought unto our homeless poor,
Who pass you daily on the street, and starve beside your door.

When Dame Fortune smiles upon you, and her favours freely lend,
So that you have not a trouble what to eat, or drink, or spend,
Are you mindful of the message that the Master left for you,
"To do towards one another as ye would be done unto."

When your children play around you, never wanting for a friend,
And health, and strength, and comfort, fairy-like on each attend,
Are you never once reminded of the wretched waifs and strays
Who never had a parent's love to sanctify their days.

When you feel quite happy-hearted, and a stranger unto woe
When all things seem to prosper you wherever you may go,
Do you think about the saddened ones, the trodden, and downcast,
To whom the game of life beseems a harvest that is past.

Oh ! could we only view ourselves whilst blessings are in store,
Perchance we should appreciate and utilise them more,
But duty bids us look around, or whether high or low,
For each according to his lights some sympathy may show.

Nutshell Philosophy.

To you I write,
And now indite
Herewith, by way of greeting,
These lines to show
That you may know
In spirit we are meeting.

I need not tell,
I love you well,
Because I never flatter,
But this is true,
'Twixt me and you,
To love is no small matter.

True Friendship may
Have much to say
Without such empty bubble,
And if each one
Let this be done
We should not have much trouble.

Why should we try
To wander by
A plain and frank admission,
Since it is best
To be at rest,
And hold a straight position.

There is no peace
Without we cease
This roundabout invention,
And I would scorn
To thus adorn (?)
A good and true intention.

So, having said,
And thus far led
Your sympathies apace,
I fain would move
Beyond this groove,
And state another case.

Suppose some friend
Were now to send
Due token of regard,
Well knowing you
Were well-to-do,
And needed no reward.

And, if in time
(To make it rhyme),
Your circumstances failed,
And you had need
Of help indeed
As nothing else availed

And should he then
Remind you when
You lacked no friendly aid,
And with a frown,
Though you were down,
Of friendship seem afraid.

How would you fare
If he should dare
A traitor thus to turn,
And tell you plain
Your hope was vain,
And all entreaty spurn ?

And, if in truth,
He should, forsooth,
Insult you, bold as brass,
Would you again
Respect him, then,
Or whip him, by the mass ?

I think I know
How you would go
And tan his brazen hide,
For he's a cur
Who would not dare
To spoil a traitor's pride.

Just so I've seen,
And treated been
By one I once admired
And this I say :
Alack-a-day !
My passion soon he fired.

And here I own
To you alone,
I tendered swift receipt ;
For nought in life
Occasions strife
So much as bold deceit.

The while I prayed
For kinder aid,
Yet this I fain would tell :
With wounded heart
I took my part
And punished him right well.

Then quick he fled,
And from me sped,
Ere I my reason lost,
Or he had got
What he did not,
No matter what the cost.

I truly hate
To hear the prate
Of underhanded folk,
For I contend
He is no friend
Who treats it as a joke.

And, if some day
Upon your way,
You come across the kind,
Pray let them know
You deem them so,
And thus have easy mind.

The world is small,
But large withal,
For all who love the right ;
So try your best
To oust such pest
Away from honest sight.

I would not own,
Or wish it known
That I had two-faced friends :
For I delight
In acting right,
And there all friendship ends.

Do all you can
To prove a man,
As on through life you go ;
Avoiding strife
Wherever rife--
Allowing love to flow.

And then, indeed,
You hold a creed
To bear you bravely on,
And he is wise—
Though I advise—
Who sees his duty done.

Helene.

(A MEMORY.)

It was summer time. The noon-day sun, in bold relief, shed its refulgent rays o'er the earth ; Nature wore its brightest garb, and the birds carol'd their sweetest. The children ran merrily from school, and the busy world for the time being hurried to their various homes, and everything seemed glad. Everything, did I say? Yet not everything, indeed ; for in her chamber, stretched upon her bed, lay the dying form of the once so bright and lovely Helene. Nineteen summers had passed over her head, and just now, when life seemed the brightest, she had to yield to the grim Conqueror and die. King Death was waiting for his prize : and though so very young in life, she was old enough to die. I had known her long and well, for as children we had romped together. I knew her at school also, when her smile was the brightest, her step was the lightest, and her form was the fairest of any. Companions next we became, roaming the fields and lanes together ; and at length, to my great joy, she had placed her heart in my keeping. But now, alas, at this grandly beautiful noon hour, when all seemed so happy around, she whom I valued more than life itself was surely passing away, and her flickering spirit battling with death for the mastery.

What an awful ending to all our aspirations it seemed. Of what avail to us now was the sunshine ! How could I feel any pleasure ? What mattered anything, indeed, so long as the light of my life was dying, and nothing under heaven could save her ? It had pleased the Almighty so to order it, and mankind could not change the verdict ; although it was inexpressibly sad thus to have all my hopes and schemes frustrated and scattered at one blow. I pressed my hand to my burning forehead, and gave vent to the grief that filled my soul. Poor Helene ! loving and clinging to the last, she could not bear to witness my distress, and feebly she entreated me to "cheer up, and promise to meet her in heaven." But I could not answer her, for I only too well remembered how very small indeed were my hopes of heaven not so very long before, until her constant pleadings curbed my sinful progress. Thoughts of religion I had banished completely, until she broke the evil spell, and spoke to me of repentance. And then I vowed, God helping me, to try to act rightly; and she, my beloved, aided my endeavours. The poor darling richly earned a better fate; nothing was too good for her; loving and beautiful, trusting and true, no man ever possessed such a jewel as my Helene, and I had honourably striven to deserve her. Of what use to me was anything now, if my loved one couldn't share it? When everything looked so promising, and a happy future seemed to lie before us, here at one fell stroke our lives had become desolate, our plans unavailing, and my beautiful love was dying. And whilst I stood watching her thus—sinking before my very eyes, my thoughts reverted to the happy time when she was instinct with cheerfulness and hope, and trouble was a perfect stranger. How different now were the surroundings, indeed! We had never calculated upon opposition to our happiness in any way, much less to anticipate cruel death. "Man proposes, but God disposes." Although the sun shone brightly above us, and all around seemed gladness, yet to me it was terribly dark and oppressive, for the queen of my heart was dying. There may, perhaps, be some stern beings who could witness such scenes, and bear such sadness, unruffled—there may, perhaps, be those who are numb and dumb with impressive awe at the approach of death, but in my inmost heart I bitterly resented it, for, in spite of all our hopes and desires, my dearest one was doomed. Sinful I know it is to rebel against our Maker's decree, very wrong it was to harbour such feelings as then possessed me, but in my wilful selfishness I could not resist railing at her fate. Love such as mine was madness indeed, and most bitterly did I bewail it; but notwithstanding the lavishness of affection displayed she sank gradually away. Ye whose infatuation leads to such utter forgetfulness of right and duty as mine, beware indeed that punishment fall not upon you. "The earth is the Lord's and the fulness thereof;" and presumption is an awful crime. It is truly said that "though our way may not be His, yet the Lord will provide." And as we stood sorrowfully by her bedside, with a dear friend repeating the ever sublime Requiem, slowly and sadly, commencing "Rock of Ages," the torturing chastening to my soul was indescribable. "Helene, my darling," I cried in my agony, "live for me, love, live for my sake." I had ever been forgetful of the fact that death is the penalty of sin, and that sooner or later all must pay the forfeit. Thoughts of death I had shunned as a bore, but now, in the very presence itself, I prayed with a fervour unceasing that still she might escape it. "Whom the Lord loveth, He chasteneth." How very hard indeed it was. We were both young, the pleasures of life seemed so inviting, and we had meant to be so happy. Ah! well; the blight had fallen, and I was indeed awakened. Tearfully I caressed her, lovingly I held her in my arms, gently she clung to me, and solemnly, slowly, but surely, each precious moment passed, never, never to return. Thank God, she was ready to die; better far than I, she had learned resignation; confident and expectant of a blessed resurrection, she waited patiently for the message that bid her to immortal light, "where sorrows never trouble, and the tired are at rest." It was only, indeed, for my sake she was anxious, and she whispered me to hope; but the end had come. Clasping me fervently unto her, with an effort she pressed her lips to mine; then, pointing with her finger upwards as if beckoning me to meet her in the realms beyond, she lay gently down again, and soon all was still. And then—they told me that she was —dead. So peaceful, so quietly still she lay, but Death was king at last. I would have given anything to have died also, but it was not thus to be; and the darkest hour of my existence was when they told me Helene was dead, and I was left alone in the gloom. And still, the summer sun was shining, the busy noon time had not passed away, the same work-a-day world was joyous; but for me, my life was dead. Never again for me will life seem so bright: never whilst I retain memory shall I forget my lost one; never whilst upon earth shall I meet such another. Helene was my idol, Helene was my all; but, alas! Helene is dead. So passeth away earthly hopes and glory. We buried her shortly afterwards, and a simple little stone, with the one brief word "Helene," is all that marks her resting-place. As for me, what matters now? any place or every place is alike in the universe; and so I bid adieu to the home of my youth, the scene alike of pleasure and of pain, bound for another shore, to battle alone in the storms of life until I meet her in heaven.

A Woman Forlorn.

God help a poor woman forlorn,
    Whose heart is all shattered and torn,
The world cannot tell, how her bosom does swell,
    With grief over-much to be borne.

Despairing, dejected, and sad,
    A stranger to all that is glad,
She drags out her life, neither widow nor wife,
    Mankind a worse fate never had.

No hope on life's journey has she,
    No prospect could drearier be,
Lamenting the cost, of a happiness lost,
    O would that such martyrs were free.

We may not and cannot surmise,
    How hopeless it is to disguise,
The pangs of each day, as they hasten away,
    With grief welling up to her eyes.

Should ever you meet such an one,
    Have pity, and harass her none,
Just one simple word, if in sympathy heard,
    Is much to a woman forlorn.

————

Here's a Health.

SONG.

Here's a health unto he, that does plough the deep sea,
    With a heart that is light as a feather,
Who leaves a fond home, through the wide world to roam,
    Away from his life's dearest treasure ;
For a brave one is he, although humble he be,
    Who so ready proves true to the core,
O'er the ocean to sail, disregarding the gale,
    True to Duty and Love evermore.

Here's a health to the tar, on each stout " man-o'-war,"
    And our valour who strives to sustain,
Who will stand by his flag, and will die ere a rag,
    Any traitorous fingers shall stain,
For he faces grim Death, and with latest of breath,
    Still he urges his comrades the more,
Yet undaunted to stand, nor abate one demand,
    Until Honour is bright as before.

Here's a health unto sailors, their sweethearts and wives,
    May each one steer wide of all sorrow,
And may they have happy and prosperous lives,
    Without any fear for the morrow.
Then away o'er the seas, with the health-giving breeze,
    Will they speed with each heart brimming o'er,
And will cheerily sing, till the echoes shall ring,
    " Here's to Duty and Love evermore."

Soliloquy—On Reflection.

What is there indeed in the nature of man,
Tends more to ennoble his fitful life's span
Than when in a turmoil of doubt and despair,
He bends to reflect on his burdensome care,
He may be oppressed—or, he may be cast down,
He may have lost heart o'er the giddy world's frown,
He may seem bereft of all comfort and joy,
Yet sober Reflection will drive the alloy,
With the passions at bay, and his manhood at stake,
Reflection will ever true *reason* awake.

When living seems useless, and all else a ban,—
To every endeavour of unlucky man,
When the gloss has "*gone hence*," and a chaos appears
Inducing repinings, exhaustion, and tears ;
There's a light lies beyond all the darkness and dread,
When his selfish indulgence and bigotry's fled.
Reviewing his case, calm and careful, and plain
He rises refreshed in his manhood again.
For Reflection enables the weakest to cope
With ills that disperse with the dawning of hope.

Reflection will ever grant peace to the soul,
Compelling the forces of mischief to roll,
Reflection lifts higher the curtain of hope,
Imparting new strength and enlarging its scope,
It cleanseth the brain from all spurious taint,
Conceiving a *wisdom* of love and restraint,
It yields to the mind a new impetus born
Of honest desire from *self* to be shorn.
Then however you be, or too fast or too slow,
Submit to Reflection the way ye should go.

―――――

Our Willie.

Dear reader, if you are partial to startling romances and adventurous themes, I can hold out little hope that this humble life story will seriously impress you. It is not at all sensational I admit, but this much can be said of it, that it is a faithful record in every particular, and I can heartily recommend it to your sympathy. The subject of this narrative was one of three children, whose advent to life was under anything but auspicious circumstances. There are some fortunate people in the world to whom misery is a stranger in their youth, but "Our Willie," as I shall call him, was unluckily familiar with it from his youth up. Whilst only a toddling child, and, along with his brother and sister, very poorly attended to in consequence of the quarrelsome bickering of ill-matched parents, the news was carried home that he who should have proved their earthly protector, had "joined the Regulars" and enlisted as a soldier. Under certain circumstances such a step would have proved a blessing to his poor wife, as it would have been the means of ridding her of what proved to be the bane of her life, but he, being the only bread winner, and so cowardly deserting her and the children, only increased her difficulties, and exposed his own heartlessness. When cruel want haunts your footsteps, and a thoughtless world derides your efforts ; when undeserved shame and remorse takes hold of you, and starving children are pleading for bread ; it is then indeed only a short step to despair. And very soon—too soon, alas ! the poor young mother, with such a fate to battle against, fell into despair ; and by and by, and step by step, unaided all too cruelly by the too stern moralists of that town, she drifted slowly, but surely, into loose habits and conduct, until getting at length into the drunken courses which are inseparable from depravity, she became the inmate of a prison. During her confinement there, her poor children were looked after by one and another of her kindly neighbours, who had more of charity than justice in their hearts. Reared as she had been in the habits of comfort and industry, and feeling bitterly how her sad plight would affect her old parents who were fast journeying to their last home, who will doubt that those grim walls drove away from her every vestige of duty and self-respect ? If only a helping hand had been offered to her when the villainous husband had deserted her, if only indeed half as much care was exercised in discovering such cases as hers as is done in detecting crime, how different it would have been with her, and how much better would it be for civilisation generally. But it was not so, alas ! and very often indeed in our advanced morality of modern times, the sin of taking the one and first false step is made the medium wherewith to wreck and blast the character and career of a whole lifetime. Upon her release from imprisonment she was changed completely from her old self, and having become unfortunately lost to the gentler feelings of her nature, she left the neighbour-hood to tramp about the country, dragging her children with her, as it were from "pillar to post." Ruin is imminent enough in all seriousness when things come to such a pass, and all too soon she lost herself and became despised of her sex—an abandoned woman. It is easy enough, God knows, for those who live in comfort and contentment to express and feel deep abhorrence at the vagaries of a fallen woman ; but in very truth we are bound to admit when pressed, that it is anything but easy for a deserted woman (who is still young, with good looks to recommend her, and who sees her children starving whilst she herself is penniless) to keep in the paths of rectitude. If we would be honest as we ought, we must confess that there is so much sin and mischief inherent in human-kind, that verily the saints of yesterday only prove the sinners of to-day. We are none of us blameless, however good we try to be ; and it is a grievous presumption—which is an equal sin with any other—to constitute our-selves judges over our weak and fallen brethren. I shall not attempt to depict the character of this wicked life in its glaring hideousness, for unfortunately such instances are not rare now-a-days. But one result of it was that her children were taken away from her, and Willie became a pauper before he was six years old ; being destined as it happened never to look upon his mother's face again. This, I contend, is the greatest misfortune that can befall a child, for "come weal or come woe," the tenderness that sanctifies the association, and which occasionally gleams out so prominently under even the most adverse circumstances, is a possession of itself that nothing else can ever atone for. It was not a pleasant lot to be a workhouse lad in Willie's day, and nothing nearly so choice then as it is now, when philanthropists of every grade vie with each other in striving to make such a lot bearable ; and it is also true that a poor boy's life was more wretched in proportion than the other inmates, for what with bullying, cramming, hungering, and flogging, it was then one ceaseless round of arrant intolerance. Not one gleam of sunshine entered his boyhood, and yet although of stinted growth and anything but robust, by some subtle elasticity indi-genous to that period of life, he managed to reach his tenth year as presentably as the majority of lads around him. There were no pence and pleasant trips for pauper lads then, everything indeed partook too much of the doctrine that existence was a bounty ; and children, in common with older heads, were taught to be humbly thankful for such a blessing. What a paltry travesty of life does such a doctrine present, when calmly considered ! one cannot avoid surmising what weight of hypocrisy underlies it. It is very certain that this workhouse life was anything but a Paradise, for within there, indeed, more than in any other place perhaps, Bumbledom reigns supreme ; and man's ingenuity succeeds in initiating a system of inquisition and torture, com-parable in its completeness to a fine art. But when Willie had turned his tenth year he discovered that the real troubles of life were only commencing, for, being then con-sidered old enough to work for his living, he was hired out, or "parish placed," to a collier, who required a lad to assist him in the mine. So with his parish outfit, he was bundled off to get along as best he could, once more amongst strangers. There was not, perhaps, a more harassing life to be found than fell to the lot of a collier's pauper lad, for they had to work half naked in grimy rags amongst mire and puddle, in a crawling position, exposed to many unhealthy, tiresome, and often dangerous conditions: and in addition were only half fed. Brutality there had its full bent, and what with the long hours, the thrashings, and varied accompaniments incidental to such a dangerous occupation, it would not be amiss to describe it altogether as diabolical. Whether it has improved in this year of our Lord, 1887, from what it was in Willie's time, I cannot say, but this is undeniable, that it cannot be at any time a desirable occupation. So much for life in a deep coal mine. Willie's "master" was a low, vicious, and brutal fellow, a veritable Shylock or a Legree in fact ; and it was quickly apparent to the lad that he had got "out of the frying-pan into the fire;" for if any doubt ever existed upon that point, the frequent beatings and bullying treatment he received soon dispelled it. There are colliers, I dare say, who are as manly and true as any gentleman can be, but in perpetration of rank mischievous conduct, and more especially in the past, the dare-devil collier "carries the palm." Before a few years had passed over, Willie's body was "black and blue" with scars and disfigurements, caused by accidents or design : and to make his bitterness complete he had not one good friend in all the world. Kindness he never experienced, and had it been possible for his poor lost mother to have seen him in his sixteenth year or so, she would have gone crazed, such an object had his weary life made him. Stunted, deformed, and rugged, he presented little appearance to a creature in the image of God. Poor Willie ; how many to-day there are in as pitiful circumstances, God alone knows. If only men and women would think a moment, how thankful they would be in having such refuges as our Ragged Schools, and Homes for the neglected and homeless waifs of society. There is not, and cannot be, a more practical and elevated form of Christianity in the whole known world of schemes for man's salvation, than is found in this glorious work of rescuing, housing, and training the helpless crowd of long suffering and puny mankind. Who indeed can say how vast a work is theirs ? and what devil's mischief they curtail. May we then not bestir ourselves more in this noble direction? Does it not in truth behove each of us to warm to the work, whether gentle or simple ? I feel sometimes that it is almost a work of martyrdom for the very few, who so perseveringly, in spite of many reverses, have yet the Divine love so implanted within them that they will not yield in their enterprise. Reader, do what you can, however little, to help such good work, and who knows, maybe more than one, as desolate as "our Willie," may through your means live to return benefit and blessing to his fellow-men. At eighteen, Willie received a visit from no less a personage than his father, who, having left the army, had taken it into his head to look up his son, and see what he was like. There was no affection prompted the visit, nothing but heartless and idle curiosity merely to satisfy himself of the identity ; and no sooner did he behold the miserable form, than he departed with as much speed as he could respectably muster. Had Willie been a fine, muscular, well-developed and manly figure, he would doubtless have "done something," for him, but his appearance horrified him. Oh, what a burning shame to betray such an unnatural disposition as that, a father indeed, whose heart should have brimmed over with affectionate yearning for the poor unlucky lad, scanning him as though he was a brute, and as coolly as if he was not himself responsible to Heaven for his desolation. Ye who understand the pitiful, wordless, pleading of children, think how much that lad would suffer, then, and afterwards, at his father's loathing and cold neglect. Would he not, think you, youth though he was, and distorted ever so badly, yearn and repine for one word of love ? God grant that when that father reaches the judgment seat he may receive different treatment ! Friend, whoever you may be, I ask you was that not enough to finish any lad, with one spark of natural craving in him ? And I can assure you, that so truly as night follows day, so surely it broke Willie's heart. It is not an idle or meaningless story I am relating, it is every word as true as Gospel, and not long afterwards he was found a stiffened corpse—cold and dead—upon his rude couch. Better far indeed was it to leave such a cruel world, for if ever a lad's history revealed a tale of horror, most certainly it was his. Poor Willie ; neglected, despised, and maltreated, from his cradle right to the grave, a home at last he would find in Heaven. Fathers, mothers, sisters, and brothers, if ye are blessed with a loving and happy home circle, do not disdain to shed a tear for Willie ; and when your family is safely in the fold, pray God that none of them experience his fate. He was only a pauper it is true, he was only an unfortunate waif, we know, but in the sight of Him who rules the heavens and the earth he was as precious as any in the universe. Bitter, hard, cruel, and undeserved as was his brief life here, yet at the great Atonement there cannot possibly be a brighter sphere of glory, than will prove to exemplify the Saviour's love for "our Willie."

Recitative Commemorative.

Since Avon gained, through Avon's bard,
   Her grand historic fame,
The world of letters well regard,
   The Grand Preceptor's name ;
Not all the wealth of history,
   Or chronicles sublime,
Reveal a name more famous,
   Or an Oracle so prime.

And well it is that fertile mind
   Can estimate such worth,
Since none more gifted or refin'd
   Has sprung from Mother Earth ;
It needs no zealous phantasy
   To prove his teachings true,
Morality has ever been
   The dowry of the few.

Then banish every mean excuse,
   And hasten due regard,
Away at once with vile abuse—
   Where merit wins reward ;
Discuss him when and how you will,
   And ponder him well o'er,
An honest verdict proves him still,
   As peerless as before.

In homage to his high estate,
   I proffer true report,
And with all votaries will pay
   A due and proper court ;
So Literate a company,
   Full mindful of his fame,
In evergreen festivity
   Perpetuate his name.

So, Shakespeare ! still, we bow to thee,
   For precepts like to thine
Shall rule the world in destiny—
   The human heart refine ;
Thy native worth, thy native shore
   Shall publish o'er and o'er,
And Father Time shall manifest
   Thy virtues evermore.

'Tis thus in Harmony we meet,
   Thy Natal day to hold,
Commemorative of a mind
   Brimful of letter'd gold ;
Respectfully before thy shrine
   Unprejudiced and free,
We yield the honours truly thine
   And tender them to thee.

The Tug of War.

The Scene was in a canvas tent, with lumb'rous vans around—
The cabin'd homes of quadrupeds in distant countries found ;
Ferocious ones, and tame ones too, were held in bondage there,
Divided from the people with the greatest skill and care.

The day was done, and flaring lights were hung around the place ;
The Exhibition had begun, and anxious seemed each face.
The people stood in groups intent, on Massarti's display,
To prove the iron will of man above the beasts of prey.

This Massarti the Tamer was intrepid, cool, and calm ;
Possessed of matchless courage, though alas ! he'd but one arm.
A sword hung ready by his side, against the time of need,
For well he knew he had to deal with savage beasts indeed.

Then, marching to the lion's den, at once he entered in,
And hounded them till nought was heard, except their horrid din ;
He made them march, and crouch, and leap, before he turned away,
As they retreated panting and excited from the fray.

No sooner had he turned his back, than, with a hideous yell,
The boldest sprang upon him, and upon his knees he fell,
But swiftly by manœuvring he deftly burst away,
And, sword in hand, did face them, like a warrior at bay.

The maddened brute did loudly growl, then sprang at him again ;
He tried his best to frighten her, but tried his best in vain ;
He slashed about him with his steel in that unequal strife,
For while she fought for mastery, Massarti fought for life.

A panic then amongst the crowd of gazers did ensue,
Each recognised his danger, yet knew nothing what to do ;
'Midst screams of terrified dismay, and many a cry of pain,
The vicious beasts did seize him, and entrap him once again.

Full resolute with every stroke, he dealt a horrid gash,
And, nimbly holding on his feet, at them full tilt did dash ;
They danc'd and howled in agony, retreating as before,
Whilst he beheld advantage, and essay'd to gain the door.

No quicker than he reached it, than with fierce and awful yell
Again they dashed upon him, and alas ! again he fell.
They carried him across the den, and bruised his body sore,
Until, with giant's effort, he enfreed himself once more.

Than slash at them, with might and main, he fought in dread despair,
Exclaiming loudly for some help, but little help was there :
The people were dumbfounded, and seemed rooted to the spot,
The while his life blood oozed away—a sad, ignoble lot.

Feebler then his blows did fall, and feebler still he grew :
His strength well nigh exhausted, yet no one knew what to do,
A strong partition then was found, to thrust inside the bars,
To part him from the lordly brutes, and foil them unawares.

Awhile enfeebled he held on, till he could hold no more.
Then, bleeding and unconscious, he fell down upon the floor ;
The barricade was jamm'd within, but hope for him had fled,
The Lion Tamer was no more—bold Massarti was dead.

System.

System rules the universe. It is the clockwork of time, the finger of health, and the soul of existence. To be without a system is to be without a head, and they without system have no guide. A system in life, or a system in business, is the surest means to success, for men without system cannot succeed. A system in government and a system in religion is absolutely necessary for advancement. No confusion exists in system, but without system confusion always. Cultivate then a daily system, a regular system, and a life system, but pray you let it be a system for good. No order exists without system, and method is the attendant upon order. Be guarded in speech, be upright in your dealings, be merciful and true. Be patient and plodding, be tender and kind, The world may move slowly and fortune may lag, but all comes right to him who waits. Contentment is great gain, and duty lies next to us. Whatever of good thou canst find to do, do it with thy might. Do all things in reason, and do all things well. Cleanliness is essential to reason, and reason essential to system. Be honest and be true, then you have a system that will honour you in life, and bless you in eternity. Hold fast to that system.

A Song of Emotion.

(ILLUSTRATING THE GRIEVOUS CONDITION OF VERY MANY OF OUR " UNEMPLOYED.")

I will sing you a song of a heartfelt emotion,
   And strive to enlist your pitying grace,
Since pity expresses the truest devotion,
   A suppliant I will unburden my case ;
Alone on the hearth I unceasingly ponder,
   Wherever, indeed, shall I light upon aid,
If in truth it will be " the big house " over yonder.
   Alas ! that it may, I am sadly afraid.

Ah, well ; should it be that nought else should befall me,
   But the grim workhouse door prove my ultimate fate,
I'll hie me and hide with dull grief to appal me,
   And wait for the next and a happier state ;
Cruel hunger and want here triumph around us,
   And jeeringly mock our reputable pride,
To be lacking a crust and the money to buy one,
   Is bearding a death which is galling to bide.

The cup of misfortune is now brimming over,
    And dear ones perforce are bedabbled with me,
The once-a-day happy and light-hearted lover,
    Stands now as forlorn as a body could be ;
The weary worn face of the poor wife and mother,
    Still trustfully beams at my immobile mien,
In vain though I try every feeling to smother,
    My heart she discerns when my eyes she has seen.

Oh, God ; can it be that dread poverty's victims,
    Must ever be dragged to the verge of despair,
Shall innocent dears in a vortex of madness,
    Sink thoroughly broken with anguish and care ?
Where, where, is the vaunted good Christian feeling,
    From pulpits proclaimed and well published around,
One true human heart deserves better of Heaven,
    Than all the stern moralists ever was found.

Then welcome, thrice welcome, the love of the lowly,
    With sympathy true and with warm grasping hand,
For they of a truth are most earnest and holy,
    Though wretched they lie and benighted they stand,
The scum and the refuse of civilisation
    Can never be termed our vast " *unemployed*,"
For these are possessed of praiseworthy ambition,
    Which cuts to the quick when all hope is destroyed.

Where is the good of disclosing my story,
    Since little indeed the harsh world would believe,
Not even though aged, and feeble, and hoary,
    I could not convince whilst so many deceive ;
Nor ragged, nor blind, nor yet begging or croaking,
    No sycophant ever, or hypocrite I,
'Twould be too good a theme for the fun and the joking,
    To crave the relief they would smoothly deny.

What careth the world for an unit so humble,
    What matters indeed any quantity such,
When I and my kin from the earth have departed,
    Though no one will gain, there will none lose so much ;
To have and to hold seems the standard of honour,
    To need and to starve is the opposite code,
To scheme for success and then hold fast upon her,
    Are maxims renowned in the world's royal road.

'Tis useless ; I cannot—nor would I endeavour,
    To win at such cost although easily got,
So I languish away and most likely will never,
    Recover from this my unfortunate lot ;
But I hope—yes, I hope—when the warfare is over,
    That those left behind may have fortune in store,
For long with reverses have I been a rover,
    And I shall have rest when the struggle is o'er.

The Work of Drink.

A TEMPERANCE RECITATION.

The kind of work that drink can do
    (As brevity's the soul of wit)
Quite briefly I'll portray to you
    The dread results that come of it.

It does its work extremely well
    At every opportunity,
And cultivates a track to hell
    By snaring the community.

Its tempts the innocent and young
    With blandishments quite various,
And garnished with a jovial song
    It renders them contrarious.

It rouses mischief and dismay
    With flattery and babble ;
It overcometh reason's sway,
    And fascinates the rabble.

It makes a man forget himself,
    And those unto him nearest ;
It steals his hardly-earned pelf,
    And love from friends the dearest.

It robs the infant of its milk,
    By making mothers careless ;
It turns its vendors out in silk
    And drunken folks delirious.

Creating wife or mother soon
    Despondent, sad, and weary ;
It makes a thinker a buffoon,
    And turns bright prospects dreary.

It makes the young and tender child
    To want and crave provision ;
It renders peaceful people wild,
    And kills good admonition.

It makes a honest man a rogue,
    And causes rogues to flourish ;
It brings a many things in vogue
    Uprightness cannot nourish.

It changes man into a brute,
    And makes a woman shameless ;
It covers both with ill repute,
    And renders reason aimless.

It fills our workhouses and jails
   And thrusts folks into prison,
Compelling bitter tears and wails
   When mischief has arisen.

It robs the people of good health,
   Disgracing every history ;
It gloats o'er poverty and wealth,
   And causes endless misery.

It robs a man of worldly store
   And swallows all his riches ;
It strips his coat, and —what is more—
   His very shirt and breeches.

It flatters virtue same as vice,
   And lures with enchantment ;
It pictures even devils nice,
   In breeding discontentment.

It robs a man of homely joy,
   His comfort and contentment,
And damages his girl or boy
   With scorn or mean resentment.

It ruins everything in life.
   And steals the senses given ;
It causes misery and strife,
   And robs a man of Heaven.

It turns the man into a fool,
   And makes the fool despise him ;
It blots away each golden rule,
   And very oft belies him.

It greedily devours his meat,
   And craves for every earning ;
It casts him homeless in the street,
   And mocks his every turning.

It fills each dirty street and slum,
   Or filthy habitation,
With victims sick at heart, or glum,
   Through cursed ruination.

It humbles men and trifles all,
   That righteous men hold dear ;
It binds its victims with a thrall
   Of recklessness and fear.

It values nought and knows no care ;
   'Tis Satan's direst curse,
Creating only black despair ;
   No torture can be worse.

Doin' Weel.

A MIXED DIALECT DITTY.

I'm sitting at whomm in mi chair,
   Withaat an odd penny on earth,
Yet free fro' ill-nature an' care,
   Enjoyin' mi quantum o' mirth.

We've spent every copper we had,
   In buyin' sich things as we could ;
I think at we've noan done so bad,
   But, could we do better, we would.

Some folks as I know, poo a face,
   Just 'cause they moan't hev all they want,
But I'm varry content in my place,
   Although what we hev's nobbut scant.

What fooils is some fellows, for sure,
   To mope, an' to bother, an' fret ;
Yo' never know'd anyone poor
   As ever improved wi' it yet.

We've getten some pratoes an' flaar
   An' a fine pair o' kippers as weel
A drenchin' an' all, in a shaar,
   'At's gone throo' mi clooas, I feel.

We've getten a good haif-a-paand
   Of butter, besides a ham shank
Wi' a good bit o' meit all araand,
   But t' shopman for that I've to thank.

We've bowt some nice pot-herbs up yon',
   Some turmits an' carrots an' all ;
Wes' hev' some good broth, I'll be bon',
   Soas who ever happens to call.

Ther's some drippin', an onions, too,
   Some meil, an' some sugar, an' tay ;
Wes' manage for one day or two,
   Befoor it's all shifted away.

We've a pint o' new milk every morn,
   For t' babby, an' Jack's porritch too,
Some fellies their noses uptorn,
   As nothin' no better can do

I managed to buy haif-an-aance
   O' 'bacca, to keep me i' toit,
So I oather can use it, or baance ;
   I hev it at hand in mi coit.

A chap 'at's content wi' his lot
  Is t' happiest man under t' sun,
An' should yo' believe it or not,
  He'll sing when them tothers hes done.

A bowl o' meil porritch is reight,
  When t' appetite's sharpened wi' want ;
It 'ud set mony invalids straight
  To bid a farewecl unto cant.

A boil, or a roast, or a fry,
  I can order an' hev in a trice ;
Ther's lots as is woss off nor I,
  For ony o' t' three's varry nice.

But I hevn't a penny in t' haase,
  For all I can jabber an' sing ;
I couldn't sit here like a maase,
  While feelin' at heart like a king.

Disappointments.

Sad things are disappointments. Broken hopes, futile wishes, and blank desires,
these are all disappointments.   It is very hard to see one's aims and hopes all
shattered and dispelled, but we cannot prevent disappointments.   Life is fitful, and
disappointments will ensue.   We need not break down under them, let us bear them
manfully, and reflect that very often they are of our own shaping.   Death we cannot
avoid, but much of misery, sorrow, and sickness we may.   Don't fret too sadly, for it
only increases trouble.   Be mindful of one another, cheer the disappointed ones, but
avoid aggravation.   Be steady and prudent, be careful and sober, and you will greatly
lessen disappointments.   Don't be cast down by a disappointment, still look
onward and strive again.   God is the arbiter of our destiny, and we cannot dispute
His will.   Love God, and when trouble comes, He will help you to bear it.   Cultivate
a forgiving spirit, and love your fellows.   Do not faint, or frown, for that is a hindrance ;
and experience proves that in the long run, such a disposition is fruitful of disappointments.

Turning Teetotal.

One day as I rambled the streets up and down,
  Undecided whatever to do,
I met with a friend from a neighbouring town,
  Who invited me with him to go.

Said he : "My old friend, I'm delighted we've met,
  "For an hour together we'll pass.
"With pleasure," said I, "and, dull care to forget,
  "We will go and indulge in a glass."

So in the next tavern we stepp'd arm in arm,
  And seated ourselves near the bar ;
Then ordered a liquor quite pungent and warm,
  As liquors, you know, often are.

We tried to be merry, the truth to confess,
  And chatted along with the rest,
But of pleasure, I vouch, we never had less ;
  'Twas making-believe at the best.

We scarcely could hear what each one had to say,
  Such a hubbub and noise they did make ;
The harmony certain had wafted away,
  And our heads with the worry did ache.

The whole conversation was meaningless too,
  Though joined in by both old and young ;
The gossiping tattle could never be true.
  Whilst the songs were unfeelingly sung.

So we quickly arose, and went out from behind,
  Confessing ourselves much the worse ;
For we'd fondly imagined a comfort to find,
  Instead of the very reverse.

So we walked up the street, and we noticed instead
  Just straight, as it seemed in our face,
A grand Coffee Palace did rear up its head—
  A rich and a beautiful place.

My friend, very soon, with a look full of joy,
  Pass'd himself through the half-open door,
And, drawing me after, said he, " My dear boy,
  There's nothing can beat this, for sure."

'Twas so of a truth, ; a quite elegant place,
  With cleanliness everywhere ;
And people admired every comfort and grace,
  Partaking the while of the fare.

The waiters were smarter and nicer by far
  Than what is the usual run ;
So obliging and willing they served at the bar,
  My friend would have flatter'd each one.

The food, too, they sold, was substantial and cheap,
  No better could anyone buy,
And of dainties besides I beheld such a heap,
  I felt I must give them a try.

There was Cocoa and Coffee, besides Milk and Tea,
  Just to suit any customer's taste ;
No danger, we felt, but that all would agree
  Avoiding all riot and waste.

And then, after meals, you could study the News,
For I read half an hour or more ;
And in various ways we ourselves did amuse,
And I never felt better before.

There were various games, and a chance for a pipe,
If anyone wished for a smoke ;
Convenient rooms for a wash and a wipe,
With comforts for all kinds of folk.

So when I reached home I explained to my wife
Each place I had seen up and down ;
She vowed and declared for the rest of her life,
She'd go there herself when in town.

Blackburn's Greeting to T.R.H. the Prince and Princess of Wales,

ON THE OCCASION OF H.R.H. THE PRINCE OF WALES LAYING THE FOUNDATION STONE

OF A TECHNICAL SCHOOL, AT BLAKEY MOOR, MAY 9TH, 1888.

Welcome, Albert Edward, Britain's heir, and Prince of Wales,
Welcome, doubly welcome, where true Loyalty prevails,
Here we gladly meet thee, as befits thy Royal part,
And Blackburn's children greet thee with affection in each heart.

Welcome, Alexandra, unto Blackburn's busy scene,
Welcome, dearest Princess, of true womanhood a Queen, .
Welcome to each heart and home, a lustre there to shed,
Welcome to the homage that by Love is only led.

Welcome, Prince and Princess, for your happiness we pray,
And hope your Silver Wedding may beam Golden from to-day,
We offer you true feeling, and we tender you good cheer,
And trust we'll long remember this glad auspicious year.

Then hail ye and God speed ye, in your noble task this day,
A nation needs must prosper that is led in such a way,
In Blackburn's name, for Blackburn's fame, we greet you with delight,
And tens of thousands tongues will sing your praises ever bright.

N.B.—Their Royal Highnesses were gracious enough to accept a couple of copies from the author, and also deputed Sir F. Knollys to tender him their thanks for the same, which he was honoured by receiving, by letter, on the 17th inst. following.

Only One.

Whether the subject of this sketch had ever any home at all, or wherever such a home was situated if he had one, is entirely beyond my knowledge ; but after having known him well for many years, off and on, as the saying is, I can state emphatically that he never owned one to my recollection. From the first moment of our acquaintance I was most strongly impressed with his manner, which, judging from his rough exterior might reasonably have been expected to be rude and uncouth, but which to my agreeable surprise was gentleness itself. Hugh, or Hughey, as we familiarly termed him, was a poor and destitute street arab, who lived solely by his wits or his luck, when nothing more definite availed. If work could be had he never shirked it that I am aware of, but at once applied himself willingly and diligently unto it, no matter of whatever kind it chanced to be. And varie I indeed were the tasks he undertook, anything from going upon an errand to labouring and living by the sweat of his brow. Kind and quiet, civil and obliging always, it was a revelation to me to witness such characteristics under oftentimes the most adverse circumstances. Of brute strength he possessed a good share, although I never once saw him in a fighting mood, nor even thoroughly defiant ; and yet he was a grand fellow, well built, healthy and muscular, but simple withal. It is a common but unworthy characteristic of the world generally, that a penalty must follow simplicity, however and wherever found ; and whenever the slightest indication of natural failing, or brain weakness is visible, then and there is a tax imposed as a matter of course. This is a most cowardly trait in the human character, to say the least of it ; and like many another poor creature, Hughey was a continual victim thereto. Not being as exactly acute in his perceptive faculties as other men, but being always submissive and deferential to superior in- telligence, he has often been an easy prey to the cheater, and has performed many a hard day's work only to be swindled out of his wages at the close. On such occasions he was rendered almost beyond the power of speech and expression, by what to his view was the enormity of the meanness ; and yet whilst possessing abundance of strength for the purposes of successful retaliation upon the rascals, he has been im- pelled to seek sympathy from myself by the mere narration, and ultimately to surmount his misfortune in tearful ejaculations. He was troubled only little by either sentiment or prejudice, and so was never long despondent. If questioned concerning his parentage he would at once explain that he knew little about it, and that his ideas were developed in a " *free school* " until his thirteenth year, from which time he had to face the world on his own behalf. Then his pilgrimage began ; and in his buffetings about he wandered from town to town, and place to place, until by the time he arrived at man's estate, he was tolerably familiar with most of the highways in the country—and thoroughly conversant with a vagrant's life. To beg he was not ashamed, but was at all times as willing to give as to receive charity, and begging was his last resort. Portering, carrying, and jobbing about, he was only too glad to be of use in either direction, and if by chance his employer was a friendly one, he would serve him as faithfully as a watch dog. I have known him in my illnesses to serve me without any recompense, and though at such times of a most irritable disposition, he has cheerfully and meekly put up with it all. In fact, he would consider me upon such occasions as entitled to growl at him, and so perverse is human nature, I have actually growled at such forbearance, and behaved rudely enough, in consequence. But no one could appreciate him better, and the poor fellow knew after all that I did not really wish to be unkind, and I always regretted such indiscretions. A real kindness occupied his memory always, and his childish mode of recognising the same was peculiarly modest and affecting ; but familiarity he despised. A word, or even a look, was sufficient at any time to quell the ardour of his attachment, and he was mightily jealous on occasion in maintaining a due appreciation of his dignity as a personal friend. He had his faults and foibles, of course, but, as he often expressed himself, " A principled man I like," and so far as in him lay, he honestly strove at imitation. Perhaps his chief ambition was to possess a watch and chain, and it was something to remember when fortune so favoured him, and he ushered himself into our presence the proud possessor of a cheap timepiece, which was safely secured to a gaudy brass appendage which swung prominently across his vest. There could not be any two opinions then as to Hughey's dignity and manifest importance, and with something like a decent suit upon his person to complete the rig-out, I verily believe that he fancied himself a highly placed personage indeed ; and he fairly endeavoured to maintain the position. This, however, was beyond his power to do, and consequently the watch, &c., were often entrusted to the custody of a pawnbroker for the means of livelihood. It was a great fall for Hughey whenever that exigency arrived, and it seemed as though all his importance vanished with the watch, never to return in anything like the same measure without it. It could not be the watch, and it was not wholly the man, but the two together completed a personalty at once ludicrous, and decidedly original. It was plainly evident whenever he shared our rambles under such circumstances, that his was the patronage bestowed ; and because we understood the poor fellow, we heartily appreciated his goodness, and permitted him the pleasure of observing it. Many people there are who will deem us faulty in our likes and dislikes, but even so we prefer simplicity at all times to false upstart arrogance. Nay, I am very often dubbed simple myself, but as the poor children of lost humanity are always with us, it is a pleasure no less than a duty to mingle sometimes amongst them, to promote harmony and contentment in their station, and persuade them into loftier paths. If by so doing I become dearer to their hearts and clearer to their understanding, then to remain simple will I be happy indeed. It is barely possible for the firmest of the poor to get out of the rut, hemm'd around as they are with so much that is depressing, demoralising, and objectionable ; and yet the very unhappiest and lowliest of them all may not unprofitably claim our kind attention. The shifts to which they are driven by the sheer force of circumstances are strangely varied indeed, and Hughey could relate his experiences as to sleeping in various fashions, in different haunts, on beds, hammocks, boards, hearths, barns, hay or straw shake-downs, and sometimes under hedges, or in the open fields. Snow clearing in winter, coal storing as occasion offers, and handbill distributing when obtainable ; together with harvesting, hop picking, and odd jobs at farm labouring, are only some of the methods employed by such as Hughey, wherewith to earn the necessary requisites to keep body and soul together. Thus the aid of such " *unfortunates* " is necessary for the development of progress and civilisation, and scouted although they ignorantly are, it cannot be denied that they prove as useful in their sphere (if not more so) than the better dressed loungers who frequent the places of public resort in our towns and cities. It is all very well to talk of dirt and depravity, and to stand aghast in pious horror at the shortcomings of our very poor ; it is high and fine to advocate prosecution for charity seeking ; but for every one bad character who is laid hold of, there are nineteen destitute and deserving people who receive the punishment designed for him. What should a poor man do who rises penniless and hungry in a strange house, in a strange neighbourhood ? He must not starve. Let him only do as Hughey has been compelled to do, when necessity taught the way, simply to walk down the centre of a respectable street, chanting in as musical a fashion as he can command, some tune or hymn, evolved from loving memories of the dim past, and which performance is intended to provoke symptoms of Christian charity. For this even is a man sent to gaol, often by a minister of the gospel indeed, and a life's prospects, hopes, desires, or ambition, as the case may be, is blotted out for ever, and he becomes a criminal. Ah, well ; let us hope for better things to come, for better hearts, for purer minds, and for cleaner consciences, What Hughey will come to I cannot say, but the odds are greatly in favour of this, that a miserable life ends with a miserable death. He is still living, sitting even in my presence whilst I pen this, a strong, robust, and not ill looking young man of about 24, and were I a man of means he should never with my consent leave my service. But such is life ; and poor Hughey, gladdened as he is by having seen me once more, must perforce travel on from face to face, and place to place, until time and fate bring us again together. I can well imagine as his wanderings lead him, after a few year's absence, back into our neighbourhood, how he yearns for another meeting, wondering as to my fate ; and when Providence guides him at length to our door, and his familiar features come into view, his glistening eyes, his kindling smile, his glad greeting, and his hearty hand clasp, are only in truth a faithful reflex of my own emotion at seeing him once more. Poor fellow ! knowing as I do his trusting and ingenuous nature, I often pray that he may escape in some degree the harassing accompaniments and perils inseparable from the condition of a forlorn and friendless waif. The privations endured, the exposure to inclement weather, and the want of good nourishment, cannot fail in the course of time in undermining the constitution ; and the number must be very small, indeed, who wilfully and permanently commit themselves to such undesirable and bitter fare. Hughey is only one of the vast army of our willing unemployed, and with such as would willingly work if they could, the bitterness of the position must be acute, for poverty compels them to be associates with the veriest scum. However, it is a pleasure to see our poor friend in any guise, and it often happens that when he arrives his wardrobe is as weatherbeaten as his countenance, and experience has taught us to be ready for the occasion. His visits are prolonged at our wish to holiday duration, and no matter how dilapidated and tattered he appears, he is generally re-rigged before his departure. He knows and feels that with us he is right, and our humble cot is made his harbour for repairs; and if our store of cast-off raiment be not always fashionable, he knows there will be sufficient wherewithal again to face the world. There are, alas, too many Hugheys in this world of ours, and every reader of this short sketch may without difficulty grant to some one of them, his or her friendship, and thereby illustrate fully their service to that Master, who of His great love declared that, "Inasmuch as ye have done it unto one of these My children, ye have done it also unto Me."

An Open Heart.

Some people think a man's a fool
    Who shows an open heart,
As though it were the better rule
    To act a double part ;
Yet I love best to see a man
    Display a nature kind,
For he, above the others, can
    A useful purpose find.

You need not whisper unto me
    His failings, not a few,
It is enough for him to be
    A man both good and true ;
Amidst a horde of reprobates
    A man soon loses fame,
E'en though his usefulness creates
    A blest and honoured name.

Then, heedless of the Cynic's frown,
    Live out your useful life,
Unselfishness begets renown
    For good amidst the strife.
The brighter looks, and brighter hearts,
    That follow in your train,
A thousand times the bliss imparts,
    That e'er attends the vain.

Slow and Sure.

A simple country couple journeyed once to London town,
With cash enough to live upon, whilst strolling up and down ;
They had not spent a single day from home since they were wed,
And both of them agreed 'twas time by pleasure they were led.

So, lover-like—in rustic style—they wander'd arm-in-arm,
While ev'ry little thing they saw possessed a novel charm ;
He murmured, "Lawks-a-daisy me ;" while she exclaimed, "Oh, my !"
And both of them did thus maintain a constant parrot-cry.

The swain had donn'd his swallow-tail—a garment he did prize—
A relic of his grandad's days, and priceless in his eyes :
Its colour was of faded green, with buttons made of brass,
And just the coat to take the eye of rustic lad and lass.

His breeches were of corduroy ; his vest was made of plush ;
For fashion he had ne'er a thought, nor cared a single rush ;
A jaunty billycock hat he wore, with half-a-foot of rim,
And a gorgeous crimson necktie, which accorded with his whim.

His pretty partner was array'd in quite a taking way,
For flounces and for ribbons she was Belle of all that day ;
Her rosy cheeks and coal-black eyes made everybody stare,
But all agreed that he and she were quite a Model pair.

He swagger'd with his walking-stick, and she with parasol ;
No other couple there could match with country Job and Sal ;
Contented with simplicity, and seeking no renown,
They envied none with whom they met in famous London town.

They were but young in years, and had nothing to deplore,
Their wedded life was happy, and they sought for nothing more,
Their income was sufficient to supply their every care,
And most o' folk were glad to know the happy country pair.

In dress and manners each did try the other one to please,
For marriage was but courtship still, with ownership and ease ;
Obliging and good-tempered, each endeavoured to appear,
And Love maintained supremacy within their humble sphere.

And so this homely country pair were innocent of shame,
And home to them was just a home—deserving of the name ;
They sang away their little cares, and kissed away each frown,
And Job and Sal, though simple folk, were higher up than down.

And as they wandered through the streets, surveying all around,
The idlers tried in vain to guess what errand they were bound ;
And whilst the Cockneys laughed in fun, our rustic pair did smile,
But never dreamt their style of dress was curious the while.

To Crystal Palace first they went, its famous sights to view,
And many wond'rous things they saw—surprises old and new—
But what the most astounded them about the Sculpture there,
Was, that the want of modesty caused everyone to stare.

It was not shame, since virtuous minds might truly wonder why
Such insults unto decency were bare to every eye,
For every eye ought not to see designs that may unnerve,
Lest they who falter by design, from innocence may swerve.

To Baker Street they ventured next, the Waxwork Show to view,
And gaze upon the novelties, as country people do ;
But Job no sooner got inside, than he was shaking hands
With the smiling Chinaman in wax, that by the doorway stands.

Then both of them did loudly laugh, that thus he was deceived,
For Job declared quite earnestly, 'twas human, he believed ;
They promenaded round the room, and noticed all within,
Attracting the attendants by their rustic style and din.

Into a handsome Music Hall they next did wend their way,
And listened to a song or two, and heard the music play,
But when the Ballet dancers came, they caused the pair to blush.
So, running to the doorway, they into the street did rush.

The Theatre, likewise they found, was anything but pure,
And fast young libertines tried hard to stare them out for sure ;
In very shame they blush'd to think they patronised such sights,
For everywhere it was the same, and wrongs were turned to rights.

Upon the Stage the Drama played was of triumphant wrong,
And words of double meaning were in every toast and song,
A brazen tone was all the rage, which caused them great surprise,
And Virtue there was bought and sold, before their very eyes.

All joy was gone ; and their sole wish, was quickly to reach home,
And both declared that when they did, again they would not roam,
They had started out for pleasure, but they found much more of sin,
Effrontery upon the streets, and shame and vice within.

So Job unto his wife did say, "When I get home again,
" I'll rest myself contented, lass " ; and she replied " *Amen,*"
"To think," said he, " we dressed so gay to travel here and back,
" If we're obliged to come again, we'll dress ourselves in black."

And so between them they were glad, to start the journey home,
Determined ne'er to London town, in future would they come ;
The sights—so called—had sicken'd them, though both escaped the ban,
So he kissed her, and she kissed him, a good, time-honoured plan.

On reaching home they changed their clothes, and placed them out of reach,
Resolved they never would forget this lesson they would teach,—
" That homely pleasures are the best, and greater comfort makes
" Than rambling aimlessly abroad, and playing ' *ducks and drakes.*' "

Thus country cousins shew the world that Town Life is a sham,
And scenes of which we brag so much, morality does damn,
So cultivate more homely joys, and perhaps in time we shall,
Entice again, to London town, true-hearted Job and Sal.

A Debating House Celebration,

AT "THE OLD SPREAD EAGLE," BLACKBURN, JANUARY 13TH, 1885.

The fire is quenched ; contention's dead ; the wordy war is o'er ;
Philosophy and Sophism have fled from out the door ;
Each solemn air and gesture strange, the hobbies learning bring,
Is laid aside, to seek repose, beneath the Eagle's wing,

The Chairman's bench, that honoured seat, which constitutes a throne,
Is relegated for awhile to regions lesser known ;
The bell, with all its glory, has been banished for the time,
And mirth usurps authority, where learning reigns sublime.

Sages, legislators, and the whole assembly then,
Hobnobbed, and broke the dull reserve, peculiar to such men,
Old age and youth, their merry quips, together they did crack,
And peals of laughter witness bore, that none did humour lack.

The goodly and substantial fare, with which the tables groaned,
Cemented a new fellowship that only friendship owned ;
Mind and matter, generated scope for more research,
And matter gave the mind a turn—the mind did matter much.

The festive board, the cheerful scene, and ever joyous song,
The loving cup, the merry tale, and happy go-along,
The soberest brain, the stoutest heart, relaxes 'mid such fare,
And thus the " Eagle's " protégés enthusiasm share.

What matters who shall call it wrong for wranglers to agree ?
Such recreation proves a boon to frail mortality.
It cannot be that noble minds will woo disastrous plight,
And so reprieve is granted for the " Eagle's " festive night.

Then, Hail, ye brothers, one and all ! for ye I breathe a prayer—
May the sunshine of prosperity attend you everywhere.
Full honesty of purpose in a honest cause must win,
And happy days will smile upon " The Old Spread Eagle Inn."

Good Owd Yorkshire.

There are many homes in England, and a many people too,
But none surpasses Yorkshire, nor is anyone more true.
You cannot find a better or a worthier renown,
Go where you will, I say it still, than Yorkshire's, up or down.

A Yorkshireman is jolly, and a Yorkshireman is plain,
He barters melancholy for a more substantial gain,
Though oft-times deemed a rustic, and as simple as you please,
He can buy or sell, your tip-top swell, and manage it with ease.

A Yorkshire girl is pretty, and a Yorkshire girl has taste,
She's happy and she's witty, and is careful not to waste,
She can bake and sew, I'd have you know, and leads a useful life,
And men-folks tell, they come off well, who win a Yorkshire wife.

There is no finer scenery than Yorkshire's acred Shire,
No better favoured country, for good health, or to admire,
There are hills, and dales, and moorlands, with many a hedge and dyke,
And honest-hearted ever, is a homely Yorkshire Tyke.

The natives of old Yorkshire are the bravest of the brave,
They never brook an insult, and a favour never crave,
The hold aloof from meanness, and no matter where they roam,
They earn a fame and honoured name, for a model English home.

Then here's success to Yorkshire, and to Yorkshire people too,
My love for you will never fade, whilst heart and mind are true,
The grip of honest fellowship unto each one I extend,
And fondly greet, whene'er I meet, a hearty Yorkshire friend.

The House of God.

When unbelievers feet have trod
   Beyond the walks of grace,
Still I within the House of God
   Delight to take my place.

What though the sceptical and vain
   Its proffer'd shelter scorn,
The House of God shall still remain
   My Refuge night and morn.

To me it is a precious spot,
   A tabernacled realm,
Where Peace abides and sin is not,
   When Faith directs the Helm.

I love to hear the Preacher's voice
   Repeating psalms of life ;
It makes my troubled soul rejoice,
   And quells all inward strife.

I like to hear the Organ's swell,
   And feel the magic power
That prompts my trembling lips to tell
   My failings every hour.

Beneath its well appointed roof
   I lift my voice in song—
A tuneful burst which tenders proof
   Of singleness and wrong.

I value not the Learning, which
  Evolves distress of mind ;
Let me a clearer doctrine teach
  Which gives me Hope to find.

'Tis in the House of God alone
  This doctrine can be found,
And gladly do I there atone
  With reverence profound.

Then let my lot be good or ill,
  Whilst uppermost the sod,
I'll plead for Mercy, Grace, and Will,
  Within the House of God.

Muggleton's Tea Party.

I went to a tea party, the other day, at my old friend Muggleton's. I dare say you have heard of Bobby Muggleton before to-day, for it is a noted fact that when he got married to Joan o' Dykes he became celebrated all at once. Joan was no common woman in any sense, and when Bobby jumped into partnership with her so suddenly, he surprised everybody by his bravado. If ever a prize had been offered for a right-down virago, and Joan could have been entered, she would have won it very easily, for she was as awkwardly cantankerous as anybody could be. I don't blame her for being ugly, although she was not so handsome that I could be tempted to flirt with her, but really she could have no occasion for being so awfully snappy and ill-tempered. It is all very well for some folks to shout for women's rights and sing "Rule Britannia," but at Bobby's house it was Joan who ruled the roost. Certainly this rule was never disputed, for against a vicious looking, big, brawny handed, and muscular six-foot woman, Bobby appeared a mere stripling. At any rate, whenever any knotty argument was waging, Joan would clinch it at once by ordering him off to some job or another, and for quietness' sake he used to put up with it. He was a tackler, or a weaving overlooker by trade, and could earn a comfortable salary; and being of economical pursuits his wife reaped the advantage. As it happened, there worked under his supervision at the mill, a nice, buxom young woman, just out of her teens, and between her and Bobby had grown apparently a mutual liking. In fact, it was the deepest occasion for remorse with Bobby, that he had never met her in his single days, and, unfortunately for his peace of mind, Betty spurred him on by appearing at her loveliest ; and both of them got deeper in Love's gilded meshes, until a perfect infatuation took possession of them. Now, Betty was really a good-looking young woman, and beyond this attachment to a married man, which could not be kept within proper bounds, there was nothing could be said to her discredit. But, somehow, it happens that the best intentions, as the Scotch poet puts it, "oft gang agley," and the heart that should have been sacredly true to his wife, yearned, alas ! for another. It does occur sometimes in this unlucky sphere, that we discover, only too late, "what might," alas, only so well, "have been." When Joan received the news of Bobby's unfaithfulness, bitter feelings possessed her, and the same boded ill for his welfare. Of all sad things in life, nothing is truly sadder than to see a tied couple travelling contrary ways, and each bent upon spiting the other. However, the commonplace routine of Bobby's life was one day changed by the breakage of some engine machinery at the mill where he worked, and, of course, as it would take a considerable time to repair it, it necessitated a holiday for the general hands, Bobby and Betty amongst the number. So when he reached home and told Joan of the affair, she very quietly arranged to visit some friends, and bade him to remain indoors and mind the house. Of course, like a proper termagant, she did not even then leave him without plenty restrictive regulations as to the conduct becoming to a married man whose wife was from home; and such a state of melancholy did her attitude inspire within him, that it was fully an hour after her departure when he arose from his seat. But for once in his life he had arrived at some sort of determination, and settled in his mind what a godsend her absence would prove, in promoting a scheme of enjoyment. And enjoyment he meant having, in some shape or other, to celebrate such a happy release from thraldom, and being undecided as to the manner thereof, he walked over to consult me in the matter. Thus did I get mixed up in the affair. Undoubtedly our friendship demanded such a display of confidence in such an important matter, but, speaking frankly, the avidity I displayed in urging him forward in his scheme was not altogether free from a malicious feeling towards Joan. So we studied the matter carefully, and finally decided to have a "tea party" at Bobby's own house, the company to consist of three couples only. Of course, in our own way, we did not forget to take measures to have a perfect clearance of everything before his wife's return, ourselves included. We arranged to have Betty with us, with also a chum of ours, and our sweethearts; so that altogether we might enjoy ourselves without stint, and be safe from prying eyes. The prospect of Betty's smiling loveliness gracing his hearthstone in reality, fairly entranced Bobby, and whilst he busied himself in the necessary preparations for the event, I went round and got the company together. He knew one or two nice little "tips," did Bobby, and when we arrived at his house he had the kettle boiling, a nice spread on the table, everything cosy, and a large bottle of "short stuff" to keep the steam up. Of course there was a little fluttering when we all got together, but it soon wore away, and before we left the table we were as merry as lambs. It was a splendid affair all through, and a drop of rum and tea is a wonderful reviver. At any rate, we laughed and chaffed, told tales, joked with one another, and behaved altogether the same as children. It takes a wonderful effect in a good company does rum and tea, and if you help yourselves too freely to it, you won't be long before you show an attack of "simples." Well, before so very long, there was some rare rosy cheeks and smiling faces, and every one of us felt fairly frisky. Bobby forgot all his troubles for once, and as he sat there in his arm-chair, with Betty next to him—one arm round her ample waist, and her beaming face nestling against his manly shoulder—they were truly a picture worth seeing; and I shall not easily forget it. They looked for all the world as soft as hot butter that melts itself away as you look at it. I often think about the "carryings on" that night, for what with song singing, and a moderate share of sweethearting as well, we fairly eclipsed ourselves. There is no one fonder of a little boisterous fun in its proper place than I am myself, but the lively and expressive style of that occasion must very nearly have approached a misdemeanour. A shrewd observer will often note the simpering and cooing peculiar to such meetings, and ours was no exception to the rule. It is a moot question, indeed, as to what becomes of the sober senses of an unusually philosophic mind in this condition of things, for verily there are very few specimens of this class even, who upon such occasions do not seem to change their character completely. However, Bobby and Betty "carried the palm" upon this occasion, and what with spooning and frolicing, I never knew such an "all gone" party as we then proved. An arrangement was made to sing a song each in turn, the rest to join in the chorus, and after a time it came to Bobby's turn to sing. With it also came the climax. Standing side by side in the centre of the room, or as near standing as they were capable of, he in a fond caressing attitude, and she leaning lovingly against him, with one arm clasping his neck, he rose grandly to the occasion, and with much feeling rendered the opening strains of "Good-bye, Sweetheart, good-bye." You might imagine, friend, but will never know, how strangely blended were the impressions produced thereby; for with her strong lung'd and unsteady assistance, the disjointed sentences and starting tears of the twain, accompanied by the audibly hysterical results of the unusual "fuddle" from everybody present, it was striking enough for a "patent right" application. No one watching the performance, such as it was, could have doubted that the farewell was realistic, and such, indeed, it proved to be. Just when the second verse was finishing, and Bobby's feelings seemed about to overflow; just as Betty (owing to the prolonged and uncommon strain upon her nervous system) was preparing carefully to fall in a convenient swoon: and just as the onlookers were experiencing unwonted thrills; just at that moment the door opened wide and very suddenly, and in walked Joan. In she stalked like an avenging fury, and at the sudden apparition, one loud and continued yell rent the building. In one moment there was a tremendous bustle ; screaming, screeching, declaiming, and bewailing, such a scene as I never wish to witness again. Bobby and Betty were fairly mesmerised, and there they stood in solemnly endearing attitude, with eyes fixed upon Joan, unable to stir either hand or foot. Beyond the ever changing pallor of their faces, which alternated from sallow to crimson, you would have thought them both thoroughly petrified. Joan took in the situation at a glance, and a peculiar sneer about her cruel lips gave me the impression that she enjoyed her triumph. It was really a pity to spoil our pleasure so unnaturally, but truth to tell, we had ourselves aided in our discomfiture in forgetting prudence, and overstaying the limited time arranged upon. Seeing how matters stood, Joan walked coolly to a slopstone in the kitchen and returned with a bowl full of cold water, which she very deliberately and diabolically emptied over Bobby and Betty together, heedless of the spasmodic cries of the thoroughly bewildered victims. But why need I relate the details of the terrible undoing they received ? Suffice it to say they deserved commiseration in their plight. Such a change in our programme was never anticipated, and we wished heartily to turn our backs upon it, which we did not manage without the aid afforded to us by the household utensils which lay convenient to the injured wife's reach. In fact, so desperate was the case that the aerial flight of a three-legged stool had miraculously missed ending my discomfited career, and I vowed inwardly and heartily as I ran, never again to risk an encounter on similar terms with an Amazon. What dire punishment befell the unfortunate love-lorn couple, pity forbids me to say ; but this I can vouch, that for their very fleeting term of joy, they suffered most cruelly, morally and physically. What happened precisely I never knew, and never had the heart to enquire ; but it is certain that Betty did not return to her work until three days had expired from the starting time, and then she bore evidence of much sundry and vicious ill-usage. As for poor Bobby, the suffering victim of an ill-starred marriage, sure his injuries were palpably evident to any beholder, for, not to mention the colouring process his face had undergone, he carried scratches and scars innumerable. He also lost his employment in consequence of enforced absence from the mill, and when I happened to see him in the street one day, his features looked so downcast, and of such a pallid hue, that I truly grieved for his sake. He suffered much for the adventure, but in spite of all remained true to Betty ; declaring solemnly that nothing should compel him to live one day longer with Joan than law permitted, and that an action for divorce was pending, which, if successful, would ensure his own and Betty's happiness for life. And folks certainly pitied his hard lot, having noticed how lightly and cruelly Joan had treated him. I told him that they had my best wishes, and many of them, for success ; but sincerely besought him for all our sakes not to be rash whatever he did, and not to let Joan hear one word of his intentions, for I felt sure if she got to hear of it, poor Bobby's life would not be worth the insuring. Naturally, I do wish that all folks who are devoted to one another should come to a happy condition, but whether or not my friends ever do so, I know that I shall never forget for a long time to come, that unexpected denouement at Muggleton's Party.

Looking Back.

Alone in my study one cold winter's evening,
    I sat and I pondered on incidents past ;
The cares of the day had dispers'd, to my seeming,
    And calm retrospection engaged me at last.

I pictured the friends who had long since departed,
    And lived once again in a beautiful world ;
The scenes long ago made me feel happy-hearted,
    As innocent pleasures were quickly unfurl'd.

The youthful *lang syne* even yet did attract me,
   As carelessly free with my fellows I played,
Till Time, the uprooter, yet farther did track me,
   And drove me athwart, where the wanderer strayed.

Some strange ups and downs were revealed to my thinking
   As over life's sea I was driven and toss'd ;
Betimes fairly calm, and sometimes almost sinking,
   'Tis hard to believe what the journey has cost.

But angels of mercy once more did attend me,
   And sunrise adorned the horizon at last ;
Though humble and frail, yet a few did befriend me,
   Till at length—happy day—is the misery past.

And now, may the rest of my days be contented,
   'For the vision has gone, and my work starts anew ;
I would that no further of life be lamented,
   So, facing my lot, I will strive to be true.

The Blackburn Poets, 1888.

ODE IN RESPONSE TO WILLIAM BILLINGTON'S "WHERE ARE THE BLACKBURN POETS GONE !"

There's a question of late that has often been put,
And the answering which proves a troublesome nut ;
But if you will grant me one minute of time,
I'll venture to give you the answer in rhyme.
"Come, tell me, O Muse," sang the Patriarch Bard,
"Where the Poets have gone whom we deeply regard,
"And why are they silent in tuning the lyre,
"Whose genius burns with celestial fire ? "

This query in truth held an ominous tone,
As Billington perfectly well would have known ;
But he, with a heart overburdened with zeal,
Spoke out from his fulness for Poesy's weal.
Devotion alone led the tip of his pen,
And made him deplore the dull quietude then ;
So, in plain, homely strain, he expressed a desire
For the music of those whom the Muse did inspire.

And wherefore should he not the question ask,
Since surely it offered a cordial task ;
For his compeers truly had fallen away,
From constant endeavours to edit each Lay.
But now that the Querist has journeyed hence,
There cannot remain any cause of pretence
For silence, or rust, or witholding the strain,
And so to his question I'll venture again.

There is Yates and there's Chippendale, Abram, and West,
With those dialect rhymsters, and locally best—
The two brothers Baron, whom nought seems to tax,
Self-styled " Jack-o'-Ann's," and again, "Bill-o'-Jacks."
There's Hurst and Joe Baron, with dry " Aker-Whitt,"
Remain with us still, and as votaries sit :
These all were renowned in a practical way,
When Billington penned his sweet Lyrical lay.

We have Duxbury, Clounie, and Edgar and Hull,
Welcome singers each one, and of harmony full ;
Surely these will succeed in creating renown,
And guarding the fame of our poetic town.
A many besides, in addition we've got,
Too modestly shy, although sterling the lot.
In defence of our honour the gauntlet is thrown,
That the shades of the dead may our Brotherhood own.

There is Walker, a name we sincerely admire,
Still sings, though with Jardine, transplanted each lyre ;
But the Querist, alas ! has pass'd into that bourne
(With poor Richard Rawcliffe) from whence none return.
May his name and his fame ever verdant remain.
And may we sweet singers for ever retain.
That a page to the glory of this, our loved town,
Be found in the annals of England's renown.

———

At Last.

[A gentleman, having served in a subordinate position for many years—a position which was irksome to his feelings—very suddenly became rich through the decease of a wealthy relative, and invited the Author to consider the circumstances, and celebrate the occasion by writing this farewell to his surroundings.]

  'Tis o'er at last—the galling yoke—
   The bondage now is past,
  The chain is loose—the fetters broke,—
   And I am free at last.

  'Tis sad to picture all the years
   Of bitterness and care,
  To think of all the sighs and tears
   Evolved from deep despair.

  I cannot own one little pang,
   Because my task is done ;
  I'm heedless now of every clang,
   For now—the Battle's won.

  Farewell, to all ye books and pens ;
   Farewell, ye Ledgers too ;
  Farewell to everything that lends
   Remorse unto my view.

Farewell, to all ye hateful scenes—
A jubilant farewell ;
A service with you only means
A servitude in hell.

Avaunt, ye spectres of the past !
Away, from out my view !
For time has vanquished you at last,
And life is leased anew.

Never again do I wish to see
Ye symbols of disgrace ;
Not any charm remains for me
About the wretched place.

I leave you all in sweet content,
Without one small regret,
Beyond the wish that luck was sent
Ere you and I had met.

So, once again, a last adieu
My patience is run o'er ;
A life mis-spent begins anew ;
Farewell, for evermore.

A Tale of Love.

Two Lovers together were strolling one day,
And fondly conversed in an amorous way ;
Each one did endeavour the other to please,
Desiring the while to appear at ease.

They tarried at length in a quiet retreat
Where mossy-grown hillocks provided a seat,
And Will with his arm clasp'd around Maggie's waist,
Of true lover's rapture enjoyed a rich taste.

But she, though indeed very happy just then,
Possessed but a sorry opinion of men ;
And though in her heart she was honest and just,
Of him she had always a little distrust.

She could not explain this condition so well,
For Love runs astray, as its vagaries tell,
But yet she displayed quite a tremulous fear
Though he was as constant as days in the year.

Young Maggie was timid and shy as could be,
From lover's sweet joys she would shrinkingly flee,
Full dreading lest Will in his ardour would poach
And cause her a future of lasting reproach.

But never indeed had he proved so inclined,
For he valued her person no more than her mind ;
His fulness of course might entice him astray,
But never beyond any fond lover's way.

And thus did they reason whilst cozily sat,
The *pros* and the *cons* duly measured in chat,
And handsome young Maggie she fluttered and sighed
As Will begg'd for favour becoming a bride.

And little by little his arts overcame,
As he in his fervour redoubled his claim,
His low murmured pleadings and kisses so sweet
Consumed every fear with fire and heat.

A Mad Adventure.

A very interesting acquaintance of my younger days was a person whose sobriquet was "Old Nepper." Not that he was so very old in years, for he could not have exceeded thirty, or so; but considered as he was—half idiot and half knave—his peculiarities entitled him to rank as "old." There was no mischief afoot he was not a party to, and whether concocted by men or boys, no surer way of securing his friendship existed than by such a paltry bribe as a piece of tobacco. For this consideration, you could command him unreservedly for either fun or vengeance, if not otherwise engaged. Add to this peculiarity an uncouth figure, short limbs, and a certain facial deformity, with a habit of developing too suddenly somewhat alarming fits, and you will have a fairly accurate description of Old Nepper. Considering the fits and the idiocy combined, it is true to say that I always experienced a certain awe of him ; and I am positive that the mad animal style, in which he kept the very young village children in justifiable terror of him, aroused in myself feelings of a similar, though more subdued nature. But with all his drawbacks he was very popular, and an acknowledged institution in our midst ; and I verily believe that in one way or another, every inhabitant had cultivated his acquaintance. In common with the rising generation throughout the country at that time, there was no day in the year so dear to the hearts of our village youths as the Gunpowder Plot (bonfire day). Upon that day and night, mischief held high jinks, and many a blazing pile gave testimony to the plundering depredations upon fences and in woods, by organised gangs, banded together for the occasion. If ever there was one time more than another when our hero's services were in request, it was on these occasions, for his daredevil ventures and simplicity rendered nothing safe that came in his way. Fences, trees, plants, and anything else that was combustible and movable, were all purloined and added to the bulk that was stowed away in some out-of-the-way place ready for the carnival. And it must not be forgotten that each separate gang of youths kept its own separate store, and, being in rivalry with each other, it not unfrequently happened that successful raids were made upon their respective stores, thus occasioning and maintaining a malicious spirit abroad. It was no wonder, then, that this "progging" time, as it was called, was an excitable period in our village ; and when, in addition to the plundering, contributions in coal and coin were levied upon the neighbours in each district, it may very easily be surmised what mischief resulted, and what an important event was Bonfire Day. These bonfires were no child's play, but great, fierce, blazing piles that illuminated the whole district, and kept burning for a couple of days, and around which roughly sported, with firearms, fireworks, beer barrels, dancing, smoking, and flirtation, the various members of each proprietary band. Amidst such scenes as these, of course, Nepper would revel until he lost his head completely, and it was little wonder that the orgies were to him ineffaceable, for in them he achieved great distinction. Upon one certain occasion, Nepper's gang had prepared a great stock of combustibles, and being desirous of obtaining a little diversion at the idiot's expense, they determined upon a line of action. Following out their plan, they were not long in informing him that, from information received, they expected to receive a visit from a certain gang of rival plunderers, and thus prevailed upon Nepper to remain all night upon the premises, and keep watch over their possessions. This information alone was sufficient to make Nepper prick up his ears, but when, in addition, they primed him well with beer and tobacco, he could not have withheld his approval. So he consented to keep guard over the storehouse yard, and plainly let them see that he was fully determined to attack anything or anybody that offered to lay unlawful hands upon their spoil. There was really no danger whatever of such an occurrence taking place, and they knew it very well ; but being mischievously inclined, they considered themselves entitled to have some entertainment. Nepper, therefore, thoroughly befooled, took up his position as arranged, and with a stout cudgel in his grasp waited seriously and patiently for the depredators. Now, it also happened that a certain frolic-loving policeman, having been an unseen listener to the gang's arrangement, resolved within himself to use the occasion for his own relaxation, and Nepper's discomfiture at the same time. So, keeping his project to himself, and having provided a white gown, cap, skull, and mask for the purpose, he waited until midnight for the efficient carrying out of his scheme. Nepper, in the meantime, having taken up his quarters in the yard, waited until he almost despaired of action, but curbing his impatience as well as a vigorous enjoyment of a smoke could express, he quietly seated himself in a corner and awaited developments. It may possibly have been that during his prolonged inactivity his ardour had somewhat abated, but whether that was so or not, a sudden sound at the opposite end of the premises, occurring simultaneously with the then closing midnight chimes, full quickly aroused him into a proper sense of his position ; and he strained his eyes in a vain effort to pierce the intervening gloom. Soon, again, he heard the same sound repeated, and thinking to surprise the daring intruder unawares, he cautiously crept towards the place, keeping very close to the wall. Now, curiously enough, the policeman—for he it was—having donned his disguise and made himself look as ghostly as possible, was pursuing similar tactics to Nepper himself, and creeping along the wall side ; and, as a natural consequence they met full tilt on the way. Whether it was the suddenness of the affair or not, I cannot tell, but certain it is that Nepper's terrified shriek and the rustle of retreating robes were startling sounds that quickly broke the midnight stillness. It happened also, at this juncture, that the moon began to shed her light upon the scene at the same time that Nepper's comrades were returning to release him from his task and chuckle over their sharpness. But, upon hearing the shriek and cautiously peering over the wall, they became witnesses of an interesting sight indeed. In one corner of the yard, trembling with an awful fear that possessed him, they beheld their victim staring with dilated eyes at a white figure which was surmounted with a "death's head," leering at him from the opposite corner. Intuitively they felt that every occasion for joking had disappeared, and that for the poor fellow, at all events, it had become a most serious matter. However, curiosity overweighed every other consideration ; and they anxiously awaited the issue of events, whilst taking the precaution not to be seen, for, knowing their comrade's peculiarities as they did so well, to expect a " battle royal " was not too much under the circumstances. What to think of such an unearthly visitant Nepper did not know, but it is certain that the figure fascinated him, and completely held him in check. With anything earthly he could grapple to some purpose, but against such as there appeared, to expect it was out of the question. Had " his ghostship " then departed, all would have ended well for both parties, but when it began to handle the precious "plunder," as if to take it away, that was a proceeding that the poor fellow would not and could not allow to pass unchallenged. Even to the idiot there seemed to be a great gulf 'twixt ghosts and thieves, and the moment that the wood was handled, he at once boldly shrieked in defiant tones a warning to "put it down." There must surely have been some determination in Nepper's looks at the time, for the figure immediately dropped it in an unceremonious manner. Such a demand, and in such tones, had rather disconcerted the intruder, but he applied himself to such ghostly artifices as in his mind seemed associated with the character, to such good effect, that so long as the "operation" lasted, Nepper was helpless,

With one arm of spotless white, strikingly uplifted, and the other solemnly waving him backwards—his whole form in an attitude of stern impressiveness—it is no wonder that he mesmerised Nepper ; for I make bold to say that any other person would have exhibited similar effects. Nepper was completely under his sway, had he not handled that wood ; and the poor fellow could readily have suffered annihilation rather than have borne such an insufferable indignity. But such a result was averted for even a second time, and this fact becoming irradicably impressed upon Nepper's mind, and his cunning being of a certain order, he quickly decided that *Ghost or no Ghost* he would make a stand for it, if he dared to touch that wood again. And so indeed it happened, for in a very short space of time, his horrified comrades, peering anxiously over the wall, saw him, frothing with passion, make a savage onslaught upon his opponent. And very quickly then it was known by the sound of a muffled but angry voice, that the end of the struggle was not so distant. The ghost impersonator was in a sad dilemma when he found himself at such close quarters, and he felt that the tug of war, the most serious item of the evening, had reached discussion. He knew his man's prowess only too well, and thoroughly appreciated Nepper's instincts when aroused ; and for the very first time he felt an earnest desire to avoid contingencies. Keeping as clear of Nepper as possible he backed freely towards the door, hoping thus to leave the place ; but a sight of the cudgel which our hero had grasped, and was preparing to wield, at once determined him to make a more serious and final effort. With this view he resorted once more to his trickery and raised his arm, but every trace of terror having been dissipated by that time from Nepper's mind, down went the cudgel upon the unlucky hand with a swinging, sacrilegious, whack. One muttered curse, one hurried move, and the skull and head gear were quickly deposited upon the ground, whilst the policeman's well-known but exasperated features were exposed to view. "D——n thee, tha wrong head," he lustily shouted, " give it up, will ta ? I'm not a ghost, tha gret fooil, be quiet." Had Nepper been at all argumentative, the matter might even then have been settled amicably, although it had reached the acute stage ; but the strange, and to him unaccountable denouement, only increased his perplexities. " I don't care what tha art," retorted he in the same vernacular, " tha munnot come steilin' my prog, an' I'll noan stand it," and with that he applied himself to waving his cudgel dangerously near to the policeman's head. Of course, after that, there was nothing for it but to have a regular set to ; so, knocking the idiot's weapon from his hand, they were soon quickly struggling, wrestling, and rolling about, locked in each other's grasp, and in justice to the policeman it must be admitted that it was an unequal contest, for Nepper was a monster in brute strength—as such people often are—but the policeman was certainly no child in his hands. Nepper's comrades perceiving a pressing necessity for interference, they hurriedly decided to part the two combatants ; and not one moment too soon. First one down and then the other, howling, pommelling, and cursing alternately, it was no wonder that the unusual noise roused the whole neighbourhood, and brought other police officers upon the scene, and then only was the officer rescued from the idiot's clutches. And it must be confessed that the practical joker, when safely released from his grasp, presented a most pitiable appearance, while as for Nepper himself he was loudly hilarious and declaiming hideously. The whole truth oozed out at last that the poor fellow had been victimised by both his chums and the policeman ; and for the honour of the village, and out of respect to the police force, it was resolved to let the matter rest, and never to try conclusions with him again. To this day there are certain villagers who entertain the highest admiration for old Nepper, and who firmly believe that the true explanation is only a concoction to deprive the idiot of well-merited honour, and they cling to the opinion that Nepper really did encounter, and actually overcome a real ghost, but was finally undone by the policeman. It is only fair to add that no one ever since has attempted familiarities with him, for the officer has often declared that he was thoroughly worn out, and expected annihilation as the only possible ending to his mad freak at the same moment that he was rescued. They are great friends now, and there is little danger of Nepper being in want of tobacco or beer again so long as he can supply him. Need I tell you, reader, in conclusion, that, popular as the poor fellow had always been previously, his ghost adventure made him more popular still ; and when the Bonfire day arrived, and the whole band congregated round their " burning record," the feather decoration in his hat proclaimed that if one spirit more than the rest was triumphant, that one was indeed " Old Nepper."

The Lost Story.

[FOUNDED ON A POPULAR ANECDOTE.]

An antiquarian—old and grave,
　Of Vandalism jealous—
Employed himself to trace and save
　Traditions—mighty zealous.

For Legendary lore, our friend
　Had got capacious swallow,
And for his facts did much depend
　On circumstances hollow.

Thus time, and space, and money—he
　Had never mind to reckon,
As boldly—but peculiarly,
　To any one he'd beckon.

And so a pile of uncertain Lore
　Had Fogy in his sanctum,
And if he had heard some things before,
　Why then—he simply "Yank'd " 'em.

Disinterested in all his aims
　To benefit the million,
He noticed not the numerous games
　To make him look a silly " un."

And when the learned (?) man had found
　Some tumble-down old ruins,
He, quite entranced, said, "I'll be bound
　" Here's been some awful doin's."

So calling to his aid a man,
　A very Hodge in bearing,
The antiquarian soon began
　To exercise his daring.

Said he—" This Ruin,—do you know
　" Of any likely Story
" That Warfare or Romance can show
　" Connected with its Glory ?

" If so you do, you may depend
　" I'll recompense the trouble,
" And should it prove surprising, friend,
　" Why then I'll give you double."

Then the Yokel spoke with an eager tongue,
　As though he'd earn'd his crown,
" Ther' wor one once, sir, when I wor young,
　" *But that Story got burnt down,*"

How it Happened.

Whether it was that Harry and I were different to other people I cannot say, but certain I am that we were very similar in our likes and dislikes. Whatever scheme or enterprise might be on the cards, sure enough it happened that each of us was interested in it ; and as he and I were of about the same age and build, we somehow came to join issue in every venture, and became boon companions and bosom friends. Young and thoughtless, we were nearly always ripe for mischief, and it became a proverb in our village that wherever one of us was to be found, the other was never far away. It is true to say that very often we received blame for things of which we were entirely innocent, and also got many physical inflictions which, although being of a salutary nature, were still undeserved and unappreciated. It could not truly be said that Harry was vicious, or mean, or even wilfully destructive ; but that he was boisterous, rich, and kindling in enthusiasm, no one ventured to dispute. What I was myself, must of course be inferred from our association ; but when we arrived at man's estate, an event occurred which in some mysterious fashion became the first but certain occasion of our drifting apart, and taking a course of our own. This puzzled me very much at the time, and as our lives had been wrapped in each other for so long a period, it was with considerable pain that I set myself the task of discovering the why and wherefore thereof. And I discovered it to my cost, for I found myself deserted to my great surprise in order that he might follow a girl who had stolen his affections from me. At first I could have laughed aloud at the thought, for I could not suppose such a state of things to continue ; but after a time the conviction was driven home to me that never again should we be lads together, and that our manhood had begun. Ah, well ; it is thus with everyone, and yet it seemed to me to be as great a punishment as any that could have befallen me, for I was made to feel my loneliness in a very bitter fashion. So we drifted apart, and as time wore on I yielded to circumstances, and became ere long a wanderer. From place to place I rambled and strayed, here one day and there another, earning a livelihood as best I could, until after a year's time I returned to the village, weary and thoroughly heartsick. Then, of course, I learnt the news, and as nearly every villager knows a good deal of his neighbour's affairs, it turned out that Harry's affairs were discussed very freely far and wide. The girl, for whose society he had jilted me, was really a nice and respectable person, but being of a highly romantic disposition, she had easily fallen in love with him. I knew her, of course ; and although I had always been on speaking terms with her family, yet I had never felt anything of so amatory a nature, as to become particularly interested in her. But Harry was always impulsive, and so he yielded easily enough to Cupid's machinations when his time arrived ; and Emma and he were really a model pair. Young, shapely, and attractive, both, everyone in the community spoke well of them, and in addition to wishing them well, took a decided and proprietary interest in them. This, of course, by the way ; but from the moment of my departure from the village, it was naturally expected that a marriage betwixt the pair was only a question that required mooting, and, once mooted, would be as easily settled. And so, upon returning thither, I expected nothing else than seeing them married, settled, and comfortable ; but what was my astonishment to learn that the wedding day had actually been postponed three times ; that Harry was very undecided, and that poor Emma, alas ! was in a most interesting but unfortunate condition. Latterly, so the rumour ran, he had begun to evince a desire to shirk responsibility ; and as folks dared not rail against him through fear of driving him clean away from the place, it may easily be imagined how matters stood. Once more, however, I felt drawn towards him, and on meeting him soon afterwards a few miles away from home, we renewed our companionship, and exchanged confidences. He seemed entirely changed as it were, wore a hunted, distressed, and haggard look, as though he suffered from great mental affliction ; and when he hinted, as he did, that together we should travel away from that neighbourhood and from all who knew us, I thought only of him and our friendship, and for his sake I agreed. Those happy days of the past haunted me still, and I felt, wanderer and lonely as I was, that for a return of such happiness to my life, I would have risked a great deal. I thought nothing of others, and in my selfishness was for the time incapable of so doing ; yet had I only considered a little, I might have seen the folly of my conduct. We decided to go home for some changes of linen towards evening, and then, under cover of the darkness, to make for the railway station and off. I must surely have been mad to have consented at all, for, would you believe it, reader, that on that very day he had turned traitor to his vows, and actually deserted Emma on what should have been her wedding day? He had arranged to meet her at a certain place in the next town, a distance of four miles off, where the marriage should have taken place, but instead of going at the appointed time, he had taken the contrary direction, where I chanced to meet him. And in that next town she was waiting, possibly hoping against hope, that a way would be found out of the difficulty. She had taken along with her, as witness to the nuptials, an old friend of her own, and what must have been the feelings of both to find themselves in such a dilemma? But we didn't trouble ourselves about those things, and so, feeling sure that they would have got back home and out of the way, we found ourselves at 8 p.m. waiting on the platform for the down train. We had booked for a long journey, and hoped by to-morrow to be far away from all home associations and scenes. I think it was I who was the most desperate and determined of the two, for, to my thinking, Harry only seemed downcast, undecided, and melancholy. Truly he had got himself into a mess, and although he had behaved very badly to his sweetheart, it was very plain that he loved her, although he seemed to steer farther and farther away from his duty. I didn't at all like to see him thus, and somehow or other began to feel oppressed with a presentiment of trouble that seemed to be impending ; but, putting a bold face on the matter, I shouted him to hurry along towards the centre of the train, which was then puffing into the station. Opening a carriage door, and trying by laughing banter to cheer him up, we were about to step inside, when out came two females ; and we instantly were accosted by them. Wonderful powers! it was *Emma and her friend*, returning heartbroken from the town ; and there the four of us all stood for half a minute gazing into each others faces, paralysed, as it were, in the doorway. Never whilst I live shall I forget my sensations at that moment ; for with the first glance at the poor girl's careworn and tear-stained face—and meeting at the same time the pitiful, pleading, and yet surprised gaze—I felt intuitively that I should do nothing more to divide them, and that I would rather suffer death than attempt it. If ever shame took possession of a man, it did of me then absolutely ; and forgetful of all but the miserable meanness of the enterprise, I was rendered powerless. Not so Harry, however ; for no sooner did he realise the fact of their presence than, with a yell that seemed wrung from his very heart's core, he retraced his footsteps at a run and hurried from the station. They were dressed quite nicely indeed, in robes which were symbolical of a marriage ceremony ; but the silence of death possessed me until Emma broke the spell, and in broken accents implored me to follow him and plead her cause ; and I resolved to do it, to put away the mean desire which had possessed me, and try what one man could to repair the breach which had been effected. So I closed the carriage door, and bidding them stop at a little wicket-gate close to, I hurried after Harry, and found him waiting disconsolately a short distance away. I at once informed him of my change of front, and tried by every persuasion to induce him to come into consultation on the matter ; but he stoutly declined to alter his views, and roundly abused me for my folly — as he called it — in addition. There was nothing for it, then, but to let him see that I was in good earnest, so, tearing my railway-ticket into pieces and flinging them away, I told him the serious nature of the offence. I am not at liberty here to detail all that I did tell him. I know that if the girl had been my sister I could not have done more for her than I did. Apart from every other consideration, I told him of her very visible approach to maternity, and conjured him to believe that Providence would not endure such cruel and unmanly conduct on his part. I bore with his reproaches, and explained that even then he had time to make reparation, and prove her honest before the world. Whilst we were in the heat of it the two girls approached us, and no sooner did he see the look of manifest love and forgiveness in Emma's face than he broke down completely, and expressed his great sorrow. This was more than I could stand, on my part ; and whilst they embraced and made it up, I and her friend took occasion to stroll further away, and discussed as to how matters might be righted between them. And when we returned, the twain had settled it all, so that I undertook, with their permission, to see everything carried out. Enjoining strictest secrecy upon the friend, it was decided that they should go home to her parents' house together for the

night, and never attempt to deny or affirm anything, other than that they were
married and wished to retire early, as they intended to take a journey on the
morrow.   And in celebration of the marriage, a general festival was already being
held by the assembled friends, and whilst they partook of the good cheer Emma
retired to rest in the company of her friend, who was asked to stay until the knot was
tied ; whilst I and Harry visited the Registrar privately to arrange for the morrow.
Afterwards we spent the night together, and before ten o'clock the next morning they
were lawfully made man and wife, greatly to every one's satisfaction, and their own
respect.   An hour's ride in a cab got them home safe and sound, but as certain
symptoms began to manifest themselves soon afterwards in connection with the affair,
a doctor was brought, and before noon my friend's wife was delivered of a fine boy.
Everything prospered with the pair ; and, as for myself, I was made so much of
by both of them, that I felt very proud of my share in the matter, and became highly
popular.   If I state, in conclusion, that at a certain ceremony with a certain baby, in
a certain church, on a certain subsequent Sunday, there was no happier man than
the godfather, and that the godfather was very like myself, you will, no doubt,
understand it.

A Winter's Night.

'Twas a bitterly cold winter's night,
   All the streets were deserted and bare,
Ev'ry house had its glimmer of light
   And nought seemed without but despair.

As I hurried along towards my home
   In a shiver with chill and the cold,
I wonder'd to think who would roam
   Abroad from a sheltering fold.

Even topers were scarce to be seen,
   And "night-walkers" too, had gone hence,
A good sign that the weather was keen,
   Too much for a hollow pretence.

Encased in warm clothing and shoes,
   I hasted along on my way,
Determin'd no spare time to lose,
   Anxiety at home to allay.

The baby was tuck'd into bed,
   And mother was darning the hose,
Whilst time only slowly had sped
   On landing in sight of repose.

But quick when I reached to the door,
   Wide open in greeting 'twas thrown,
I was slipper'd and settled before
   Any bachelor *how* could have known.

Enfreed from my wrappings and hat,
   The chair being drawn to the fire,
My darling quite opposite sat,
   A woman to love and admire.

A thankfulness rose in my heart
   For a partner so loving and true,
Whose presence alone could impart
   A joy and a blessedness too.

And there by our own fireside,
   Quite gladsome and happy were we,
Content in our lot to abide
   Ever trustful, and loving, and free.

Thus sitting with love in each eye,
   And softness the while on each tongue
No reason gave scope to deny
   A pleasure through all our life long.

'Twas grand to remain seated there,
   With hearts beating faithful and true,
Secure from the blight of despair
   And kindred unhappiness too.

The pitiless storm raged without,
   The wind moaning weird and wild,
No signs of a lull were about,
   No hopes of a morrow more mild.

The hisses, the whistles, and groans,
   Whilst swiftly careering along,
Resembled in shriekings and moans,
   Cadenzas of mischief and song.

The howling, discordant and strange,
   The *whirr* and the *swish* of its might,
Were startling and sudden in change,
   Enough to put one in a fright.

So life, with its infinite sounds,
   Can harass a mind ill at ease,
While falsity's measure rebounds
   On those who iniquity seize.

No Rock like the sound one of Truth,
   No Blight like the depth of Despair
No Hope so inviting as Youth,
   No Canker so bitter as Care.

Though Tempest, and Blight, and Despair,
   Surround us the worst and the best,
Yet trusting in God's gracious care,
   We calmly retir'd to our rest.

And so then to be happy and free,
   Like a many through life who have trod,
Their evidence—the token shall be,
   " Live closely unto Nature and God."

My Birthday.

Once again has Father Time
   Another year unroll'd,
And once again I hear the chime
   That tells I'm getting old.

Short, indeed, the years seem,
   Retracing o'er the time ;
Stranger, too, than any dream,
   That I have reach'd my prime.

What have I done good in life?
   Or has it been well spent ?
How have I gone through the strife ?
   And am I now content ?

That's the question ; is it well
   Or is my record bad ?
Would that I could truly tell,
   I've reason to be glad.

Still the answer I should know,
   Since mine has been the task ;
Yet would I not answer " No,"
   Because myself I ask.

Creatures of the earth are we,
   So I intend no harm,
Humbly wishing to be free
   From vain presumption's charm.

Can I improve? That's the test,
   Which reaches to my heart ;
Each one may attempt his best
   To act a better part.

Am I willing ? I say, " Yes ;
   "And will do right away."
Frail, yet I can venture this,
   From now, on my Birthday.

So each one may do the same,
And strive with better grace ;
Keep the conscience free from blame,
And bear a smiling face.

This is all that man can do,
Throughout his fitful life :
Prove himself upright and true,
Engaging in the strife.

Indecision.

A great hindrance to man is man's indecision. Forgetful of the proverb, "God helps those who help themselves," how prone we are to ignore our own responsibility. Many is the time when a decisive character would have led us on to avert evils that otherwise have attended us. I would not say be rash, or impetuous ; but many instances occur, where, without study, a firm, manly decision, gains success. In any questionable undertaking, be backward enough, but in a right or reasonable cause, decide at once. Men should be manly, and in manly work not slow to decide ; and whatever is unmanly reject at once. Not in idleness or wrong doing, not in worldliness or dishonesty, lies man's duty ; and all the gloss and glitter of life should make no man shirk his duty. The duty of man is clear to all men, his responsibility light as day, and the path of duty is the path of honour. Be honourable in all things, be just to all men, and true to yourselves. When sorely tempted, think of your honour, and decide at once. Remember all those who depend upon you, and trust you ; and never by any omission of duty, or indecision of purpose, cause any trouble to be accounted for afterwards. Fortunes have been lost, and hell has been won, many a time and oft by indecision, as well as indiscretion ; but look calmly before you leap. Delays are dangerous, but don't always kill. Second thoughts are sometimes best, but generally the way lies straight before us. Judge fairly, but beware of hypocrisy. Always cling to fair honest principle, and be sure in all your atonings you owe none for indecision

An Hour in "The Sun."

"Twas in a town of some renown,
In a Tavern styled "The Sun,"
Whose Host, from all frequenters,
Had a high opinion won.
I ventured late one afternoon,
Determin'd to enjoy
An hour's strange society,
And business to defy.

The tables were surrounded
By a troop of merry blades,
Whose characters were various
As their respective trades.
Each one for mirth was well inclin'd
Upon that afternoon,
And told again his favourite joke,
Or struck a lively tune.

The player sat upon his stool,
  And freely strumm'd away,
When suddenly the landlord came
  And unto all did say :
" Let us have some sport, my Lads !
  " And sing with hearty cheer,
" And each one who neglects his turn
  " Shall forfeit pay in Beer."

No sooner said than seconded,
  And quickly then 'twas pass'd,
That everyone should sing around,
  In turn—until the last.
The " Items " and " Ahs," from many a throat,
  Resounded through the place,
As bold or nervous warblers then
  Became possess'd of grace.

Along " The Banks o' Bonnie Doon "
  Did stroll " The Yorkshire Lass,"
And "Blue-eyed Nelly " sang " Good-bye,"
  As " A friend in need " did pass."
" Give me the man of honest heart ! "
  Exclaimed " Bold Pat Molloy ; "
" Long life unto your honour,"
  Said " The Connemara Boy."

" What are the wild waves saying ? "
  To " Dick Turpin's mare Black Bess,"
That " Jonathan, James, and John " should raise
  The laughter to excess.
" The Waterford Boys " went mashing
  With " The South Carolina Gals,"
On " The rocky road to Dublin,"
  Along with " Dear old pals."

The Forfeits were collected then,
  Midst many a hearty laugh,
And voices lately harassed were
  Reliev'd with many a quaff,
Some were crack'd and broken quite,
  And others all but done,
But I turn'd away delighted
  With—an hour in " The Sun."

" Veritas odium Parit."

A curious subject is this of mine ; from its very nature, as it were, compelling me to criticise truthfully any body or any thing that may perchance attract my attention. I must do myself the simple justice to state that were it not for my business peculiarities, very possibly I should have had no tendency to outstrip Nature with my wondering propensities. Certain it is that more than half of my business hours I have little else to do than gaze through the window, or content myself with the contents of some book or newspaper. Now when it happens also that across the road there is a flourishing pawnbroker's shop, and that customers are continually passing in and out all the day, whilst I have rarely any business to transact ; such a fact renders one of a more contemplative turn, than perhaps would otherwise be the case. That being so, I am positively certain from my vantage ground to notice scenes and occurrences that help curiously but materially to swell the curiosity in my composition. Certainly, my eyes were originally intended for observation, just as my brains were intended to support them ; and while, at the same time, many people base their faith on simple rumour, I am myself convinced that nothing for a positive fact can surpass ocular demonstration, although certain vulgar expounders of proverbial wit declare most boldly, that only feeling is the naked truth. This is scarcely admissible, seeing indeed that science has to account for much that is not literally tangible; neither would it apply to any person's case who might be blind or deaf, as then it would appreciate one of the senses to the detriment of the other. Let that be as it may, it has often struck me as a curious question, why the three gilded balls should always hang so conspicuously over the pawnshop door, for they would undoubtedly explain themselves far more clearly if upon each one of them were inscribed an initial of £ s. d. There is no denying that they present a very close relationship to those magic signs, in whatever light they may be regarded ; and perhaps it is a truth that such establishments are a very useful institution in a crowded commercial country. At any rate, for my part I am sure that they are much preferable to the money-lending dens which abound now-a-days, and which businesses, so-called, only thrive themselves in many instances out of the exorbitant and extortionate *fees* that needy and unwary applicants are swindled out of. It is a pleasant thing, I know, when one can rid themselves of trouble at any time and under ordinary circumstances, but it must be infinitely grander still to be enabled to bundle it up, and getit changed for cash deposits. Such is the case, however, for I can see folks with worn and weary faces, patiently waiting their turn at the door, with bundles of all shapes and sizes, and then after a time come away without them, nervously grasping the much required change. It is good to see some of them come away, with a happy glitter in the eye and a lightness in the step that contrasts greatly with their previous moods. I have often watched them walk away thus, sometimes, indeed, joining a friend in waiting, and the pair smiling gladly at the knowledge of possession. O, this money ! what it can both do and undo ! It is with great pleasure I sometime revel in the hope of a cheaper and commoner commodity for purposes of existence, in the future sphere to which we are undoubtedly accredited. But there, I must not digress ; on and away they go with the money upon their various errands—some maybe to comfort a poor sick sufferer, some to prepare nourishment for the toiler, some only to hand over the money in settlement of rent or some other obligation, and some others to spend it in a drunken spree. You can very easily sort out the drunken class, by one or other of the several distinctive badges or "trade marks" peculiar to them, for it is characteristic of them that they make little effort to disguise their identity; and, as a matter of fact, I have very often seen them in the open streets actually and unblushingly doffing coats, skirts, shawls, shoes, &c., and carefully bundle them up, preparatory to disposing of them, for the pittance that the broker in his discretion chooses to lend. When things get to that pass, it needs very little discernment to know that the Drink is having its innings, and it often happens in such circumstances that those who drink freeest of the spoil, will finish the day's carousal by thrashing the spoiler. How else, indeed, could it be otherwise ? for it is undeniable that as a rule the chief actors in such orgies, have also immoral tendencies apart from drinking, and only the most depraved, vicious, or idle characters, will cling sufficiently long to the vice to become, as it were, bold enough to push it to desperation. Thus we see that if we would be just as we ought, it is not alone the drink that is responsible for all the mischief that ensues ; for if you notice a person with good moral character, or who is honest and hard working, indulging in a drink, you will invariably find that, if let alone, he can attend to his business without being tainted with an inclination for becoming either an imbecile, a criminal, or a pauper. This is the case all the year round, in many thousands of instances, and there is very little justification for the attacks made upon moderate drinkers as a body, for they will most favourably compare with any body of total abstainers of equal number, for either virtue, charity, or respectability. It is true, however, that the indictments always flow from an interested or prejudiced source, which cannot, therefore, be accepted as arguments ; for, besides being entirely unjust, they are in point of fact as misleading as they are unwarrantable. It must be understood that there is no evidence to support the righteousness of total abstinence over moderation, which is half so convincing as that which supports the righteousness of moderation, in the fact "that every night, through all the year round, the most respectable, honest, and hard working of our citizens, together with thousands of the best wives and mothers, can consistently and beneficially use it without abuse, or to the neglect of their obligations. Tons of statistics cannot overcome this honestly plain and palpable fact. If you desire to trace this argument in its entirety, just ask any experienced Detective the Life Story of a drunkard, and you will hear of vicious and rakish tendencies before the drink, at least seven times out of every ten. A law to prevent thieves, prostitutes, and criminals of that class, from frequenting any licensed house or drinking bar, would do more towards sobering the community than all the preaching and raving possible. The Detective knows as he passes in and out of the pawnshop, or the drink shop, which is the depraved and which is the unfortunate customer. A guilty career seldom can pass unseen ; it may for a time evade, but it is only a question of time after all. A good thing to remember always is, that those who pay little or no regard to their own character and capital, will never care to regard other people's ; and so it is very often far preferable to cultivate a love of your own company only, than to have connections with such worthless trash. I positively hate loungers, and unhesitatingly vote them a great public nuisance idling about, their chief hobby being to hang upon other people's sympathy or simplicity. I know it is not right to hate anyone, the instinct within us of right and wrong is sufficient to tell us so much without any Bible ; but when men will so far forget themselves as to be always moping and preying like brutes upon their fellows, for the contemptible purpose of easily swindling them out of their hard-earned money, whilst they themselves never try, or care to earn one cent by their labour, I cannot help hating them. And so it is ; a man cannot think long without money getting mixed up in his thoughts. Whoever first invented money must surely have had hard neighbours, or else there would never have arisen any necessity for current change. That first commercial speculation did more to cause an upset in the world than any cause or combination since, barring women. Religion and Politics, Money and Women, have everything at stake. It is greatly conducive to serious reflection to notice how easily and thoughtlessly men as a rule can blame women for the mishaps of life, when we know them to be in reality the dearest and truest helpmates that ever mortal man possessed. This is not easily nor creditably to be accounted for, and although I may be laying myself open to the charge of partiality, I really must say a few words in defence of women. Things have gone very wrong indeed with a man, when he thus forgets his due to womankind, and I am curious enough to imagine that if poor women laid claim to one half of man's vindictiveness, the time would not be far distant when it would be " God help poor men." How prone is man to take advantage of a woman's weakness, and yet how prone is woman to forgive after all. Is it not a shame indeed that man's superior strength should be arrayed against the innocent arts and devices of inoffensive woman ? How grand it is to witness, not to mention enjoy, the loving devotion and cheering influence of a pure and noble woman. In times of strength and prosperity we are only too apt to think lightly of the tender sex, but just watch carefully, how, when the crash of misfortune comes upon us, what a true, trusty, and invaluable friend we possess in a beloved mother, wife, or sister. And then again, is it not ten thousand pities to see this sex, the mainstay of our existence in fact, from whom we select our partners and helps, often in large numbers, and amongst the lower classes increasing alarmingly, led and reared in vice and sin at very tender ages. It cannot be the drink that is responsible for this ; if the truth must be stated, and the sooner we face it the better, it is the laxity of morals we display, and a total disregard of correction, and real pride we evince, that in great measure must be blamed for such a state of things. How else indeed can we account for the abomination ? The recent revelations of Modern Babylon were not one whit too strong in depicting the lustful carnality of the age, and it is certain that if only half the truth was told of the trafficking in immorality, it is truth to say that the public would not believe it. I have no desire, as some writers have, to pander to an unfair spirit of class partiality by condemning the higher orders, for it is of no use, and it would not advance the interests of morality one tittle to do so. In spite of the strong statement lately volunteered by a Lancashire operative deputation to the Home Secretary, " That the conditions imposed upon workpeople, and especially females, by factory employers, in continuing a system of mixing sexes in hot rooms where it is necessary for both to work half naked, is conducive to immorality," which is certainly true in inference if it be a fact, there yet remains the startling and damning evidence, that childhood and the years of puberty, exhibit very degrading tendencies. It is not unknown among scholars, even in Sunday as well as day schools, and this can only be accounted for by the assumption that rigorous surveillance on the part of parents and teachers is neglected, and example becomes infectious. The working classes can not rid themselves of responsibility on this head, for they are equally guilty (if not more so) on account of greater numbers, with the rest. High wages and reduced prices of life necessaries, together with increased facilities for false pride and questionable amusements, seem to have developed the lurking evil propensities of nature ; and no one dare assert to-day that there remains in the lower orders, anything like the amount of civility, indebtedness, gratitude, and humility, which shone out so conspicuously, and often very creditably, a few generations ago. So much for morality. Is it not a disgrace upon nineteenth century civilisation that women should have to sink so low as we now see them, when even young girls openly solicit prostitution in our streets ? Is it not a shame that the common lodging houses of all our towns should contain so many of those unfortunate fallen ones, who turn there as a last resort to avoid starvation, and there lose the last shreds of virtue and modesty that might perchance cling to them ? Is it not a shame that our police records at Petty Sessions should in the main be one long string of infamy on the part of these our sisters ? And is it not a shame that our prisons should have to hold so many of these victims to a nation's bestiality ? If the Law that establishes prisons only employed its resources in establishing a Code whereby it became penal to have *suspicion of character verified*, and also in providing Refuges for homeless and ill treated females, there would soon be an improvement. There is no denying that to a certain extent the Law, recognising this sin of fornication as a necessary evil, has grown more lax in repressive measures, until finally we are overrun with it and its attendant evils. It is high time, indeed, that women, the same as men, should be allowed also the privileges of training for special work, so as to grasp advantages that may render them in time secure from the dominant association of any mean, dissolute, or criminal connection. There are those, undoubtedly, who fancy that if such were the case, our homes would suffer, but in my opinion such a fancy is utterly ridiculous. Women know very well that in neglecting our comfort they increase their own discomfort, and I suppose that however learned they may become, they would remain, materially, women still. Before closing this paper, and seeing that I have drifted thus far from my starting-place, I will just say one or two words concerning a question that has often occasioned much comment in recent years, namely, the withdrawing of Grocers' Licences to sell intoxicants. I have tried hard to consider this question carefully, and cannot resist coming to the conclusion that if grocers have invested their money in a lawful business, and in a lawful manner, and if they conduct that business lawfully, it seems to me a sheer act of confiscation to deprive them of their licenses, at anyone's bidding, without a reasonable compensation. To my mind, no other conclusion is possible, and although drunkenness is deplorable enough in all seriousness, yet it will not do to match sentiment against honesty and fair play. It must not be assumed that all rights are on the side of sentiment, for they are most certainly not ; and it very often occurs that sentiment has revolutionary tendencies. It has been said that these licenses promote drunkenness in women, but this is in reality—as a rule—not the fact, for it is asserted that according to the returns of Petty Sessional cases, not one of every twenty female drunkards, are proved, or known to have got their drink at such shops. Neither is there any proof that such shops create a taste or pander to it, but it could be proved that very often, indeed, they present opportunities for respectable women to purchase this requisite in a proper and becoming business fashion, safe from contamination. The majority of drunken women are loose or abandoned, whom we always know where to find, and who get their drink where they cannot buy groceries, and where they don't expect to do. Therefore, having, as I think, travelled pretty considerably since the commencement of these remarks, and having no doubt whatever but that many will consider me, in some instances, rather wide of my argument, I leave you to decide upon it. A settled conviction impresses me that I can never hope to please everybody, and so I never intend to try to do ; but as I have handled each subject honestly, and according to my lights, I trust sincerely that I may give no offence, in spite of the truism I take as my title, which, translated means, that truth often causes hatred.

Tekkin' t' New Mayor tut' Church.

Come, stir thi, my lass, if tha can,
   Tha knows 'at I munnot be late,
An haar sin at first tha began,
   Tha seems as tha'd just geet agate ;
Ise ne'er manage up tut' Taan Hall,
   Unless I can put on a spurt ;
I've to wesh me, an' dress me, an' all,
   Beside changin' flannel an' shirt.

Just look at aar Jacky's new whim,
   He's pushed mi clein front off at chair,
Ise t'hev to be stricter wi' him,
   He's woss nor a cat I declare ;
So hand me them shoon ovver here,
   An' find me mi collar stud, too,
I only feel useless an' queer,
   So push thisel forrad, nah do.

Fasten this collar, if tha will,
   For raylee I'm fitted for nowt,
If I don't ged off sooin I'll be ill,
   An' I wodn't miss t' walkin' for owt.
Nah brush mi new hat, theer's a lass,
   An' gie me mi walking-stick, too ;
Just stir, while I look intut' glass,
   By gum ! mi owd daisy, Ise do.

Tell Jacky to ged off at step,
   Soas I can goo aat on mi way ;
His face is as red as a hep,
   Through what he's a wantin' to say.
He fancies Ise tak' him wi' me
   A marchin' int' ranks, I declare ;
Dost think as I'm lettin' folks see
   A "monkey up stick" after t' Mayor ?

By gow ! but ther's plenty o' folk,
   An' Riflers, an' Pleecemen, an' all ;
Musicianers too, 'boon a joke,
   Just framin' in order to fall.
I wodn't hev missed sich a seet,
   An' nah I'll not leave 'em int' lurch ;
I'll follow them top-nobs int' street,
   An' join int' procession tut' church.

Theer's t' childer, just landed wi't wife,
   An' t' new married couple next dooar ;
Sich craads I ne'er seed in mi life,
   Ther's double as coom t' time befoore.
I might as weel do it quite grand,
   An' keep up tut' Mayor if I can ;
No better a chap lives int' land—
   He looks ev'ry inch like a man.

Theer's t' Parliment members beside,
  An' Caancil chaps, polish'd as steel ;
Theer's t' Aldermen, puffed up wi' pride,
  An' t' Lampleeters walkin' as weel.
I'm fond of a gradely turnaat,
  An' I fancy we look up to snuff ;
Although but for me bein abaat,
  They *might hev* looked badly enough.

Theer's t' bugler saandin' his note,
  An' t' drum gies a regilar bang ;
Then like a "Great Eastern" afloat
  We start wi' a musical clang.
I hardly dare look to one side,
  Mi collar's that stiffen'd wi' starch ;
But as straight as a gaslamp wi' pride,
  I like a bold Briton did march.

Mi walkin'-stick stuck in a hoil,
  An' it brak' as I strided along ;
Mi blood it set on to a boil
  To notice 'em laughin' int' throng ;
But I marched wi' t' stick handle in hand,
  An' tried to look sanne as nowt wor,
When a hoss, as geet startled wi' t' Band,
  Just made me soas I dussn't stir.

Them gentry as walked next to me
  Kept shaatin' for me to ged on,
But I felt noan so wishful to be
  Weel slatted and trampled upon ;
So I hurried misel' aat o' t' rooad,
  An' mi hat tumbled daan ontut' flooar
Misfortune oft comes in a load,
  An' pitched me heidfirst at a dooar.

A lump just as big as mi fist
  Arose on my heid in a crack,
An' varry soon then I geet hiss'd,
  An' wished in mi haase I wor back.
Yo' talk abaat laughter an' fun
  I caused 'em wi' my sorry pass,
But all mi ambition wor gone,
  So sharp I piked off wi' t' owd lass.

Int' church that unfortunate morn,
  While t' Parson wor readin' his prayer,
A misrable figure, forlorn,
  Set burden'd at hooam wi' care ;
But nah its a good while ago,
  An' noanb'dy's no reason to search
As to haa, when, or wheer, yo' know,
  I walk'd wi' t' New Mayor tut' Owd Church.

Blessed Moments.

When the shades of night are falling
And the work of day is done,
When the Memory is recalling
Hopes departed or begun ;
There is magic in that hour
Which dispels the inward gloom,
Making Home a fairy Bower
Where the Love-light does illume.

When we trace again the History
Of the period gone before,
When we know we've solved the Mystery
That can never haunt us more,
Then, perchance a source of profit
Unto each one may accrue,
If we take a lesson off it
In the Gloaming's brief review.

Blessed moments ; sad and aching
Though at times they prove to be,
Still their influence keeps waking
Chords of tenderest Harmony.
O, if such could only linger
In our work-a-day concerns,
Love would be the welcome Ringer,
Yielding as our Manhood earns.

"Dei Gratia."

A CHRISTMASTIDE REMINISCENCE.

A hard, unthankful life is the life of a tramp. In this happy land, as in every other, there are many people whose fortune or misfortune, leads them or drives them, into what is not incorrectly described as a career of vagabondage. or a life on the tramp. Years ago it was my misfortune—bereft of parents' care—to be living a life on the tramp. Why I tramp'd I knew not, and where I tramp'd I cared not, so long as I might keep body and soul together, and ultimately find a settlement. I was only a youth, and though too often in extreme danger and inured to hardship, yet I had occasionally tasted the sweets of life and the comforts of a settled home. True, it never had been my own home, and only too often indeed did I feel it, and bear as bravely as I could with the contending influences. Yet even those varying periods of content I remembered keenly as happiness indeed, and the hope of at some time, however distant, finding again a haven of rest, sustained my spirits wonderfully. Somehow or other, in all my wanderings I seemed ever to make towards a seaport, and on the occasion under notice I was bent upon reaching Hull. Why, I cannot say, only that the sea connection in my idea offered a better chance of employment. What I really knew of seafaring was next to nothing, but impressed somewhat by reading stories of adventure, I expected in some way or other to meet with an opening of good luck. So I plodded along, hungry and weakly for want of nourishment, my bare feet encased in an old pair of shoe-tops from which the soles had entirely departed, but which I retained and wore as some excuse for decency. The rain had fallen incessantly all the day, and on until midnight, when it cleared away, and the moon shone out most brightly, lighting up the distant Humber, and acting as a beacon to my path. I was thoroughly saturated, and presented a woe-begone appearance, I dare say, for my heels being blistered and sore, they bled freely, and I had not even a rag to cover them. The previous night I had slept underneath a wall on the roadside near Selby, as I could not proceed further in my lame state ; and I could not beg for the life of me, fearing to meet the consequent scowls, refusals, and unjust criticisms, which follow the act. But in some degree I could tell when I saw a kindly person, and such I asked relief from, and consumed it as I got it. However, I pulled myself along, feeling as though I should drop every minute almost, until I reached the Hessle road. Hessle is but a few miles distant from Hull, and being a nice level country, the highway served as a kind of promenade for pedestrians, and seats of a garden pattern were ranged at convenient distances from each other alongside the causeway *en route*. From other tramps I had learned that it was Hull pleasure fair on the morrow, and so when a policeman met me pushing along, and asked my business, I replied that I was for Hull fair, and inquired the nearest way to the ground. Of course he directed me, and ordered me also to hurry indoors as soon as I could ; so, very tired and wretched I limped along. I did not get much further before I stopped to rest on one of the seats provided, and gazing away o'er the wide expanse of water beyond, I bemoaned my lost and desolate condition. I could have slept soundly, wintry and wild though it was, but prudence forbade ; and so rousing myself with a great effort, I again hobbled on. I reached the town at last, but not knowing my way about, I wandered up street and down street, lost entirely. Of course, all streets were alike to me then, for I did not care where I was if I could only find shelter until morning. But of shelter I saw no hope, and tired out, although the moon was shining brightly, in despair I crept into an alley, and fell down on the cold frozen flags, thoroughly worn out. I might have slept an hour or so when I awoke and looked about me. It must have been the intense cold that disturbed me, for it seemed to have reached to my bones, but shivering all over, I managed to get up, and shuffled away. Two policemen were at the street corner, so, thinking to be directed to the Fair-ground, I enquired of them the way. As bad luck would have it, one of them was he I had encountered on the highway, so he gruffly threatened me with gaol if I did not clear off at once. I turned sadly away, and after rambling about for some time, I saw a light from a fire over a wall close by, and I asked the man who stood by—a watchman—to let me sleep in his hut until morning. I was crying bitterly then, and being frightened, and beyond further exertion, I must have looked a pitiable spectacle indeed. He instantly assented, and helped me over the wall ; then spreading some old mats on the floor near the fire, he bade me sit down and have some remains of his supper to eat. But indeed I was past eating, and even whilst he was yet talking, I had dropped down and was fast asleep. He awoke me in the morning when his time had expired, so eating the few mouthfuls of food that he offered me, I thanked him and hobbled out once more. The old mats on which I had slept having been damp, my joints and limbs were as stiff as could be, having also had my wet clothes on ; and what with my lame feet and my aching joints, with my miserable prospects, my condition may be much better imagined than described. All through that day I wandered about like a lost wretch as I was ; and when darkness again came on, I felt that I must either beg or die before morning. Seeing a benevolent-looking gentleman, I plucked up courage and asked him to assist a poor lame stranger boy who was in the greatest need. He replied very kindly, and after bestowing a few coppers on me advised me at once to find lodgings and get to bed ; adding that it was his duty to arrest beggars, being a member of the detective force. I took his advice, sought out cheap lodgings, and hastened inside. Paying threepence for a bed, I was first ushered into the backroom of the house, which was set apart for lodgers and furnished for their convenience. Round the room was a high-backed seating, crescent shaped, the centre falling backwards and the ends approaching inwards. The right centre and the arms were the seats of honour, and generally occupied by those who had most eloquence or audacity. A way behind the settee led to the tables, and over these and around the room were the shelves for food, and no responsibility was to attach to the landlady of the house, as, of course, characters of every degree constituted the assembly, and she could not be expected to spend her time in looking after them. There were altogether about thirty lodgers of both sexes in the house, some few of them toiling daily at regular work, but lodging in such a place for the sake of mixing with, and enjoying, the society of adventurous tramps and outcasts of every description. One of them, who turned out to be a quack doctor, noticing my distress, kindly provided me with some clean hot water to bathe my feet in, and wrapped my heels in some clean greased rags; offering me also some bread and milk afterwards, which I very gladly accepted, and which in fact constituted my only refreshment for that day. A big, warm, roaring fire made the place quite comfortable, and on the mantel over the fire were ranged ready for individual use, a quantity of small tin tea-urns, in every degree of cleanliness from a brightly burnished gloss, down to 'a thick sooty coating. I then went to bed, sleeping by invitation with the quack doctor, who seemed to fancy me as being likely to prove less troublesome than any other bedmate. Both sexes undressed and slept in the same rooms, and beyond the more modest female who undressed in the dark, that was the only exception to the rule. For myself I didn't trouble much about such a circumstance, although I had some misgivings at first about my bedmate; but being too wearied for much reflection, I was soon soundly asleep. I afterwards learnt that any one could have a bed to themselves for a trifle extra, which plan gave great satisfaction. I slept heartily during the night, and was much benefited by it; and so, after attending once more to my heels and redressing them, I partook of a few mouthfuls of breakfast, and hobbled at my leisure during the day around the docks. I managed to live on for some time by the generous help of a friend, to whom I had written, and who forwarded me a remittance by return. When I was able to walk comfortably, and·my heels were better, my money being exhausted, I turned out to seek some labouring work at the docks. But my hopes were speedily dashed, and I could not get any on any terms, as, it being severe weather, the rivers were frozen and work was very scarce. So I managed as best I could, doing some little service at my lodgings now and again for a meal, and doing without when I could get none. To add to my distress, I had been unable to pay my lodging money for a few nights, and I knew that such a state of things couldn't last; so I worried and fretted considerably, until the days passed on, and Christmas Eve came round at last. I shall never forget that Christmas Eve whilst I live, for I truly expected the landlady to turn me adrift, seeing that I could not pay my way, and I was then indebted to her for several nights. I had tasted nothing at all that day, and felt naturally very faint, but fearful of being outside in the bitter cold and fog. I determined at all hazards to remain indoors as late as I possibly could, whatever might be my ultimate fate. Some idea may be formed of my predicament when I mention that, sickened at the sight of more fortunate people returning cheerfully with their stocks of provisions and good things for the morrow, I had seriously contemplated the possibility of ending my despair in committing suicide. It was a desperate resolve I know, and wicked; but indeed I had scarcely the heart to live, for I was thoroughly nauseated with misery and woe. One thing I could not account for, and that was that everyone seemed to be cheerful as could be, although some of them I knew had very little indeed to be cheerful over. By the time that all were assembled, it had got eight o'clock, the time when the landlady usually collected her money; and I was studying the matter over whether by slipping out unobserved I ˈmight avoid the being driven out, when the door opened suddenly and she appeared. Behind her walked a couple of men, each having hold of a basket full of rich Christmas loaves cut in halves, which they placed in the centre of the room; whilst she made her way right to the hearth, where she turned and faced the company. The sight alone unnerved me, for I thought the old lady had given them permission to try to sell a seasonable commodity, and I inwardly bewailed my unhappy lot. However, there was then no help for it, if such was the case, as repinings could do no good, and tremulously I awaited the course of events. Expecting to hear her voice making the accustomed demand upon all to "*pay up*," I tried to calm myself to meet the unlucky inevitable. But, God be praised, it was not to be; for, standing in renowned Yorkshire fashion before the fire, she wished us everyone, old and young, in her dear old Irish voice and gesture, "*A Merry Christmas*," and many of 'em; inviting each one present at the same time in the heartiest of tones, to partake of the Christmas cheer at her expense. It was also intimated that anyone who cared could have a pint of beer free in addition. And then such a joyful cheer rose up to Heaven for her kindly and timely assistance. As for me, I was thoroughly unmanned, and would have nothing whatever until I had seen her and explained my position; so following the good woman into the passage privately, I told her as earnestly as I could the true facts of the case, and asked her to allow me to be indebted to her for one more night. The bliss of that next moment I'll never forget, for, looking at me in a kind motherly fashion, she put her hand into mine, and with tears in her eyes replied, "God help ye, my lad, it's all right, darling," telling me that it was an annual custom of hers to treat all her lodgers to a *free night* and *good cheer* upon Christmas Eve; and, she continued, whilst patting me on the side of my head, "*Go inside lad, go inside; you're somebody's poor bairn, go and make yersel comfortable, an' God be wid ye,*" and hurried herself into her own room. Cynics may sneer if they will; but just at that moment I felt so truly happy and so blest that I was rendered speechless, for they were the very kindest words I had heard for a long time. Tears were in my eyes, and I could not keep them back, try as I would; and what with the choking sensation in my throat, and the relief to my mind, I was powerless. But I could not go inside just then for the world, so when she had gone into her own room, I went out into the yard behind, and cried like a child for very joy. I felt that God had extended His grace to me, and that he had proved to a poor helpless outcast a Friend indeed. Ye who are heavy laden and bowed down with trouble, never despair; for this proves that the Almighty taketh note of you. Then I went inside, and ate and drank my share with the rest, sang as lively as any of them, sang from my heart for joy; and amongst all that lot, hearty and happy though they were, none of them I know were more truly happy than I. My tears were chased away, my sorrow had flown, my heart had grown light, and—like a bee humming amongst that rough and ready throng—I spent a contented, happy, and thankful Christmas time. I cared nothing for my rags indeed, I thought nothing of my sad plight; such things seemed as nothing then, compared to the great end gained in enjoying a Christmas Eve as of yore. My rags were bad enough, God knows; but what mattered rags, indeed, in Poverty Hotel, where there was scarcely an exception to the rule? No one present went short of food or comfort on that night, I can vouch; for happiness in a measure is contagious, and each one tried in a simple fashion to forget dull care. And then later on, whilst the Christmas bells were ringing, and through the streets the choristers went singing—when peace reigned supreme, and all the assembly lounged cozily around the hearth, some smoking, and all listening to the ready stories from some one or another of bygone Christmas associations—the tears of some, and the murmurs of others, told plainly enough of a holy, soothing, and cheerful influence; and although in many other places and around other hearths, the celebration might have been more robust and inspiriting, yet to me one of the happiest Christmas Eves that ever I spent, was that amongst the dregs and drones of society in the "*puddin can.*" Ye who have not suffered so extremely cannot imagine such a state of mind. I felt renewed as it were, and when midnight arrived and the last chime had struck clear, I hurried out of the house cheerfully to again traverse the docks, and see if any vessel had arrived for unloading. As good luck would have it—and it often comes in lumps—a large ship from Hamburg was just being moored; so along with several other poor fellows, I got started to work at once. That was the turning point, and cheerfully I toiled away, and put in as many hours as I could reasonably manage, in overtime as well. I wanted no more tramping, for I had had enough of such a life, and I felt determined that if it were possible to realise the necessary expenses for the purpose, I would return to my native village, and find work and shelter amongst the people whom I knew. I was fortunate enough to secure a full month's work here and there amongst the shipping, and afforded myself such apparel as my circumstances allowed. I settled with my generous hostess for so much as she would accept, but not one penny piece would she receive for my indebtedness during Christmas week; for, as she feelingly observed, I was at liberty to consider the same as a gift. And in return for her kindness I have endeavoured ever since to remember substantially the wretched waifs of outcast humanity, and sometimes I am fain to imagine with a similar result. At any rate, I returned to my native village, was successful in my desires, and before so very long afterwards, had come to learn to forget on occasion, the unutterable perils and privations, I had found during my wanderings, to be inseparable from the life and condition of a "tramp." Such an experience is not inspiriting I know, but whenever Christmas comes round, I am forcibly reminded of that time, many years ago, when my misery was so crushing, and emancipation so unexpected, but which surely gave evidence of the Grace of God.

Love.

What is love ? Is it a thing
   To gather, or to choose ?
   To either find or lose ?
And to order, or to bring ?

Do you deem it something born
   Of artificial aid ?
   An article of trade,
And of higher glamour shorn ?

Do you fancy Love can flow
   In measure or demand,
   Or that you can command
Either touch, or taste, or glow ?

Is it something you can check
   Or quicken as you will ?
   To create, or to still,
And to hinder, or to beck ?

Has Philosophy a guage
   Its eloquence to sound ?
   Or can a thought profound
Its dominance assuage ?

Is it ever bought or sold
   For cash, or style, or place ?
   Can you equal its grace,
Or define it, young or old ?

Have you once felt its power,
   And known its kindling rays,
   That brighten'd darkest days,
And cheered the lonely hour ?

Has it sparkled through your soul,
   Or aroused you with its fire ?
   Has it purified desire,
And yet magnified the goal ?

Has it made you more refin'd,
   And caused you to be good—
   To live just as you should,
More careful of your kind ?

   *   *   *   *   *

Or whence, or how, or reason,
   True Love has Honour's place,
   It animates our race,
Or high, or low, or season.

A Smiling Face.

When a friend I meet, upon the street,
    Who shows a smiling face,
When I come to stand, and grasp his hand,
    Or fervently embrace,
There's a wondrous spell, I cannot tell,
    Possesses me awhile,
For the friends are few, I count as true
    With glad sunshiny smile.

There's a something nice, that in a trice,
    Goes straight unto the heart,
And the loving act, proclaims that fact,
    Where words could not impart.
Should a man deceive, and in his sleeve,
    True innocence beguile,
Yet the traitor's eye, will oft belie,
    His self-complacent smile.

There's a genial glow, does ever flow,
    Within an honest breast,
And it seems at once, to give response,
    And set the mind at rest.
How I do enjoy, or man or boy,
    In greeting him the while,
To denote the truth, of friendship's youth,
    And win his cheery smile.

Then howe'er you be, take this from me,
    Or whether late or soon,
Do the best you can, to prove a man,
    For friendship is a boon,
Ever cultivate, this happy state,
    Be high or low your style,
That a loving friend, until the end,
    May greet you with a smile.

Five Minutes with a "Medium."

It is not often that I trouble myself about mediums or familiar spirits now-a-days, for those whom I have hitherto encountered in the "professional" line have never conducted themselves as became desirable acquaintances ; but an old friend of mine, named Mr. Bowdle, got so mixed up with them that ultimately Spiritualism, with all its evils and phenomena, settled on his brain. I do not mean to infer that Spiritualism is an evil, because I am not so positive upon that point, but without a doubt the clap-trap and humbugging manifestations which are believed in by the common people in connection therewith, I do heartily denounce as an imposition and a nuisance. The affinity of loving spirits, the influence of sacred memories, and the inspiration of reminiscences, are circumstances that I acknowledge ; but these are another thing entirely from the glaring and often bungling manifestations of the present day ; and however my friend had embraced such notions surpassed my understanding. He was far from being an ignorant man, although a little peculiar upon certain doctrines and beliefs ; and at the same time was moderately well-to-do, which made his conversion more remarkable still. This will be best understood when I explain that, on account of his wealth, his hospitality was taxed considerably by the fraternity, who travelled professionally from place to place, and required housing. I have often wondered at this trait in their character, since all are affected by it ; the common blight of impecuniosity, like some distinguishing brand, claims mediumship as its very own. I had made some little acquaintance with one or two members of that ilk, and was not, therefore, entirely ignorant of their pretensions and peculiarities, which I thoroughly appreciated at their proper value : at any rate, from my point of view. In fact, I have received more than one invitation to private séances, as their experimental sittings are termed, and I must confess, seeing that " truth is the only flower that never decays," that never but once was anything done by any medium that was either startling or uncommon in any degree.

The exception was in the case of a so-called Medium, who was described as an illiterate country blacksmith from the Border neighbourhood. Whether that description was correct I cannot say, but as to his ability "under influence," there could scarcely be two opinions. I cannot think of his name, as it is some years since ; but I can say this, that in a very quiet way, I tried by conversation and social chat to discover off-hand what art he possessed. But I could not manage it, for he was very reserved and shy in his remarks ; so, as his quiet silence was too much for my inquisitiveness, I perforce had to content myself with observing his stolid demeanour and guise. He was young, sallow-looking, and very humbly dressed ; and although I could gather little enough of his history, beyond that he was married and slightly consumptive, there was that about him which betrayed very clearly a studious disposition. However, he showed little polish, and certainly, unless it was his part to play, was wanting in even the commonest civilities. His "business" was to give "Trance Orations," and upon any subject put to him, at a moment's notice. The chosen topic on the occasion under notice was a classical one, dealing with ancient history ; and whether he was in a trance or no, his handling of the subject for an hour was uncommonly surprising and able. His language was eloquent and cultivated, but I remember very well the sensation that unconsciously overtook me at the close, to the effect that if I liked, and possessed nerve enough to sham inspiration and to keep my eyes closed, I felt that I could play a similar part, although not an easy one. My great objection to it all was that we were compelled to accept everything without argument. This was the only drawback I could find, and I distinctly remember that it made me as ill prejudiced after all, as if I had discovered a flaw. But I had no real right to such an assumption, and would gladly have banished it had any person present attempted to put its genuineness to the proof. However, this case has been the only one, hitherto, where I could not clearly doubt the honesty of the matter ; therefore, on that account, I will not show bravado enough to oppose the point as to whether certain minds can or can not, be strongly influenced upon occasion ; but this I do deny heartily, that certain noises, freaks, or cute applicable words, set to mean anything or nothing are related to real Spiritualism.

Anyway, my friend Bowdle firmly believed in all these things, and by his championship thereof, created in me and my friend Tomkins profound regret. Certainly he could hold his own in any little argument we had, but it was in his own way ; and a very peculiar way it was after all, for he stoutly believed himself surrounded with spirits, and that he was more or less subject to their influence. Thus he grew quite restless, and a victim to the most idiotic hallucinations. Tomkins and I, of course, were always at loggerheads with him, because we would not see things in the same light, and fall into his views headlong.

So things went thus until one day it happened that a famous Medium paid a visit to the town, and private "circles " became, amongst that community, the order of the day. And it happened that Bowdle invited my friend to one of these, and he went accordingly. Now, if Tomkins had one characteristic more prominent than another, it was in being devout, and frank in his disposition ; consequently he was rather startled when the lights were turned down. We had previously understood that mediums varied in capabilities, but this particular one, it seemed, professed almost anything ; a matter which caused Tomkins to whisper to Bowdle " that he must have been a blood relation to ' Old Harry.' " However, they all clasp'd hands around the table, and waited anxiously for the alarm, passing the time in singing, &c.; and after half-an-hour's patience, to his great surprise, Tomkins felt something covering his head, and clasping his shoulders. In my friend's dilemma there was only one remedy to his way of thinking, and he embraced the opportunity of earnestly and inwardly engaging in prayer.

There is not the slightest doubt about the efficacy of prayer, experience and expediency alike support this view, and so our friend prayed accordingly. But alas ! the fates were against him, and his prayers failed lamentably upon this occasion ;

whether or not upon account of his having wilfully joined the transgressors I cannot say. One thing is certain, a "smack" upon his mouth, which cruelly set all his teeth upon edge without any warning, and considerably staggered him, put an end to his prayers instantly. When, in addition, some hard substance collided with his nose, causing his terrified shriek to mingle with other strange noises then in vogue, poor Tomkins, thinking that his annihilation was intended piecemeal, threw up his hands and turned on the gas, just in time to catch a malicious grin stealing o'er the medium's phiz. But nothing more. That was enough for my friend however, and very quickly they got to high words, and Tomkins was in a fair way to become a blasphemer, when Bowdle interposed and enticed him homewards ; thus ending a most discreditable transaction. It cannot be denied that an unbeliever, who is known to be stubborn, can get grossly assaulted under the conditions imposed on such occasions. I may here be allowed to state that this one complaint I have heard made very often since then ; and I declare that such brutal conduct is tantamount to stigmatising the whole doctrine as a huge piece of blackguardism.

But the time came at length when both I and my friends were invited to an exhibition, and for our friend Bowdle's sake we decided to go, so that if it were at all possible we might venture to expose his infatuation. So the three of us set out together, and duly arrived at the place where a certain notorious Medium was engaged to illustrate the wonders of *second sight*, or clairvoyance. Tomkins and he had met before, it seemed, somewhere, and they could not "hit it" in consequence, as my young friend, after a warm argument. had openly dubb'd him as an imposter. Slanderous abuse is not argument, and I do not for one moment wish to screen my friend's indiscretion, for I maintain that he had no right to say so much, even if he had thought it.

The room was quite full upon our arrival, and consequently we had a little difficulty in procuring seats, but with the help of Bowdle, who was a committee-man, we managed very comfortably indeed. The audience were mainly females, and of these a good proportion were elderly ; but here and there were scattered about a few representatives of the sterner sex, members of the committee, &c. The Medium, who was upon his feet on the platform when we entered, noticed us going in ; and as we were rather late and our entrance caused some little stir, we were thus unfortunate in furnishing him with a cause of complaint against us ; and so he stopp'd the public performance to tender us his private opinion. However, we didn't want to miss our opportunity, so avoided recrimination by swallowing his insolence as best we could, and saying nothing. We could see his purpose very plainly, and possibly he could see ours, for he did his best to excite the people against us, and us against him, but we allowed him to keep the excitement to himself. There was nothing singular about his appearance at all, except we mention the clerical cut of his garments ; and as he was of middle height and age, and tolerably good-looking, he would readily have pass'd muster with most people as a model minister. However, there he was at his post, and it needed no Phrenologist to discover his excitability and combativeness. He was very loth to commence *business*, after unburthening himself even ; but there was no help for it, as the multitude clamoured for a commencement. His procedure was something after the manner of a mesmerist, throwing out his arms and drawing them in again with dramatic effect ; then, with a prolonged murmur and a solemn tragic air, he subsided into an idiotically unconscious position. after the stage maniac style ; and thus *the words of wisdom* fell incoherently from his mouth. And in the name of all that is sensible upon this earth, what think you was the substance of his endeavours ? It was nothing more or less than a string of guess work, and surmises upon the simplest rubbish and tittle tattle. "*If the father of some one present had lived until then, he would be so old or thereabouts ; he had such and such an appearance, and his sister had a daughter about so old, who was then present at the meeting.*" He had his eyes fixed upon a certain woman, although his tapering fingers pointed at the whole row of women ; and so suddenly stopping his jumble, he professed to ask one woman, although in truth pointing to the lot, "*if anything he had said was true, and did any one recognise the character he depicted.*" The woman he was looking at spoke at once, and very abruptly, something to the effect that she recognised his remarks, lately deceased, and that there was some appearance of truth in his remarks. And then the multitude applauded and cheered, as though some marvellous revelation had been made, instead of a piece of guess work, &c., upon some notoriety that was common property, easily obtained, and certain almost to be part correct even if haphazard. I felt ashamed indeed, for the whole thing from a rational standpoint was simply ridiculous, and nothing whatever but what would have passed muster as gossip's chat, was ever introduced either naturally or scientifically for our advancement.

Tomkins was not going quietly to allow such a demonstration without urging his protest ; and he rose at once to put a question to the Medium upon the point, but no sooner did he attempt his purpose, than the committee were appealed to, to support their representative ; and he was sternly requested to keep silence. And so it would have ended, but Bowdle and I, thinking that a civil question deserved a civil answer, taking our friend's part, the committee then, in consideration of Bowdle's position, agreed to let the matter be discussed, if the Medium would consent. But, as the saying goes, the Medium's "blood was up," and charging us with riotous intentions, he declined to proceed either to discussion or any other business. I never saw anyone so much agitated as he was ; to any ordinary person such excitement was dangerous, but to such as he, it hazarded danger and disgrace. But he stuck to his text however ; and nothing would content him but our summary dismissal from the premises, which he must have known was a very safe plan to adopt. This settled the matter at once, for some of the company having come considerable distances on purpose to hear him, did not relish the idea of having a night wasted, and so they supported the motion for our eviction. So there was really no help for us, and we received the order to disappear, which not being inclined to obey so readily, we were hauled forth by the rougher element, and very quickly got hurried into the street.

And to call such work as that Spiritualism, why it is the most senseless and idiotic tomfoolery that ever received public recognition. How can it be construed into a religion at all ? And what is its purport ? The wonder is that people will encourage such a mockery of common sense, for it could not survive calm criticism. It is no more Spiritualism in reality than is legerdemain, and not half so warrantable, because of its entire uselessness. It is debasing in its tendencies, and how it can be sustained at all, depends greatly on the frivolity of human nature. We were certainly disgusted with what we saw of it, but what new freaks were developed in our absence we cannot say. However, Mr. Bowdle never forgave them the insult put upon him by ejecting his friends, and very greatly to his credit he left them entirely. Time after time they tried to excuse themselves and persuade him to return, but all to no purpose; and the news arriving shortly after of the arrest and conviction of the same "Medium," as a rogue and vagabond, and his subsequent imprisonment for three months with hard labour, drove the last nail into Bowdle's heresy and completed his emancipation. True, his discomfiture happened in another town ; and more honour to them, say I, for their superior discernment, although his accusers were termed his traducers. Call this business by any other name, but out of respect for our enlightened intelligence, do not say that it is Spiritualism. It is just possible, indeed, that there might have been something more and deeper in it than what we discovered, but if so, it is not our fault in neglecting to remark upon it, since we were not permitted to see it ; but whether there be or not, I have not the slightest desire to see repeated the too utterly absurd and ridiculous demonstrations we then witnessed, in that well-remembered "five minutes with a medium."

A Straight Appeal.

A GOSPEL STORY.

There—the wretched woman stood,
 By Pharisees arraign'd—
Vilest of that neighbourhood—
 With guilt and evil stain'd.

Steep'd in misery and sin,
 And weighted with despair,
Not a friend had she to win
 Her soul from dark despair.

There—the humble Nazarene,
   Whom Pharisees did fear—
Noted well the vicious spleen,
   And undisguised sneer.

Thrills of deepest pity ran
   Throughout the troubled frame ;
Whilst His wond'rous love began
   The lost one to reclaim.

Then He cast a loving glance
   Upon her sullen face ;
Then the creature looked askance,
   Ashamed of such disgrace.

Then did Jesus, with a word,
   Her drooping spirit cheer ;
Then his voice each Rabbi heard,
   Commanding not to fear.

Soon her stern accusers spoke,
   With dangerous intent,
Trusting that her bitter yoke
   Might gainsay argument.

" There she stands," the spokesman said,
   " The vilest of the vile ;
" Infamously born and bred,
   " And never free from guile.

" There she is—the luckless wretch—
   " Beyond redeeming power.
" Hast Thou evidence to stretch
   " In her behalf this hour ?

" If Thou art the Son of God,
   " As Thou doth boast to be,
" And a lifetime she hath trod,
   " In utter infamy.

" What should happen unto such ?
   " And what shall be her fate ?
" Hath she not deserved much
   " Of punishment's estate ?

" Show us now Thy holiness,
   " The while her sin is bare ;
" Prove to us Thy Godliness,
   " And let the harlot hear."

   *   *   *   *   *

Silence then did reign around
   That Pharisean Court ;
No dissentient voice was found
   To question that report.

On each Phariseean face
A gleam of triumph shone ;
Such a very clear case
Admitted question none.

In mocking irony they sat,
Awaiting Jesus' plea,
Contented and exultant that
No loophole could He see.

Hark ! The solemn voice was heard,
By every Rabbi there ;
Each one hung upon His word
With most expectant care.

" Ye Pharisees," He slowly said,
" Your duty now is plain :
" By Justice only be ye led,
" Since Mercy pleads in vain.

" See unto it, that Justice now
" Retains her judgment seat ;
" Let each with heart and voice avow
" A Justice all complete.

" Hear Me, therefore, every one,
" This woman's cause espouse ;
" And so that Justice may be done,
" Your Consciences arouse.

" Though her Sin hath found her out,
" Yet Justice should be true ;
" And so, to banish every doubt,
" I now appeal to you.

" If ye—her Judges—have no sin,
" Then woe, indeed, for her,
" But if ye are defiled within
" Then further do not stir.

" If any 'mongst you have no sin,
" She suffereth alone,
" And such an one may now begin
" To hurl at her the stone.

" But if ye know a sinful act
" For which ye should atone,
" Within yourselves admit the fact
" And leave her well alone."

He said—and each judicial mind
Such Ruling did deplore—
Since none of them could hope to find
A word against her more.

So one by one they fled away,
From out His presence then
And neither one had aught to say
To baffle him again.

Yet as they hurried each without,
All accusation lost,
The wretched woman stared about
Considering the cost.

But He—the lowly Nazarene,
Remained to Duty true,
He knew how wicked she had been
And what remained to do.

So after each had gone away
He turned to her and said,
" Woman, even from to-day
" Be thou more wisely led.

" These Pharisees in Judgment Hall
" Thy sinfulness condemn,
" The while their Consciences appal
" And cowards make of them.

" Sinful, though indeed thou art,
" Repent thee of thy deeds,
" Choose a meeker, purer part
" More suited to thy needs.

" Love thy God, and every one
" Of all thy Neighbours too,
" As we would have all things done,
" So also we should do.

" Thy sins—though many—are forgiven,
" The wretched past is o'er,
" Live to earn thyself a Heaven
" Go, and sin no more."

Entrapped; or, A Mad Salvation.

It was in 187— that I made the acquaintance of my friend Jamieson ; and I will say this much, that if ever one man had a strong regard for another, I certainly had for my friend. When I first made his acquaintance through a mutual friend, he held a very high and honoured position in the town. Having a private business that provided him with lots of spare time, he devoted that time and his energies, with much assiduity, to following the vocation of an amateur missionary and philanthropist. His exact status in that capacity I never knew, nor cared to know ; it was sufficient for me that every person of any eminence in the neighbourhood both knew and respected him. I believe that as a temperance worker, a local lay preacher, a visitor of the sick, a charity dispenser, and an organiser of social meetings, he had very few equals; but temperance was his great hobby. Naturally such a position led him into society, and as a consequence there were few people with whom he was not on intimate terms. And he was certainly a creditable acquisition, for I never found any person, old or young, rich or poor, who did not consider him as a gentleman every inch; but notwithstanding all this, he was a man of little education. When I speak of little education, I allude more especially to his perceptive faculties and his judgment, for it seemed to me that very many people who were recipients of his worth, considered him as very much in the light and character of a pump handle; and consequently he was very often victimised. Large hearted, sympathetic, and impulsive, I know of a truth that he was no fit person either to dispense charity, or be allowed carte blanche to give his manual services in any project, for he proceeded in total disregard of self-interest. I have never since in my experience of life met another such a man, and probably I never shall. Not yet thirty, and of serious demeanour in dress and manners, slenderly built and rather tall, rapid gait and thin featured; his moustache, his smile, and his hearty hand clasp, were the only things that separated him from the gloom which enveloped his life. However, it is not so much of my friend as of an incident connected with our acquaintance that I am now about to speak. He and I became inseparable, and thus it happened that his deeply religious character and genial disposition, did much to promote in me an earnest desire to follow in his lines. With this view, therefore, I improved my attendance at services of his religious persuasion, and accompanied him to various meeting places. I cannot admit that my record was an exceptional or even commonly dark one, so far as law-breaking achievements went, for I had never seen the inside of a prison, and, as a matter of fact, only a Court of Justice once or twice. But as he and I grew more companionable, I discovered that the one thing lacking to render our friendship complete, was greater religious interest on my part, and so, out of pure regard for my friend, and a natural desire to act aright, I determined to cultivate it. I could not have been considered proud, since I had certainly attained a very unselfish opinion of myself, and in my mind resolved to become a more serious man. This is a most laudable purpose, if only suitably and successfully carried out, but alas! "Man proposes and God disposes." I had begun to accompany him to his private pew upon Sundays, and was finally prevailed upon to pay a visit to a "class-room meeting." Those of my readers who have never attended one of these special meetings, must understand that it is a meeting of a religious class, who are members together, in a room attached to the chapel or school, and set apart for the purpose. This class is presided over by a "Leader," as he is termed, who is generally brimful of habits and speech betokening deep religious fervour. Both sexes meet in the class, and the meeting generally consists of congratulations, hymn singing, individual prayers and praises, and fervent ejaculations. Should any strangers attend, by invitation or otherwise, it is understood that the class in various ways make them feel their position more or less acutely as the case may be, and to those who attend such a meeting for the first time, as I did upon this unlucky occasion, a strange experience is sure to await them. That is, supposing them to be ordinary human, and not adamant. I shall never forget that occasion whilst I live; and although I have had many strangely exciting and original experiences in my time, I always count that as one of the most thrilling and truly impressive. From the moment of my entrance, until I made my exit, I was made to feel the awful responsibilities of my position most intensely, and from first one and then another, from the Leader down to the female sitting near me, I found myself in their prayerful addresses, the wretched object of their supplicating solicitude. I will here admit that no sooner had I got well seated inside, and taken a rapid view of my surroundings, than I felt that I had altogether mistaken my vocation, and got into the wrong place, for I always had an aversion to being attended to and discussed from a "pious" point of view. What humility I possessed upon entering the room, was hacked out of me in a very short time, and before so very long indeed, I found myself burning with a mad desire to leave the place, and see their faces no more. The Lord knows how eagerly I desired peace for my soul upon entering, but for my peace of mind I devoutly wished to be out again. All my hopes of entering the earthly Heaven unimpressively were rudely dispelled, and yet for the world I would not, nor could not be bold enough to create disruption. I can very well imagine some of my readers saying that I was making much ado about nothing, but although some people might not be ruffled by such an experience, yet I have learnt since then that I am not alone in my peculiarities. It is all very well indeed to take a certain interest in man's salvation, but there can be no excuse for the excruciating monotony and monopoly developed in these wretched seances. The line must be drawn somewhere, and the sooner and the better for morality. Entreated from all sides to pray, I confess I could sooner have cursed, in my dilemma. I boiled almost with heat, and what with rage, perspiration and humility, I have no doubt but I seemed a fit object of pity, and in need of Grace. But sadly indeed for me, neither pity nor grace was forthcoming, and I had to bide it out in the best way I could. Sitting down blankly and appearing unconcerned, was altogether out of the question, for I lacked the power of mimicry necessary to carry it through. Again, there is such a thing in my composition as a love of fair play, and my feelings rebelled against the imposition. If I hardened myself sufficiently whilst upon my knees not to notice them, and covered my face with my hands, they had still the advantage of me, and the giving out a verse or two to sing, standing up, only increased my mortification. At one time I had a man upon either side of me, and whilst one would ask insinuatingly if I was "saved," the other would follow by asking me pointedly, "Would I wish to go to Hell?" At another time, a female would use her best endeavours in bidding me to make a good confession of my sins, whilst the voice of the Leader could be heard in chorus, "Do it now," as if the very existence of that class depended upon my undoing ; every sentiment expressed was supplemented by prolonged "Amens." And whilst I was forced to accept whatever offered ; and it is only simple truth to tell, that nothing was ever offered me of consolation that could for one moment be considered as either friendly or Christian sympathy. Some folks without doubt will consider that I must have been a wicked sinner, to feel the position so painfully, but I can only retort by saying that the whole proceedings grated harshly upon my senses, and was altogether foreign to my expectations. According to my sentiments, there was not a vestige of true religion about it. A quiet, respectful, and contrite demeanour, in every one present, would have appealed to my better nature ; but for a section to presume they were saints, and stood in no need of meditation and prayer, and to select me as the "sinner," was neither upright, moderate, nor charitable. We all entered I supposed upon common ground, and so I resented the bullying horse play indulged in. I know very well indeed, how ill becoming it was to feel as I felt, upon leaving that assembly, but when that blessed time arrived, I most sincerely wished never to enter the place again. The lightness had been taken out of my life for the time, and although repentant enough when I entered, when I left I was nearly past redemption. The numerous hand-shakings and invitations that I received to visit them again, seemed only to my thinking the usual artistic effusions born of an inordinate hankering after sport ; and the very sheepish appearance of my too solicitous friend confirmed my suspicions concerning the operation. He, I am sure, had never intended my undoing in that fashion, but I suppose the revival mania (like the dogs of war when once let loose) does not stop at trifles. If such another experience should await me in the days to come, and I receive the slightest warning of its proximity, I can here assure my friends that full preparations are made for my defence. I cannot exactly account for my repugnance to such methods, but to my mind, there seems something wholly distasteful and out of place in vulgar intrusions upon private devotions. We are certainly not every one alike in our nature and disposition, and it as well to remember always that what is fun to some people, may be punishment to others. To be termed a black sheep, a sinner, and a prodigal, is quite enough of abuse in my opinion to be thrown at any one, but to be basted as well as roasted, is beyond human endurance. The whole service from my standpoint was execrable, and most certainly a travesty of the Sacred character. No more roasting and basting in the name of religion for me ; for though I am a firm believer in the efficacy of spiritual supervision, in a proper and becoming spirit, I can safely say that outrages such as I have described are an arrant hypocrisy, and an unmitigated canting nuisance. There is undoubtedly a great need of civilization yet, even in this enlightened age, but I would infinitely prefer the blight of bluntest scepticism, to the mean and petty devices of those peculiar people who deem themselves the recipients and partakers, of what I unluckily discovered to be after all, only a mad salvation.

Modern Scepticism.

In considering this question, perhaps it will be as well to state at once that my object is not to discountenance religious life and effort of any creed whatever, for I have the deepest respect and reverence possible for true Religion, pure and undefiled. This is not an occasion for inquiry into the particular merits of the various religious idioms, and therefore it will be sufficient upon that head to consider granted any claims that each may set up. Seeing, then, that there will be no occasion for bickering amongst contrary sects, I ask the calm attention of every serious and well-minded person to the study hereof. To commence, let me state at once that Scepticism is not Secularism, and in order fairly to demonstrate my position and understand it clearly, I shall consider Secularism as on a par with every other ism, and grant it just as much consideration. Now, it is not my province in this essay to give a definition of true Religion, any more than it is to preach a new one, and therefore I request that every thinker will apply himself strictly to the subject under notice. I say at once, that to be a Sceptic is, in my opinion, no sin, so long as such Scepticism be provoked by seeming abuses or irregularity. Satisfaction is a necessary factor in the establishment of Faith, and Faith is the backbone of Religion ; so it occurs that Dissatisfaction is the prevailing cause of Scepticism. To be a honest Sceptic, from a religious point of view, is at once to show and prove an inquiring mind, and no Scepticism can be genuine that is tainted with Bigotry. The controlling element in Scepticism is Doubt, not Disbelief absolutely and in toto ; and a certain amount of Toleration is due as well from a Sceptic as from a Bigot, or Priest, or Believer. It may possibly have occurred that many doubters have gone into the ranks of opposition through sheer error of circumstances surrounding their position, and no good end could be served by denying such a fact, but it is due to such to state, that the sin of so doing, was perhaps more truly one of omission than commission. One thing is certain, and it is this : that no simple Sceptic upon any point or trimming of religious doctrine, is justified in becoming an opponent. Defence is not defiance, and it is plain that as no two wrongs can make one right, therefore it is that injury is caused by seceding, and injustice by opposing. Whilst I may excuse the position of a conscientious Sceptic upon reasonable grounds, yet it must be understood that there is no sound plea for obstinacy, since that is as reprehensible as religious Bigotry, to say the least. My object is simply to show that there are, and have been, great reasons at work in the propagation of modern Scepticism. So far from this Scepticism being detrimental to the spread of Religion, we find that religious life itself has progressed wonderfully in recent times, as evidenced by the increase of communities ; and in fairness we may note that a very striking evidence in favour of honest Scepticism, as distinguished from rank infidelity, is the fact that the children of very many Sceptics still receive pious training in our Sunday schools. There remains, then, the great question as to what causes have contributed towards the development of Scepticism, and I maintain that for this growth is the prevalence of Cant mainly responsible. Not solely, I admit, for I confess that Intolerance and Ignorance also have something to do with it, but perhaps nothing nearly so much. As to whether my assertion is correct or no, I, of course, only argue; but I feel convinced, in my mind of this, that there is truly so little of real infidelity in the land that I cannot claim for it importance sufficient, to warrant me in attaching much value to its force. And, therefore, as a natural consequence, I cannot consider it as at all comparable to such factors of Scepticism as Intolerance and Ignorance. Then what shall I say of Intolerance, and in what measure is it responsible for Scepticism ? First then, Intolerance is the natural fruit of a strained or half-hearted principle, and in religious matters generally attaches to a schism, where class distinction or personal jealousy predominates. It is impossible to particularise every instance that illustrates Intolerance, but as the symptoms are patent enough to all who suffer from it, it is unnecessary so to do. Intolerance differs greatly in its application, but under any circumstances it is the nearest possible approach to Bigotry, and is always lamentable. There is little or no excuse for its display and exercise, and good people will avoid the very appearance of it ; for it is evident that no close communion or real confidence can abide with it. Such, indeed, is its power for evil, that where ignorance might be disposed to walk reverently in a chosen but rather hazy groove, as one may say, the very appearance of dictation or superciliousness would rouse a latent spirit of opposition, that once feeling the infliction would chafe under the restraint, and finally quit its presence in disgust. So much, then, for Intolerance ; and innumerable instances of it might be noted with profit if the occasion warranted. There is never any justification for its employment, and it enters so insidiously into doctrinal etiquette, that very often where it is most painfully and profusely evident, the slaves to its passion remain in ignorance of the fact. The remedy for this Intolerance is plain, but not easy of accomplishment ; and it may easily be that there exists in it very much of mutuality, for if the heaping coals of fire obtain on the one side, and a freezing disregard continue on the other ; thus both parties remain strained, and mischief to one or both must ensue. Such intolerance as is thus manifest, is decidedly certain to provoke not alone Scepticism, but the bitterness of revolt ; and the sooner official authority steps in, and the better for religion's sake, and for the welfare of the community. There is possibly a misconception abroad as to what really constitutes intolerance, and it may be that occasionally, instead of there being any exhibition of intolerance on the part of the clergyman, that there exists an unreasonable and unprofitable expectation by certain of the flock, or even the church officials. Whenever such is the case it clearly proves that Intolerance is not confined to one section only, and it behoves us to be careful lest we deal unjustly with innocent and meritorious individuals. In the case of ministers of the Gospel as apart from others, there are indeed examples showing how most cruel intolerance can be practised by wardens, deacons, and trustees, to the great pain and complete undoing—in some cases— of the unfortunate Pastor. I merely mention this as a proof that Intolerance is not always one-sided, and to show that it is a very easy matter for a combination to act unjustly towards one or two who may fairly be called estimable individuals. It is also worthy of notice that the Faith which unbelievers deem to be the most intolerant, namely, the Roman Catholic, yet presents to the world an union and profession where charges of intolerance in reality are rare. And such a spectacle as this, which is undoubtedly the case, proves a high tribute to a Church which is animated with those holy and humble instincts so conspicuous amongst members of this ancient Faith. It proves at once, and very conclusively also to my mind, that the great antidote and drawback to Intolerance is to be found in Humility ; for no one can dispute that humility and reverence, are very prominent characteristics amongst all members of the Church of Rome. Whether or no these virtues are engendered by the diligence, benevolence, and learning of this Priesthood, is not the question : although personally I am inclined to believe so ; but the facts as here stated are evident enough to all observers. So that it is plain that it behoves us to be very careful in casting aspersions and bitter recriminations, to the detriment of any particular person or body ; for if we would be honest, as it is our duty to be, we must be prepared to "give and take" somewhat in settlement of these differences. The old adage concerning "glass houses, &c.," is always very applicable where charges of intolerance are bandied about. Concerning *ignorance* then, which is my third reason for, or cause of, Scepticism ; there can be very little doubt as to the fitness and also justice of the charge. Not that I infer such an ignorance as might be displayed in social or political matters, although it may occur that it is identical ; but I allude more particularly to a symptom that is best described as irreverent, unappreciative, unfeeling, and unnatural. This is an ignorance which is totally blind, careless, and unregardful of the real merits of the case. It cannot be denied that many so-called Sceptics are certainly irreverent, not alone of persons but Doctrine also ; and such being the case, much unhappiness befalls, for it renders them unapproachable. It may reasonably be inferred that such people are hypocritical, for they are out of sympathy with those whom they profess to be in sympathy with ; and in charity we cannot avoid putting this down to Ignorance. If they knew any better, and desired *God's Grace*, or *soul comfort*, they could not be dangerous, seeing that sympathy alone would bind them to right ; but knowing better, and having no desire for reconciliation of spirit, upon them rests the charge of Intolerance. So much for the irreverent Sceptic. That there are unappreciative and unfeeling Sceptics must also be admitted, and it must be calamitous to fall into their clutches ; for to adopt sanctimonious airs and habit for the devilish purpose of creating mischief, is brutal, dishonourable, and inhuman. These are the black sheep of Religion, the wolves in sheep's clothing, the Pharisees, and drawbacks to real religion, who would not consider themselves ignorant, but whom we know to be blindly so, nevertheless. Not alone are they blind themselves to the power of salvation, but they are powerful in leading or driving the waverers into a similar condition, and spreading disruption thereby. To be a honest Sceptic one must have a honest cause. It is no answer to impute motives, and profess solicitude also ; there must exist some plain, plausible, and tangible reason for living beyond the pale of Doctrine ; some palpable barrier to a reasonable and united Faith. Likes and dislikes should not enter into the calculations of thoughtful, earnest worshippers ; and it is very mean, even to absurdity, for any one with no better cause for holding aloof, thus to damage a good cause by separation. There always will be honest Sceptics against one or other point of Doctrine, but the man who wars with Religion *in toto,* is only stemming the tide of Progress, and is veritably a hindrance to the welfare of Society. There can be no honour in such work, and not much of satisfaction either. Therefore, this is certain, that true Scepticism pure and simple has no place for continuance, and false Scepticism of any kind whatever is dangerous. By having no place I mean, and I think it is plain, that if you are honestly doubtful concerning the fitness of any petty point of Doctrinal etiquette, you may by discussion and attention have such doubts removed by enlightenment ; and even if not in every one particular entirely dissolved, yet you may, by virtue of your good desires and conduct have them accounted for satisfactorily. This course, if followed, would put a great check upon Infidelity, and it is not alone the duty of any Sceptic to approach this end fairly, but it is also the duty as it should be the aim, of any Minister or official to meet him equally. So long as Jealousies, Bigotry, and Intolerance exist in religious communities, so long also will religious cant ; and the present attitude of Scepticism upholds it. I have endeavoured to show that there are no real grounds for separation from each other, between Sceptics and Religious Bodies ; and it behoves both parties to put an early end to useless bickering. This may easily be achieved by each person attending to Duty in a proper spirit, but with an increased desire to study more the interests of others rather than personal aims. It is deplorable that good, honest, respectable, and well meaning men and women, should, through the agency of Traitors, or their own Stiffness, deny to the world, through individual effort, the manifold advantages which only flow from unanimity, and an acquiescence in the Divine injunction to "Love one another," and preach the Gospel unto all the world.

Adieu !

How many times one little word,
  Has been the cause of pain ;
Which neither they who said or heard,
  Could e'er recall again.
And yet, alas ! it may occur,
  As now 'twixt me and you ;
To such a word, we must recur,
  This simple word—Adieu !

To you, my critical Adept—
  Or Butcher—if you will :
Should any faultiness have crept,
  Herein, beyond my skill ;
I wish you to remember, that—
  A "*Beggar*" is not you,
Yet one in cold November sat,
  Inditing this—Adieu.

For you, ye virtuous and kind,
    I own a deep regard ;
Desirous that an earnest mind,
    May merit some reward.
Could I your Friendship hope to win,
    I vow by all that's true,
I'd rather linger than begin
    To tender this—Adieu.

Amidst the labyrinths of thought,
    Where you and I have strayed :
Perhaps I may have set at nought,
    Decorum, prim, and staid :
A natural Bohemian bent,
    Is my excuse to you,
And if so be, you are content,
    Shake hands, and say—Adieu !

That "*Beggar Manuscripts*" may prove,
    Deserving your support ;
I pray, and strive by ev'ry move,
    Your sympathy to Court.
Some interest, p'r'aps now and then,
    Its pages may renew ;
And so I hope, as now my pen,
    Inscribes this fond—Adieu !

NORTH-EAST LANCASHIRE PRINTING AND PUBLISHING COMPANY, LIMITED, BLACKBURN.

www.ingramcontent.com/pod-product-compliance
Lightning Source LLC
Chambersburg PA
CBHW021123020726
47500CB00003B/895